"I KNOW ... BROUGHT ME HERE."

Scott was staring at the stars as he spoke. He snuggled closer to Cassie on the bedrolls they'd spread out on the grassy mountain crest.

"Oh?" Cassie looked at him with interest. "Suppose you tell me then."

"To seduce me."

Cassie chortled. "I certainly didn't have to come all the way up here to do that. You're easy."

"I mean to seduce me to this way of life."

"So, you admit it's seductive." Cassie ruffled his hair playfully.

"I'm beginning to understand the lure, why it holds such appeal for some people."

Cassie was silent for a moment. She heard a rustle of movement beside her, but her thoughts were on the hypnotic night sky. "You get such a feeling of being close to nature, don't you."

There was no reply. Cassie turned to Scott. He had crawled into his sleeping bag, and was dead to the world. The day's long ride had done him in. Not even a good-night kiss! Cassie sighed as she looked down at him lovingly. "Not bad for a tenderfoot...."

ABOUT THE AUTHOR

There's a down-to-earth, no-nonsense quality to
Barbara Kaye's writing that captures the rhythms
of ordinary people caught up in that
extraordinary condition called love. And this is
the charm that keeps fans clamoring for just one
more Superromance from this delightful
Oklahoma author. *Traditions* is Barbara's ninth
Superromance, and she is busy at work on her
tenth novel for the line. Now that's tradition!

Books by Barbara Kaye

HARLEQUIN SUPERROMANCE

46–A HEART DIVIDED
124–COME SPRING
161–HOME AT LAST
206–SOUTHERN NIGHTS
219–JUST ONE LOOK
257–A SEASON FOR ROSES
270–BY SPECIAL REQUEST
316–THE RIGHT PLACE TO BE

HARLEQUIN AMERICAN ROMANCE

19–CALL OF EDEN

Barbara Kaye
TRADITIONS

Harlequin Books

TORONTO • NEW YORK • LONDON
AMSTERDAM • PARIS • SYDNEY • HAMBURG
STOCKHOLM • ATHENS • TOKYO • MILAN

Published November 1988

First printing September 1988

ISBN 0-373-70332-5

To Mike Hester,
attorney-at-law and Annapolis graduate,
with grateful thanks for his assistance
in the writing of this book.

PROLOGUE

AS THE AUTUMN DUSK began to settle, a white Mercedes convertible pulled into one of the few available spaces in the country club's parking lot, and a well-built, dark-haired man dressed in soiled khakis got out. It was the last day of October, and the scores of youthful ghosts and goblins scampered toward the clubhouse clutching brown paper sacks, ready to take part in the club's annual Halloween party for its members' children. Scott Maitland paid them little attention. He had too much on his mind.

It had been a bright, warm day in Fort Worth, perfect for golf, so Scott knew where he could find his grandfather. The club's green was closing; he waited near the eighteenth green until a golf cart lumbered over the rise with the unmistakable figure of Theo Maitland behind the wheel. The cart halted, and the elderly man stepped down. Spying his grandson, he raised his club in salute, then lined up and sank a long and difficult putt. Watching, Scott shook his head and smiled. Theo was a wonder, a man of eighty years who regularly shot his age.

When Theo had retrieved his ball from the cup, he motioned to Scott to join him, and the two drove off in the direction of the pro shop. "When'd you get back?" the older man asked.

"Just did. Flew the plane in, then drove straight here. Henderson One's been plugged."

Theo digested this without expression. "Well, maybe we'll have better luck next time."

"We probably ought to make next time a long way down the road, Granddad. A few years ago Henderson One would've been a pretty good well, but with the price per barrel the way it is now, it didn't produce enough to make it worthwhile."

Theo eased into the long line of carts parked outside the pro shop, then shot a withering look at Scott. "You telling me about the oil business, son? I was drillin' before you were a gleam in your daddy's eye."

"Yeah, back in the glory days, the fun days. Now the business is on its ass."

"Nothin' I don't already know. These things come in cycles. I've been through more booms and busts than I can remember. Things'll pick up."

"Maybe," Scott said, "but in the meantime there's not a hell of a lot going on. Frankly, I'm bored. I've got to do something."

"Yeah? Like what?"

"I need a challenge. I guess I want to do what you did, take nothing and build it into something."

"Young bull contestin' the old bull, eh?"

"I guess so. Isn't that the way it's supposed to be?"

"Who told you that?"

"No one had to tell me. Around here you're measured by how much better you do than whoever came before you."

Theo chuckled. "I got news for you, son—you've got a heap of catchin' up to do if you're chasin' me. Why don't you just get married again? Keepin' a woman happy would take up your time. You wouldn't be bored then.''

Scott managed a straight face. "That isn't something you just decide to do, Granddad."

"Why not? Waitin' for lightnin' to strike? You don't learn much about a woman till after you marry her, anyway. You shouldn't live alone, son. Gives a man too much time to think about everything that's wrong with his life. Every time I start grousin' and grumblin', your grandma comes up with the drapes in the livin' room aren't right or the john in the powder room's backed up, and next thing I know I'm thinkin' about drapes and plumbin' instead of whatever it was I was worryin' about to begin with." Theo grew serious. "I'm sorry Becky's gone, sorry as I can be, but she is and has been for some time. You just ought to think about gettin' married again. I could use some more great-grandkids."

"I think my sister's handled that obligation admirably."

"That she has. I'm real proud of Judy and that brood of hers. But you still oughta get married. How old are you now...thirty-four?"

"Five," Scott corrected.

Theo shook his head. "Too old to be alone."

"And too old to be sitting around doing so damned little. In spite of what some people in this town think, I never fancied myself your heir apparent, not without earning it. And I get very little personal satisfaction out of plugging wells."

"Then go get a job." The elderly man squinted. "What was it you studied in college?"

Scott grinned. "Land management."

"Ah, yes, land management. That one really threw me. Well—" Theo twisted around in the seat and climbed out of the cart "—you say you're bored and need somethin' to do till the oil starts flowin' again. I admire that attitude. Had it m'self when I was your age. Never could stand sittin' around on my duff doin' nothin'. So...go find some land that needs managin'." Theo chuckled at his own joke. "Tell me, how does one go about bein' a land manager?"

Scott had gotten out of the cart and fallen into step beside his grandfather. "First, you have to get hold of some land."

"You mean . . . like farmin'?"

"Not exactly, but you're in the ballpark."

"You really thinkin' about buyin' some land?"

"With your permission, sir."

Theo stopped in his tracks and looked at his grandson. "Permission? Sir? Been a spell since I heard you use those words."

"I'll have to leave Fort Worth to do what I want to do, Granddad."

"Why?"

"The kind of land I'm looking for—something really run-down that needs a lot of attention—well, I probably won't find it anywhere near here."

Theo stared at the ground a moment. "I see. Your grandma's gonna hate that. What'd your mom and dad have to say about it?"

"I haven't mentioned it to them." Scott's socialite parents, jet-setters who lived in Europe most of the time, had not been the major force in his life. The tough old bird standing before him had.

The expression on Theo's face didn't change, but he was always pleased when his grandson came to him first, and Scott knew it. "Is it buyin' some land you're so hot about, or leavin' Fort Worth?" he asked.

Scott uttered a dry laugh. "Not much gets by you, does it?"

"I hope not."

"Okay, I admit it. In this town I'll always be no one but Theo Maitland's grandson unless I do something on my own. When business was booming and Becky was still here, I didn't think about that much, but lately..."

"Yeah, I guess I understand that. I might not like it, but I understand. So, I'll tell you the same thing my daddy told me when I left Oklahoma—do what you gotta do."

"That's it?" Scott asked in astonishment. "You don't mind if I scout around for some property?"

"Like you said, you gotta do something. Can't sit around goin' to seed. That's the worst thing a man can do. Just as long as you don't get too serious about it."

"What's 'too' serious?"

"Just don't go gettin' hay and manure in your veins instead of Texas crude." Giving his grandson a pat on the back, Theo nudged him toward the clubhouse. "Come on, I'll buy you a drink, and you can tell me some more about this. Sounds interestin'...in a peculiar sort of way."

As the two men made their way toward the building, Scott felt a great wave of relief sweep through him. He had been thinking about this a long time, maybe ever since Becky died. A piece of land to call his own, a chance to put his theories into practice. He might fall on his butt, but it would be his butt, and he'd be the one doing the falling. But he had dreaded telling his grandfather he was going to leave. Theo

Maitland had some pretty rigid ideas concerning family and destiny and all that.

One thing for sure: Scott had never expected this to be so easy.

CHAPTER ONE

Eight Months Later

WHEN GEORGE WHITTAKER APPEARED in the doorway of her office, Cassie Tate glanced at her watch. It was only nine o'clock, a bit early for her foreman to be checking in with her, so she immediately guessed that all was not entirely well with the DO Ranch on this bright spring morning.

"Good morning, George."

"Mornin', boss."

"What can I do for you?"

To the jingle of spurs and the stump of boot heels, George crossed the room to stand in front of her desk. "Looks like we got us a problem."

"Oh?"

"The Horseshoe's south gate's been padlocked. The boys had to ride miles out of their way to get the herd to the top pasture."

A look of total exasperation crossed Cassie's face. Scott Maitland again! There had been one "problem" after another ever since that brash oilman from Fort Worth had bought the adjacent Horseshoe Ranch. Admittedly, most were petty annoyances, like his damned airplane that spooked the dickens out of the cattle, so she ignored them the best she could. But padlocking gates was unheard of in the High Country of West Texas. Not only was it unfriendly, it went against tradition.

But then, Maitland didn't give a hang about tradition, and that was the biggest problem of all. It only reinforced Cassie's belief that outsiders didn't belong in the highlands—specifically outsiders like Scott Maitland who had bought the Horseshoe the way he would buy an object of art, then set about playing at ranching and flaunting all the traditions and values that the real ranchers held so dear.

Frowning, Cassie considered the situation and pondered the best way of handling it. The padlocked gate was the latest incident in her running battle of philosophies with her new neighbor, but it was more serious than the rest. It interfered with the DO's operation, so it couldn't be ignored.

Getting to her feet, Cassie kicked back her chair with the heel of a boot. "I guess I've put this off too long," she said. "I think it's time Maitland and I had a little talk."

"Want me to come along?" George asked.

She hesitated, but only for a second. "No, thanks, George. I want him to realize who's in charge over here. I don't think Maitland takes me seriously."

At that moment another man entered the room. He had thick snow-white hair, bushy white brows and a weathered, textured face that reminded one of a relief map, but his sturdy, ramrod-straight body belied his sixty years. He was J. B. Ferenback, Cassie's father and the DO's reigning patriarch. "Mornin', hon. Mornin', George," he greeted them in a gravelly voice.

George touched the brim of his Stetson with a forefinger. "Morning, J.B."

Cassie reached for a lightweight tan blazer that was slung over a nearby chair and slipped it on. "You going somewhere?" her father asked.

"Yes. To see a man about a gate."

J.B.'s eyes quizzed George, and the foreman gave him a succinct account of the padlocked gate incident. J.B. scowled. "Maitland's got about as much business running a ranch as I do flying that dad-blamed airplane of his. Someone oughta do something about that young man."

"I couldn't agree more, Dad," Cassie said, "and I'm open to suggestions. Got any ideas?"

"If I did, you would've heard about 'em long ago. Where's Rob?"

"Still in bed, I guess."

"God a'mighty!" J.B. fumed. "It's nine o'clock!"

"I'm aware of that."

"We're not running a rest home here."

"Oh, come on, Dad." Cassie jumped to her son's defense. "School's only been out a week. Let him enjoy vacation awhile."

"A sixteen-year-old boy shouldn't be lolling around in bed till nine. There's plenty of work that needs doing. My daddy wouldn't have put up with that from me for a second."

Cassie got her car keys out of the center desk drawer and headed for the door. The last thing she wanted was yet another confrontation with her father over her son. They only ended in stalemates anyway. "Then you rouse him. I'm a woman with a mission."

Leaving J.B. mumbling under his breath, Cassie and George left the room. The foreman walked outside with her and stood on the porch while she climbed into the new four-wheel-drive pickup. "See you in a bit," she called as she drove away.

"Don't take any guff off of Maitland," George called back, watching as the truck disappeared down

the road and was swallowed up in the rugged canyon.
He had paid alert attention to the exchange between
father and daughter concerning young Rob. He knew
it was none of his affair, and he wouldn't have
dreamed of putting in his two cents' worth, but he
thought J.B. had a point. For a boy who would someday take charge of the Ferenbach's sprawling cattle
empire, Rob took precious little interest in the DO's
operation. Some might attribute that to his age, but
George didn't. By the time he had turned sixteen he
was so enamored of horses and cattle and the whole
idea of ranching that nothing on earth could have de-
terred him from that way of life, and it was like that
with every rancher and cowboy he'd ever known. Unless he completely missed his guess, Rob just wasn't
bent that way.

But Cassie couldn't see it. When it came to her son
she had a bad case of tunnel vision, and everyone on
the ranch knew it and talked about it. Bunkhouse
gossip usually centered on the family in the big house.
This was true on every ranch where George had
worked, but it was even more pronounced at the DO
because the boss was a pretty lady. Since he was the
foreman, George knew Cassie a little better than the
other hands did, and he long ago had decided she was
the most complacent person he'd ever met—completely satisfied with her ranch, her son and, apparently, the memories of her late husband. And like the
others, he was curious about Robert Tate, the man
Cassie had been faithful to all these years. His only
glimpse of her husband had been the casual remark of
an old-timer. "They were just so well suited, Robert
and Cassie were. It was like two real good friends had
decided to get married and raise a family."

To George that didn't sound like the love affair of the century, yet Cassie hadn't remarried. He'd never ever seen any dudes hanging around her, and that was strange since she wasn't the kind of woman men tended to ignore. She looked a lot younger than thirty-eight, and she was pretty enough to make a man temporarily forget the wife and kids. George had to surmise that there had been plenty of hopeful suitors through the years, but they had been given the brush-off.

He took off his big hat, ran his fingers through his hair, then replaced the Stetson. Leaving the porch, he headed for the corral. He had been at the DO four years, longer than he usually stayed in one place. The Ferenbachs were good folk to work for, a lot better than most. But Cassie was going to have to do something about Rob, or sure as day follows night, this wouldn't be the Ferenbach spread for too many more decades.

CASSIE FOUND A SHALLOW PLACE to cross Limpia Creek; still, the water was hubcap deep. Intermittent spring rains had ended a three-year drought and sent the normally placid little creek roaring out of its banks. The first storm back in April had dumped ten inches of rain on the area in one night. Now, in early June, the countryside was at its best. Brilliant green highland pastures undulated in all directions. The floor of the valley was sprinkled with masses of yellow prairie zinnias. Atop nearby Mount Locke, the McDonald Observatory presided over all. Cassie gazed appreciatively at the scene through the windshield, and a smile touched her lips. Before the rains she had been planning to make serious cutbacks in the DO's oper-

ation, but now she was looking forward to a great
year.

About time, she thought. She'd had the bad luck to
take on the task of managing the ranch just as the
drought hit, so the profits under her directorship had
been modest. No one blamed her for that, of course,
and it certainly wasn't something to be ashamed of.
There were plenty of local ranchers who'd had no
profits at all during the past three years. But the DO
seemed to thrive in spite of hard times, and it was
Cassie's heartfelt opinion that it did so because the
Ferenbachs believed in letting nature have its way.

And therein lay the source of her displeasure with
Scott Maitland, her new neighbor. He was hell-bent on
bending nature every which way—always innovating,
experimenting and modernizing, with a total disre-
gard for the land and for the methods that had worked
for over a century. If he had kept his outrageous theories to himself, she could have tolerated him, but the
man had more nerve than an army mule. He, a newcomer with no ranching credentials, had the audacity
to stand up at a ranchers' association meeting and de-
clare that drought was the rancher's excuse for bad
times, not the reason for them. She well remembered
the shock that had rippled through the gathering after that statement.

As she turned off the main road and drove down the
dirt lane that led to the Horseshoe Ranch, her mouth
set determinedly. Padlocked gates indeed! Not only
were they inconvenient, they were unnecessary. Maitland probably didn't know it, but boundary lines in
this rugged, mountainous country were not sharply
defined and never would be. Properties meandered
along creeks, spilled into crevices and interlocked like

the fingers of two clasped hands. She wondered if her new neighbor was aware that his horseshoe-shaped property cut deeply into the Ferenbachs' own land. He couldn't even reach his own house without driving across a mile or so of the DO. How would he like it if they started padlocking gates, something she might very well think about doing if her neighbor proved to be less than neighborly.

Approaching Maitland's house, Cassie's disapproval intensified. In a few short months the Horseshoe had been transformed. It now looked more like a squire's country estate than a ranch. The main house had been repainted and landscaped, and a sprinkling system had been installed. That alone was enough to raise her hackles. Maitland was much too free with his use of water, a precious resource in these parts.

Her gaze continued to roam the scene. The old barn that had stood out back for decades was gone, but several prefab buildings had been erected. In the distance was the runway he had constructed and the little hangar where he kept that blasted airplane. Near the hangar stood huge pieces of farm equipment—including a plow. A plow! The very word was anathema to most ranchers.

But what galled Cassie right down to the pointed toes of her Tony Lama boots were the fences. For months the sound of whining saws and pounding hammers had reverberated through the hills. On the DO one could ride for half a day without encountering a fence, but the Horseshoe had been fenced and cross-fenced to the point that Maitland's property was a maze of enormous holding pens. All those fences, and to her knowledge, her neighbor didn't own so much as one cow.

The man truly was impossible. He had taken open rangeland and fenced out his neighbors, and the worst of it was, he didn't seem to think there was a thing wrong with that. He didn't understand, and that was why he didn't belong.

She noticed the sleek convertible parked in front of the house and pulled in behind it. Getting out, she went to the door. She had raised her hand to knock when the door opened and Scott Maitland stood grinning at her, his high-crowned black Stetson set rakishly low on his forehead. "G'morning, Cassie," he drawled. "Saw you coming."

"Good morning."

"Been a while, hasn't it?"

"Yes, I guess it has." An odd sensation passed through Cassie, and she recalled that the very same sensation had hit her the first time she saw Maitland. Being honest, she wondered if that initial reaction to him might be one reason she had avoided him. He might be a nuisance, he might be impossible, but he was a good-looking devil, and she suspected he knew it.

They had been introduced at an early spring meeting of the High Country Ranchers' Association, and even then she had been aware of his dark good looks, the ingratiating smile and the mischievous twinkle in his deep brown eyes. That night he had worked hard at blending in with the crowd, but he had succeeded only to a point. Some vague, indefinable quality had set him apart. Studying him carefully, she finally had placed him in a category: a man on familiar terms with fine champagne, caviar and the men's department at Neiman-Marcus. When she later discovered he was the scion of one of Fort Worth's legendary oil families, she had congratulated herself on her powers of observation.

That night he had fairly oozed an effortless charm, and Cassie supposed she had been as fascinated as the other women present. The more she heard about the man and his ideas, however, the less attractive he became. As gossip continued to circulate, she formed yet another opinion of him: he was spoiled, plastic and uncaring. Now she felt completely immune to his charm, as formidable as it was. The only thing she wanted out of Scott Maitland was a reasonable compliance with High Country traditions.

"To what do I owe the pleasure of this visit?" Scott asked.

"I hope I'm not disturbing you," she said pleasantly but coolly. "I'd like to talk to you if you have a few minutes."

"Sure." He stepped back and opened the door wider, motioning her inside. "How about some coffee?"

"No, thanks. I had my coffee hours ago."

"Then, this way. We can talk in my office."

Alive with curiosity, Cassie glanced around as she followed him into an alcove off the living room. It had been several years since she'd last been in the Horseshoe's main house, and the difference in the way it had looked then and the way it looked now was startling. The worn hardwood floors obviously had been refinished. A long sofa and four upholstered chairs stood grouped around a magnificent dhurrie rug, all focused on the stone fireplace. Above its mantel hung an abstract painting that to Cassie's unknowledgeable eye didn't appear any more artistic than some of the things Rob had brought home from the first grade. Yet she somehow knew that the painting was valuable. There were, in fact, many objects of art scattered around the room. Books, too, and lush plants in shiny brass pots. Anyone who entered this house would immediately know that its owner was no ordinary highlands rancher. After three years of drought, not many real ranchers could afford to surround themselves with such tasteful luxury.

"You have a lovely home," she said, feeling the need to say something.

"Thanks. It needed a lot of attention."

Maitland's office was an extension of the living room—restful, quietly elegant, neat and spotless. She thought of her own office, with its cluttered desk, mishmash of worn furniture and unadorned walls and windows. But then, she quickly reminded herself, the DO was a working ranch, not a rich man's plaything.

"Have a seat, Cassie," Scott said, indicating a big chair that was upholstered in a muted plaid fabric. She sank into its deep comfort as Scott sat down behind his desk. He leaned back, folded his hands at his belt buckle and smiled. "What can I do for you?"

The man's regard was unnerving, and Cassie couldn't understand why. So instead of exchanging preliminary small talk, she got right to the point. "Your south gate was padlocked this morning."

"Yes. So?"

"Padlocked gates are unheard of around here, particularly between the DO and the Horseshoe. My men had to ride miles out of the way to get the herd to the top pasture. That's never happened before."

Scott frowned. "Well, now, I'm sorry about that. Tell them to use my west gate. There's no lock on it."

"That's still miles out of the way. The DO has always been allowed to drive its cattle through the south gate, no matter who owned the Horseshoe."

Scott shook his head slowly. "I wish I could accommodate you, Cassie, but...you see, that south pasture is going to be my showcase plot."

She looked at him blankly. "Showcase?"

"I'm having it plowed up and reseeded with a special hybrid grass I've ordered from a fellow in Australia. It's a new strain—drought resistant, vitamin packed, real 'hot feed.' It's also expensive. Obviously I can't have cattle tramping across it until the growth has been established."

Cassie wondered if she had heard right. "You mean...you're going to plow the whole pasture and plant grass?"

"Yes."

She stifled a smile; he was an oddball, all right. "This entire country is nothing but grass. That's why it's so good for raising cattle. If I were you, I'd spend my money on something else."

Scott wondered if she was aware that she sounded like an impatient adult trying to explain something to a dense child. Oh, he'd known the minute he ordered the gate locked that it would bring someone from the DO running to his door. The hired man who had received the order had looked at him aghast. "Them Ferenbachs ain't gonna like this one damn bit, Mistuh Maitland," the man had said. Scott had told him to do it anyway.

So he'd been waiting, expecting to see George Whittaker or one of the ranch hands, anyone but Cassie. She'd given him a wide berth ever since the night they were introduced at the association meeting. Everyone else for miles around, even the ones who didn't agree with his theories, had been exceedingly friendly, but not Cassie.

And that was a shame. He had taken one look at her and decided he wanted to get neighborly, but so far their encounters had been chance meetings in Fort Davis or Alpine. Each time he had been struck by her fresh attractiveness. *Wholesome* he guessed was a good word for her. She had beautiful green eyes and a generous mouth that had an intriguing little indentation in its bottom lip. Her hair was the color of a chestnut pony, and it curled softly around her slightly square face. Anyone would call her a pretty woman.

But she wasn't as attractive as she could be. She used a minimum of makeup, yet with a little enhancement, she could be a real knockout. And she wore her hair pulled back and tied at the nape, instead of letting it fall to her shoulders. Scott had only seen her in jeans, but with that figure he'd bet she was really something when she got all gussied up—if she ever did.

With some effort he brought himself back to the moment. "Yeah, it's full of grass, all right. Grass that's been overgrazed for a century. Grass that's just come through three years of no rain."

"There have always been droughts. There'll be droughts again."

Scott grinned. "Well, I guess that kind of attitude is the easy way out."

"I beg your pardon!" Cassie bristled indignantly.

"Bending to nature. It's a cop-out."

"It's worked for us Ferenbachs for over a century."

"Mmm. But the DO's so big you folks can get along in spite of almost anything. I'm sure I don't have to remind you of how many ranchers around here are about to go under."

"Of course not." She wondered if Maitland knew how many of those same ranchers had received personal loans from J.B., although in some cases her father knew that the chances of the loans ever being repaid were exceedingly slim. Would a man who fenced out his neighbors understand something like that? "But there have always been hard times," she said patiently. "It's a fact of life for ranchers. There's not one of us who hasn't had to slaughter cattle rather than let them starve. But out here folks work together and help each other, and they always survive."

"Some of 'em won't this time, not if they insist on doing things according to 'tradition.' Tradition counts for very little at the bank. And why put up with that feast-or-famine rut just because that's the way it's always been?"

"I don't know what you're talking about."

"No, I don't suppose you do, and you have plenty of company. I seem to spend a lot of time talking to deaf ears lately."

"Talking?" she asked suspiciously. "About what?"

"You wouldn't understand."

"Try me."

"About employing new methods and modern science to make the land more useful, instead of using it up and moving on."

"I'd like to remind you that we Ferenbachs have been here for—"

"For over a century. I know, I know. And it's to your credit that none of you ever lost your land or ruined it, but you haven't done much to improve it, either."

Cassie felt a rush of color in her cheeks. She was so surprised at his impudence that she couldn't find her voice.

Scott's response to that was a warm, lazy smile. "I'm really glad you stopped by, Cassie. If you've got a minute or two, I'd like to show you something."

"I really must be going."

"It'll only take a minute," he insisted.

In spite of herself, Cassie was curious. In some perverse, unpleasant way, Scott Maitland interested her. "Well . . . all right. A minute or two."

They both stood, and Cassie followed Scott through the house and into a kitchen that looked like something out of the pages of *Better Homes and Gardens*. A tiled work center stood in the middle of the room, and several stools sat around it. Dozens of assorted cooking utensils hung from an iron rack above. A built-in shelf held jars of more kinds of herbs and spices than she had known existed. This was a kitchen for a serious cook, and since, to her knowledge, Maitland lived alone, she supposed he was the cook. If so, he was an unusual man. None of the men she knew or worked with would have been caught within a country mile of a stove. She doubted that her father had ever done more than walk through the DO's kitchen.

Scott opened the back door and stood aside to allow her to precede him outside. Cassie stepped onto a curved redwood deck that afforded a spectacular view of the rugged green hills. The panorama was breathtaking...or could have been, she quickly amended, if it had been left alone. As it was, the maze of cross-fencing had, in her estimation, thoroughly spoiled what had once been desirable open pasture.

Scott, however, sounded as proud as a father showing off his first-born when he said, "Every one of those pastures has been planted with a different type of grass. Most are hybrids from Texas A&M, but there's the Australian strain and another from Arizona. Grasses like those could save the Western range."

"The entire Western range? How ambitious. That takes in a lot of territory."

Scott ignored the sarcasm in her voice. "Yep. From Saskatchewan to the Rio Grande. From the ninety-eighth meridian to the Pacific Ocean."

Cassie shook her head in bewilderment. "But why go to all this trouble when the native grasses have been supporting livestock for centuries?"

A minute passed before Scott turned to her; he seemed transfixed by the sight before him. "How many cow units per section you figure the DO'll be running this year?"

The question startled Cassie. It was bad manners to ask such a thing. Might as well ask the size of a person's bank account. But Maitland wouldn't know that, so she considered the source and answered, "Oh, fifteen, I guess. Before the rains came I would have said ten, but this is going to be a good year, so fifteen's about right."

Scott chuckled indulgently. "And I intend running twice that many."

Cassie's eyes widened in disbelief. "Thirty a section? That's ridiculous. The pastures won't support that many."

"Maybe the DO's won't, but mine will. The grasses I'm planting will be so nutritious that I probably could pack 'em into those pens like a cattle car."

"No one can run a ranch that way!"

"On the contrary, my way is the way of the future. When the small ranchers around here see what I'm able to do with fifteen sections, compared to what the DO can do with two hundred . . . well, we'll see. I may start a revolution. You might not recognize this country in ten years."

A spate of anger boiled inside Cassie, then quickly subsided. She didn't like that smile on his face; she didn't like him, and she certainly didn't like the things he was doing to the Horseshoe, but she wasn't going to let him bother her. Facing him squarely, she said, "Let's get back to the reason I'm here. A padlocked gate."

"I'm sorry that's causing you a problem, really I am, but the south gate stays locked. I've got a lot of money tied up in that ground."

Cassie struggled with her composure. "I had hoped I wouldn't have to bring this up, but . . . for decades now, the DO has had the right to drive its cattle across your property in return for unlimited water rights on ours." She stopped there, not wanting to come right out and threaten to withhold watering privileges. No conscientious rancher in a drought-prone area would do such a thing.

She had expected the reference to water to prompt some kind of reaction from him, but Scott's lazy smile changed hardly at all. "I doubt I'll be needing to use your watering holes much, Cassie. I'm damming up a portion of the creek that runs through my northern section."

"You can't do that! There are dozens of ranches downstream that depend on that creek."

"Don't worry, they won't be deprived. The water may slow down for a spell, but they won't be without it. I'm simply assuring myself of enough water to run my irrigation system."

"Nobody irrigates in this country," she snapped, fully aware that she was repeating herself. She persisted in telling him what "nobody" did, and he couldn't have been less concerned.

"I'm going to," Scott said calmly. "I'm afraid I don't have the patience to wait for rain when it refuses to come."

There was so much Cassie would have liked to tell him. She would have liked to explain that the water table had been dropping for years, so water in West Texas was more valuable than gold. She would have liked to tell him how fervently she believed there was a reason for everything under the sun, and that included drought. She would have liked to enlighten this greenhorn by saying that what he referred to as a feast-or-famine rut simply was part and parcel of ranching life. But it would be useless with this man, so she would save her breath. "Well, I can see that I'm wasting my time. Obviously, you're no rancher, Mr. Maitland."

"Scott," he corrected. "And you're right. I'm a businessman, and the business I'm getting ready to go into is raising cattle."

"And just when is this new venture of yours going to begin?"

"Just as soon as the pastures are in the shape I want."

"I see. Most of us don't have the luxury of waiting for ideal conditions. Most of us have to get a herd to market or go broke. I thank you for your time, anyway."

She turned on her heel to leave, but Scott placed a detaining hand on her arm. "Just a minute, Cassie..."

Cassie disliked having him call her by her first name, which was petty and silly since everyone she'd ever met called her by her first name. But she couldn't bring herself to call him "Scott," not to his face. He was simply "Maitland," a nasty, hooky thorn in her side. "Yes?"

"I'm sorry I rile you so, but I know what's behind it."

"Of course you do. Padlocked gates, dammed up creeks..."

"Let's be honest. You wanted to buy the Horseshoe yourself. I've been around long enough to have heard the story about your great-granddaddy."

She saw no point in denying it. "You left out a 'great.' It was my great-great-grandfather who lost the Horseshoe in a poker game. The story's part of local folklore, hardly a secret. And, yes, every Ferenbach since then has wanted it back. But apparently it isn't meant to be. Every time the Horseshoe's been for sale, the DO's been without the means to buy it, and vice versa. I'll be honest with you. If the rains had come even one month earlier, the Horseshoe would no doubt be back in the fold. But I don't begrudge you that. I simply wish you were more...oh, in tune with our traditions. Out here we work together for the common good, which means we don't lock gates and we don't dam creeks."

"Hmm." Scott pursed his lips. "Quite a speech, Cassie. Tell me something—what about the bottom line?"

"Money?"

"Of course."

"Money may be important—you can't keep going without it—but it's not the whole point."

"You're wrong. The whole point of any business venture is to show a profit."

"Like you said—you're a businessman. But I'm a rancher, and I have a feeling you're going to find this country very difficult."

"On the contrary. I expect to be wildly successful."

The novice's optimism, Cassie thought. If he weren't so troublesome, it might almost be sad to see what harsh reality did to it. "Good luck," she said. "Now, I really must be going. I'll just go around the side of the house, and there's no need for you to see me to my car. Goodbye."

"Bye, Cassie. Stop by anytime. I'm always glad to have company."

Scott stared after her, noting with admiration her erect carriage and long, sure strides. *In fact, I'm starved for company,* he thought. The isolation got to him after a while. He had never minded solitude, feeling most of the time that it was a reward, but this was ridiculous. The farm and ranch broker in Fort Worth who'd first told him about the Horseshoe had described the area as big, lonely country. Then Scott had discovered the ranch was located in a county the size of Connecticut and Rhode Island together, with perhaps ten thousand residents in all. *Lonely* hardly described it adequately.

So it wasn't surprising that he had hoped to get on friendly terms with the Ferenbachs, his closest neighbors, but so far that hadn't happened, chiefly because of Cassie's undisguised hostility toward him. Normally, if an attractive woman had shown so little interest in getting to know him, she would have been dismissed without another thought. But from the beginning he had been intrigued with Cassie Tate. He disliked thinking that perhaps it was her very hostility that fascinated him so.

Scott knew that the main stumbling block to a friendlier relationship was their warring philosophies, but he understood Cassie and her ilk far better than she thought he did. He could empathize with the stubborn ranchers who clung to drought-ridden land, dreaming of the great year just ahead. After all, he'd sprung from two generations of oil wildcatters. It was in his blood to be optimistic when all the odds pointed to failure. Where he differed with the ranchers was in his feelings about change. He thought it was inevitable and desirable; the traditionalists considered it a dirty word.

And from what he'd been able to gather from local gossip, the Ferenbachs were the most tradition-minded of the lot. Of course, they had more tradition behind them than most. The DO was a legend in these parts, the kind of place city types thought of when they heard the word "ranch," and the Ferenbachs were the area's First Family.

Still, Scott hadn't been able to find out much about Cassie. He guessed her to be somewhere near his own age. She was a widow and had a son. Once in Fort Davis someone had pointed out young Rob Tate to him. He was a nice-looking boy who didn't resemble his mother. On another occasion Scott had been introduced to J.B. Ferenbach, a man who had reminded him of a younger Theo Maitland—tough, cagey, sure of himself but not impressed with himself.

But it was Cassie he wanted to get to know. She was the first woman since Becky who'd aroused more than a passing curiosity. He couldn't imagine why she, more than anyone else, had piqued his interest, but he knew he wouldn't rest until he'd found out all he could about her. Once that had been accomplished, he reasoned, he'd figure out how to get close to her. That wasn't conceit; he simply knew his own nature. He had inherited dogged determination and tenacity from his grandfather. When he wanted something, or someone, badly enough, he did his homework, followed through, then almost always got what he wanted.

His first task was to find out if Cassie really was someone he wanted.

CHAPTER TWO

CASSIE DROVE HOME in a fit of frustration, all the while chiding herself for the feeling. Why did she persist in giving Maitland a second thought? He was just another "recreational" rancher looking for new ways to spend his family's money. The highlands, being wetter, cooler and greener than most of West Texas, had seen so many of Maitland's kind over the years. They hardly ever lasted long. Once they discovered what a hard life ranching really was, they sold out and hurried back to their former comfortable surroundings, and their ranching experience became something fun to talk about on the golf course. Her new neighbor wouldn't be around long, and his departure couldn't come soon enough for her. In the meantime, she wasn't going to let him upset her.

Cassandra Ferenbach Tate was the fifth generation of her family to manage the DO Ranch in the Davis Mountains. She had assumed that position three years earlier on her thirty-fifth birthday, just as J.B. had taken over from his father on his thirty-fifth birthday, just as Rob would take over on his thirty-fifth birthday. That was tradition, and if there was one thing the DO thrived on, it was tradition. The ranch could trace its roots to 1870, when the first Ferenbach had come to the highlands from Dayton, Ohio—hence the name of what was to become an impressive empire. The modern branch of the clan did not operate in a significantly different way than those early pioneers had. Cassie imagined that some of those nineteenth-century founders would have blanched at the thought of a woman manager, but none of them, she was sure, would have questioned her ability. Her lot in life had been preordained from the cradle, and it suited her fine.

She must have been twelve or thirteen when her father sat her down and explained exactly what was expected of her. She was J.B.'s only child. Her mother had died when she was an infant, and though J.B. had remarried a few years later, the second marriage hadn't lasted. The woman hadn't liked ranching, and there had been no offspring of the union. Virtually everything in Cassie's life, including her degree in agriculture from nearby Sul Ross State and her marriage, had been done with an eye on what J.B. called "the master plan." She had followed it right down the line. The things that had gone awry—the miscarriages, Robert's death—had been beyond her control.

Of course, as with anything worthwhile, being a Ferenbach had its drawbacks. At thirty-eight she had realized that love probably wasn't going to happen to her again. The men in her limited universe seemed to fall into two groups: those who were enamored of the name Ferenbach and those who were intimidated by it. Not once since Robert's death had she met anyone who was enough his own man not to be influenced by who she was instead of what she was. Yet the thought of being alone wasn't particularly dismaying. Her life was serene and fulfilling. She had plenty to be grateful for.

If there was anything on earth Cassie wanted that she didn't have, it probably was Horseshoe Ranch. She recalled her acute disappointment when she'd learned it had been sold. Actually, Scott Maitland's property was a pretty sorry piece of real estate when compared with the rest of the DO, but that wasn't the point. Their ancestor's ineptness at cards had been a burr under the Ferenbachs' collective saddle for almost a century, and Cassie wanted to be the one to bring that land back into the fold.

She'd do it, too, just as soon as Maitland got tired of his new plaything. The next time that horseshoe-shaped piece of property went on the market, she was going to buy it, even if doing so meant going heavily into debt.

The ranch house loomed into view. Cassie parked the truck out front and headed straight for the corral, looking for George. She hadn't accomplished a thing with Maitland, and she hated having to admit it to her foreman. She felt it diminished her effectiveness. She doubted George would think so, but the feeling was there, nevertheless.

George was perched on the top rail of the fence, watching a couple of cowboys break in a pair of new horses. Cassie hoped that one of the busy ranch hands manning the ropes would turn out to be Rob, but as she neared the corral, she saw that was not the case. She climbed the fence to sit next to George.

"How'd it go?" he asked with interest.

"Not too good, I'm afraid. The Horseshoe's south gate is off limits until further notice."

A second of silence passed, then George said, "Sure, boss, whatever you say."

He sounded disappointed, so Cassie felt compelled to explain further. "It won't last too long. Maitland's something of a flake. He's experimenting with some high-powered grass seed that's going to save us all from ruin. We might as well humor him for the time being . . . just to keep the peace, you know."

"Sure."

"Tell everyone to use Maitland's west gate until I tell them otherwise."

George nodded. "You're the boss."

Cassie didn't much feel like the boss of anything at the moment, and she focused the blame for that squarely on Scott Maitland. "He was so adamant about not letting cattle trample his precious grass that I really didn't have much choice in the matter. I'm not prepared to order our men to trespass openly."

"Yeah, I know. There wasn't anything you could do. Tell me something, though—why's Maitland planting grass?"

"He says he's improving the land. The grass supposedly is packed with vitamins and . . . oh, I can't remember all of it. But get this—he's planning on running thirty cow units a section."

She and George shared a laugh, then he turned serious. "That man's gonna be a problem."

"He already is. I want all of you to respect his property, but you don't have to take any flack from him."

"Right."

There didn't seem to be anything to add, so Cassie climbed down off her perch and brushed the seat of her pants. "Have you seen Rob?"

George nodded and pointed from the ranch's hub to a spot by the edge of the creek some distance away.

Cassie glanced in that direction and spied her son. Rob was seated on the ground with his back propped against the trunk of a huge cottonwood, and he seemed to be... reading!

A flash of irritation swept through her, though she was careful to conceal it from her foreman. How could Rob laze away his time reading when there was so much work that always needed to be done? "Thanks," she muttered. "I'll talk to you later." She walked off toward the creek, oblivious to George's knowing look.

Rob was so engrossed in whatever he was reading that he didn't see his mother until she was almost upon him. Glancing up, he smiled. "Hi, Mom."

"Good morning." Squatting on her haunches, Cassie smiled back. "What are you reading that's so interesting?"

Rob's face twisted into an exaggerated grimace. "Chemistry."

"Chemistry? You mean, you're studying?"

"Yeah."

"But school just let out for the summer."

"I'm boning up for next year."

"Whatever for? As I recall, senior year will be a piece of cake. English Lit, a few electives, and that's about it."

Rob shook his head. "I signed up for the honors program, and it's going to be a killer—a full schedule, mostly math and science."

At this, Cassie sat on the ground and crossed her legs, staring at her son thoughtfully. "This is news to me. Why haven't I heard anything about it before now?"

"Oh... I don't know. A couple of weeks before school ended, the principal called some of us juniors into his office—the ones who had finished in the top twenty percent of the class—and he told us about this program. I just signed up, that's all."

"For heaven's sake, Rob, you're not trying for a scholarship to Harvard or anything like that. Your grades have been superlative. The registrar at Sul Ross will swoon with delight over them. I should think you would want to rest on your laurels a little. I thought you might take it easy next year, maybe get involved in some fun things for a change."

"Baseball and track and the student council pretty well take up my free time, Mom." He averted his eyes when he spoke.

Seeing this, Cassie was troubled, and she pondered the best way to say what needed to be said. It was true that he was something of a leader at school, and he was good at sports. He was too small for football, but he excelled at track. Yet it had often seemed to Cassie that he pursued those things more from a sense of duty than from any real passion. His only real passion seemed to be his studies.

She didn't want to be guilty of minimizing the importance of school, but she thought Rob carried the whole scholarly thing too far. His only hobby was building those intricate model airplanes he loved so, and the girls he chose to date were usually chums he'd known since grade school. He'd never even pestered her for a car. True, there were many vehicles on the ranch, so he always had something to drive, but what young boy with a driver's license didn't long for his own car? She knew there was nothing wrong with any of that—plenty of parents would have envied her—but it didn't add up to Cassie's notion of what an ordinary teenager should be. It was as though his heart and mind were focused on something far removed from his immediate surroundings.

Of course, he was only sixteen, she reminded herself, but such a serious sixteen. She began carefully. "You know, dear, your grandfather and I are enormously proud of your grades. We can't begin to imagine where all those brains came from... But there are a lot of things about running a ranch that you can't get out of a textbook or in a schoolroom."

"Shoot, Mom, I know that."

"You can learn an awful lot from the men who work here. George, for instance. There's very little about the DO he doesn't know." Cassie eagerly searched her son's face for some sign of response, some indication that she was getting through to him. Rob's impassive expression, however, told her nothing, so she pressed on. "I'd like you to get more involved in the ranching business this summer. It's time."

Way past time, she thought to herself. *Why, when I was his age, I dogged the heels of any cowboy who'd let me tag along, asking a question a minute. What a horrible pest I must have been, but I was the boss's daughter, so they had to put up with me.*

She would have given anything if Rob would show even half that much enthusiasm and interest in what, after all, was his heritage. She reached out and brushed at an unruly lock of his hair, noticing that the older he got, the more he looked like Robert. "You know, dear, to run the DO you only have to be medium brilliant."

Rob attempted a smile, but it was a weak effort. With a barely audible sigh, he reluctantly closed his book. "Okay, Mom, you've made your point."

"A couple of men are working a pair of new horses in the corral. Maybe you'd like to go up there and watch them."

Rob shoved himself to his feet and handed the text-book to his mother. "Sure. Will you take this up to the house for me?"

"Of course. I'll put it in your room."

Rob took a step away, stopped and turned around. "I almost forgot to tell you Laurie called while you were gone. Said she'd be over this way after lunch and would stop by."

"Thanks, dear."

"See you later." The boy ambled away, hands in pockets, head down.

He was going to be taller and more athletically built than Robert was, Cassie observed, but in every other respect he was the living image of him. She stared after her son's retreating figure, and her shoulders slumped dejectedly. Once again she had forced him into something that she wished he'd do because he wanted to. She knew that given his choice, Rob probably would spend the summer with his books and model planes, taking only an occasional trip into Fort Davis or Alpine to relieve the monotony. She remembered how much Robert had loved books and solitary pursuits.

Rob was so much like his father. Was that what bothered her? Robert had turned out to be an excellent rancher, but it hadn't been the sum total of his being. Ranching hadn't been in his blood the way it was in hers. Robert had dreamed of adventure, and he had talked constantly about the faraway places they would visit someday. Cassie's own dreams never took her very far from the DO.

Absently she opened the textbook and thumbed through a few pages. It might as well have been written in a foreign language, but even she could see that its contents were pretty advanced stuff. She could think of a dozen more useful things Rob could have been studying. She just didn't understand him, not at all.

Closing the book, Cassie jumped to her feet and shook her head. She had wasted most of the morning on Scott Maitland as it was, and here she sat, wasting even more of the day on all this introspection. That wasn't like her. Striding purposefully toward the house, she conveniently decided she was worrying for no good reason. There was nothing wrong with being a loner; every cowboy she'd ever known had been one. Rob was young, but he was going to do just fine. He would do what was expected of him, just the way she had. He would do it because he was a Ferenbach.

THE GENTLE LIGHT in Laurie Tyler's eyes could not mask her fatigue. It seemed to Cassie that her friend looked tired most of the time, and that wasn't right. Laurie was a good four, maybe five years her junior, but her cares and responsibilities were ten times greater than any Cassie had ever known. *No wonder she's worn out,* Cassie thought compassionately. *If I had her worries...*

The two women were seated on the front porch, sipping iced tea. They had been friends a long time, partly because for years they had been the only female members of the ranchers' association, but chiefly because their personalities seemed to mesh. "It's so good to see you, Laurie. You look wonderful," Cassie said and meant it. Despite her obvious fatigue,

Laurie looked great. She'd always had a way with hair and makeup that Cassie envied.

Laurie uttered a small laugh and brushed at a stray lock of blond hair. "Don't lie to me, Cassie. I look terrible, and you know it, but thanks for the nice words. It's good to see you, too. I keep meaning to get over here, but it's been one thing after another now that the kids are home most of the time."

"The kids" were her much younger brother and sister, Andy and Jill. Laurie had been in sole charge of them ever since the automobile accident that had killed their parents ten years ago. On top of that, she had cared for their ailing grandfather for years before his death. Although she had inherited her parents' small ranch, she hadn't been able to give it much attention. Duty had demanded she work at a salaried job, so she had been teaching in Alpine since her parents' death. It couldn't have been easy, but somehow she had managed to hold everything together. Now Andy was a recent Sul Ross graduate, and Jill had just finished her second year. Cassie knew no one she admired more than Laurie. Never once had she heard the woman complain or bemoan her fate. She could only hope that her friend was beginning to see the light at the end of the tunnel.

"Well," she said brightly, "tell me what's going on in your life. How are the kids?"

"Fine. Andy just got word that he's been accepted by a firm in San Antonio. He'll be leaving next week."

"Oh, Laurie, that's wonderful!"

"Isn't it? When he was sixteen I wondered what in the world was going to become of him, but somehow he turned out all right."

"Somehow, my fanny!" Cassie scoffed. "You're the reason he turned out all right. And Jill?"

Laurie rolled her eyes dramatically. "She's in love."

"Well, she's about the right age."

"Unfortunately, the young man in question is having to spend the summer working for his father in Midland. A lovesick nineteen-year-old moping around the house isn't my idea of a stimulating companion."

Cassie smiled. "I guess not. Do you know the young man?"

Laurie shook her head. "I've never met him, but I've heard plenty about him. He'll graduate next year, so that just might be the end of this great romance, if it lasts that long. What first love does?"

Mine did, Cassie thought soberly, but she imagined her friend was alluding to her own first love. At the time of her parents' accident, Laurie had been a pretty, vivacious young teacher, engaged to a young man who taught at Sul Ross. The marriage had never taken place, however. The man left to take a teaching position somewhere in California, and the engagement had been quietly terminated a few months later. Cassie assumed he hadn't been interested in taking on a wife who came equipped with two teenaged siblings and an aged grandfather, though she had never known what actually happened. That was one thing she and Laurie hadn't discussed.

"Are you going to school this summer?" she asked.

"No, I'm about schooled out," Laurie said with a sigh. "I'm not even sure I want that master's degree."

"But you've devoted so many summers to it."

"I know, and I know I'll never be able to teach at college level without it, but once Jill graduates, I might quit teaching altogether."

"And work the ranch?"

Laurie's brows knitted. "The thought's appealing, but the place has been neglected so long. I'm sure I'd never be able to get it going again by myself. I once harbored the hope that Andy might take to ranching, but he quickly dashed it. I never pressured him, because if there's one thing I've learned it's that you either like the life or you hate it. There doesn't seem to be an in-between."

Cassie thought of Rob, and an uneasy inner stirring began. "You really have a nice piece of property, Laurie. It just needs some attention."

"Maybe, but a realtor told me that property values around here have skyrocketed in the past few years. I almost fell down when she told me what that old ranch of mine is worth. Almost two hundred dollars an acre! It has something to do with all the new people moving in."

"Yes, I know," Cassie said with a sniff. That was another sore point. Thanks to Scott Maitland and others like him, land values had quadrupled during the past decade, and that made selling out all too attractive to a lot of small ranchers.

"Speaking of new people," Laurie said with sudden interest, "I saw your neighbor in town, yesterday. He's a real hunk."

Cassie laughed. "Yeah, a hunk of trouble. Mr. Maitland certainly makes an impression on the ladies, I'll give him that. Where'd you meet him?"

"At Annie's Cafe. He was holding court and had quite an audience. He has some rather unusual ideas about the way a ranch should be run."

"To say the least. I can't believe anyone was actually listening to him."

"Oh, not only listening but interested. Someone...I think it was Harry Johnson...suggested Maitland ought to run for president of the association next year."

"God forbid! Not that I think he'd actually be elected. For one thing, I don't expect Maitland to still be here next year." Cassie frowned thoughtfully. "Two hundred an acre?"

"That's what the realtor said."

"Laurie, you're not seriously thinking about selling, are you?"

"I don't know. If someone's crazy enough to pay me two hundred an acre, I'd be even crazier if I didn't sell."

Cassie couldn't have been more dismayed. "Lord, how it depresses me to hear you talk like that."

"Well, I have to be practical. What I own isn't anything like the DO."

And though Cassie didn't like Laurie's reasoning, she guessed she understood it. "Would you leave?"

"I'm not sure," Laurie said thoughtfully. "Once Jill's gone, I can't think of a thing that would tie me to this place, and two hundred dollars an acre sure would give me a nice head start somewhere else."

At that moment George rounded the corner of the house. Seeing the two women, the foreman did a doubletake, than gave the brim of his hat a little tug, which was as close as he ever came to actually removing it. "Well, good afternoon, ladies."

Cassie nodded in acknowledgement. Laurie's eyes brightened considerably. "Hello, George. I haven't seen you in a spell."

"Hi, Laurie. You're looking good."

"Thanks."

"Comin' to the barbecue on the Fourth?"

"I wouldn't miss it."

George grinned. "Good. See you then." Another tug on the brim, and he continued on.

"Damn," Laurie muttered under her breath. "Why do I always look like the wrath of God whenever I see him?"

Cassie shifted in her chair slightly in order to look at Laurie. For some time now she'd suspected that her friend was more than a little interested in her foreman, and she'd gently teased Laurie about it once or twice. She turned her head to watch George as he strode away from them. He was an unusually attractive man in a quiet, rugged way. Cassie particularly admired the way he exuded an aura of being his own man. He had strength of character and was imbued with old-fashioned ideals. He also could make men want to work for him. Those were the qualities that made him such a good foreman. And, naturally, they would appeal to a woman, too.

Now there was a way to tie Laurie to the highlands, but good, Cassie thought. If only obtuse George would notice and do something about it, but he was so shy around women. Truly a man of few words. She couldn't imagine him coming on strong to a woman or even engaging in a little lighthearted flirting. If Laurie wanted to get a romance going with the foreman, she would have to make the first move, and somehow

Cassie couldn't see gentle, gracious Laurie doing anything of the sort.

Maybe I'll *think of something,* she thought impishly.

THE WEEKS PASSED UNEVENTFULLY, and spring drifted into summer. Cassie noticed that activity over at the Horseshoe had increased dramatically. A steady procession of trucks came and went, and she had seen Scott's plane take off and land several times, but there were no more incidents involving her neighbor. In fact, the few times she had seen him were from a distance, although she heard plenty about him. The newcomer from Fort Worth had become the chief topic of local gossip. Some, usually old-timers, thought him peculiar; others, usually female, thought him handsome and "interesting." But no matter what their feelings about him were, everyone talked about Scott Maitland. Cassie had learned, among other things, that he wasn't married, but she didn't know if he was widowed or divorced or had never married. She disliked being even the slightest bit curious about Scott's love life. The man meant nothing to her.

She'd also heard that his grandfather was a living legend, the product of the great East Texas oil boom of the 1930s, one of those overnight millionaires who abound in Texas folklore. Learning that prompted her to wonder why a man with Scott's background had wanted a broken-down highlands ranch. If he was so crazy about growing grass, he probably could have afforded the choicest piece of land on the market. And again, she wondered why she wondered. Since all she really wanted was for him to get fed up and leave, she couldn't understand why she seemed to listen so intently whenever the conversation was about Scott.

When Cassie wasn't busy with other things, she was preoccupied with plans for the DO's annual Fourth of July barbecue. The event was another long-standing tradition, begun back at the turn of the century. Now as then, it was unquestionably the social highlight of the year. People came from miles around to attend it, and everyone on the ranch got involved in one way or another. Much to her delight, Rob seemed to be making a concerted effort to spend more time with the hired hands, learning ropes he should have learned years ago. Cassie, in turn, made a point of staying out of the way so that her son could make the inevitable mistakes away from her watchful eye. She trusted George to give her a full report on Rob's progress, but so far the foreman had said nothing. She just hoped that no news was good news.

It was the final week in June before she again had to deal with the reality of Scott Maitland. She was seated at her desk one morning, reading the market reports, when George stomped into the room, his eyes blazing fury.

"George, what on earth . . ."

"Now Maitland's gone and padlocked his west gate! I thought you said we were free to use it."

"That was my understanding."

"From the looks of things, he's getting ready to plow up that pasture, too. That'll cut us off from the top country completely."

"I know." Cassie slammed the reports on her desk. She was so furious her temples pounded. It did no good to remind herself that Maitland had the right to do whatever he wished with his own property. In her

world, a man's word was better than money in the
bank. He had broken faith, and that was unforgiva-
ble. He hadn't even had the basic decency to warn
them that the gate would be locked, something she
certainly would have done had their situations been
reversed. Apparently there was no way of getting
along with the man, so she wasn't going to try.

"George, tell the men to start carrying hacksaws
with their gear. I'm honor bound to stay away from
the south gate, but if any of the other gates have locks
on them, saw them off."

George grinned. This was more like it! "Yes,
ma'am, boss. Anything you say." And he hurried out
to pass the word along. The men were going to get a
hell of a charge out of this!

CHAPTER THREE

CASSIE FULLY EXPECTED the first sawed-off lock to bring on another confrontation with her neighbor, and she wasn't disappointed. Three days after issuing the order to George, she glanced up from her desk to find Scott standing in the doorway, arms akimbo.

"Well, good morning," she said crisply. "What can I do for you?"

She was braced for a burst of outrage, but to her surprise, the hint of a smile touched his lips, and he wagged an admonishing finger. "Dirty pool, Cassie," he said in his soft drawl.

With deliberation, she closed the ledger she had been working on, folded her arms across it and fastened her eyes directly on his. "On the contrary. Locking the west gate is my idea of 'dirty pool.'"

"Would you believe it if I told you I didn't have a thing to do with that gate being locked?"

"Frankly, no."

Scott glanced around to make sure they were alone. "May I come in?"

"Oh…of course. Please come in and have a seat."

He strode into the room and sat down in the worn leather chair that faced the desk. Even though she considered Scott a full-blown irritant, Cassie was taken by the way he looked. He wore a starched white shirt and snug-fitting jeans. The leather belt at his waist had an enormous silver Texas Sesquicentennial buckle. He propped his right foot on his left knee, then took off his Stetson and set it on his lap. She noticed that there were no sweat stains on the hat, no scuffs on the boots. He wore his clothes with ease, but no one on earth would have taken him for a cowboy. He was too crisp and clean. His hands alone, with their square, manicured nails, were a dead giveaway that here was a city-clicker, or perhaps a gentleman farmer. Accustomed to the casual untidiness of the men who worked on the ranch, Cassie couldn't help admiring his neatness. She felt that appalling inner stirring again. He was a good-looking man.

Scott creased the crown of his hat with a thumb and forefinger. "Well, it's true. One of the men who works for me has been locking it without my knowledge. He figured since the south gate was locked, the west should be. It won't happen again."

Cassie was doubtful. "Good, but George tells me it seems as though you'll soon be plowing up that pasture, too."

"If and when I do, I'll give you fair warning. That's the neighborly thing to do."

"I agree."

"And it would have been far more neighborly of you to have asked me about the locked gate before instructing your men to take matters into their own hands. I assume it was you who gave the orders."

"Yes, but it never occurred to me that one of your gates would be locked without your knowledge."

"Do you know everything that happens on the DO?"

"Of course, that's my job. George gives me a full report every day. When things start happening that you aren't aware of, Mr. Maitland, you have problems."

Scott's eyes narrowed slightly. *It's still Mr. Maitland. Damn, doesn't she ever relax?* He wondered if she ever went all soft and pliant and behaved like a woman. She had been a wife and become a mother, so she must have loosened up a time or two. For some reason, the thought of a loosened-up Cassie was unbelievably exciting. It amazed him that this woman was the first one in years who had aroused his interest. She wasn't the least like Becky or any of the women who had been important to him before his late wife. Maybe Cassie was simply a challenge. A few discreet questions here and there had revealed that she hadn't been seriously involved with a man since her husband's death, but Scott hadn't learned much about Robert Tate. *Quiet* was the adjective most often used to describe him. If she liked quiet men, he could hang it up. *Quiet* was the last word that had ever been used to describe a Maitland, male or female.

For weeks Scott had thought of dozens of excuses for coming over to the DO, but none of them had been very plausible. He'd been tickled to death when his hired hand told him about the sawed-off lock. It gave him a legitimate reason to seek out Cassie. So here he was; now what did he do?

"I'll keep a closer watch on things from now on," he said. "The man who locked the gate just had my interests at heart, but like I said, it won't happen again."

"Thanks." Cassie noticed that he had begun gazing around her office. Her eyes followed his, and she tried to see the familiar room as a stranger would. It wasn't impressive, to say the least, just a plain, utilitarian room that some ancestor had designated the office. The chairs were worn, the desk old and badly battered. No one had ever bothered putting a rug on the hardwood floor or curtains at the windows. The Ferenbachs never had been ones for spending money on frills. Walls were painted when they absolutely had to be; furniture was replaced when it wore out. Then she remembered Scott's office, its tasteful, dignified elegance. This must look like a tenement to him, she thought.

"How are things going over at the Horseshoe?" she inquired politely since he'd made no move to leave. "Have you been able to hire any men?"

"A few, not many."

Cassie nodded in understanding. "Good cowboys aren't standing on every corner, but I know a few who've applied for work here. Maybe I could send them to you."

"I'm not looking to hire cowboys. I want fellows who can run a plow and dig irrigation ditches and mend fences. And I need someone to look after one very special animal."

"Special?"

"Uh-hmm. I just bought my first bull."

"Oh? From a local breeder?"

"No, I went to a fellow I know near Fort Worth. The bull's name is Trendsetter, and I expect him to be just that. I've got to admit, though, I never thought I'd live to see the day when I'd pay half a million dollars for a bull."

Cassie's eyes widened. She searched his face for some sign of teasing, but there was none. He was completely serious. Raising a hand to her forehead, she shook her head in disbelief. She was willing to pay what she considered a princely sum for a good bull to upgrade the herd, but by "princely sum" she meant maybe seven or eight thousand. Half a million? It was ludicrous! "Mr. Maitland, there's—"

"Scott, please. We're neighbors. I hate it when you call me Mr. Maitland."

"All right, Scott. And in the interest of being neighborly I feel I must tell you that no one can raise cattle and show a profit by spending half a million for a bull. For one thing, that kind of money makes him too valuable. What good is an animal that's too valuable to turn out to pasture?"

"Oh, I never intended letting Trendy out to pasture."

"That means you have to bring the cows to him."

"I don't think I'll let him near many cows, either," Scott said, his eyes twinkling. "He might hurt himself or the cows. I plan to sell his semen rights."

Cassie's face grew very warm. She had been in the cattle business all her life and normally thought no more about discussing livestock breeding than she did commenting on the weather, but for some reason it was different with this man. She simply wouldn't feel comfortable discussing semen rights with Scott Maitland.

"I see," she said distractedly. "Artificial insemination. When the practice became so widespread we tried it for a few seasons, but the real cowboys didn't like it, and I never could see that it was all that profitable for us. So we went back to the tried and true ways of bulls and cows in the pasture. Frankly, we like it better."

As her discomfort became apparent to him, Scott's grin broadened. "Well, you probably weren't going about it right. I have an excellent manual on the subject, if you'd like to borrow it."

Cassie flushed deeper. He had a surplus of nerve. She had forgotten more about raising cattle than he'd ever learned. "No, thanks. I wasn't aware that there were different methods of going about it."

"I figure on taking a lesson from the oil business. Say you've got a well you want to drill, and say it's going to cost...oh, several hundred thousand dollars, and say you don't want to spend but a quarter of that. You get fifteen or twenty investors who could use a tax write-off and won't be hurt if you come up dry, and they put up the rest of the money in exchange for a percentage of the well..."

Cassie interrupted impatiently. "You can't run a ranch the way you run an oil business. The two aren't remotely related."

"I disagree. Good business practices are good business practices, no matter what you're doing."

"You're wrong. In ranching you have to put your faith in experience, in what's worked over the long haul. If you don't, you're doomed to failure."

Scott admired her missionary zeal, even if he thought it was misplaced. But he had acquired some zeal of his own. "I think I told you that I expect to be extremely successful, and I intend getting that way by using my methods."

"Then I'm afraid you're going to be sadly disappointed." Cassie sat back in her chair. A wild thought had come to her from out of the blue. It was totally absurd, but too delightful to let pass. "Why not let me do you a big favor, one that'll save you a bunch of trouble, money and...er, face?"

"What's that?"

"Sell me the Horseshoe."

Scott smiled. "The asking price would have to be considerably more than it went for in February. I've made a lot of improvements."

Cassie smiled back. "That's a matter of opinion, but I'm willing to meet any reasonable price."

"You want it that bad, huh?"

"I want it, yes. I admitted that to you."

He seemed to be seriously considering it. A new surge of hope swept through Cassie, one that was destined to be short-lived. "Why, I couldn't do that, Cassie. Then I'd never know if I'm right or not."

"I'm telling you, these newfangled methods of yours don't have a chance," she snapped more harshly than she intended. That, however, only broadened Scott's grin.

"I know what you think, that I'm just a rich man's son with a new toy, but that doesn't bother me. I've dealt with that kind of thinking before. I'm telling you that I couldn't be more serious about what I'm doing, and my inherent business sense demands that I make a profit. I looked at a lot of property before I bought Horseshoe Ranch, so I really don't want to sell it. But I might consider something else."

"Something else?"

"Are you a wagering woman? Do you ever take a chance on anything?"

An odd inflection in his voice suggested that the question wasn't prompted solely by this conversation. "Surely you're kidding. I take a chance on the weather every year."

"Then I'm going to propose a little bet, a very good deal for you."

She looked at him warily. "What is it?"

"I'm going to bet you that the Horseshoe's year-end profit will be—" Scott paused to give it some thought "—will be at least twice as much as the DO's."

At that, Cassie laughed heartily, and Scott realized it was the first time he'd heard her laugh. It was a delightful sound.

"Oh, I'm tempted to take you up on that," she said, "but I'd be taking advantage of you. A first-year operation make more than the DO? There's no way that can happen. You don't even own a herd!"

"I'm fully aware of what I do and don't own."

Cassie shook her head. "I'm sorry. It just wouldn't be fair to you."

"Hey, I'm the guy who came up with the terms, remember? If you're so sure I'll lose, you ought to jump at the bet."

"Okay, so you lose. What do I win?"

"I'll sell you the Horseshoe."

A second of silence passed. Cassie's heartbeat quickened, but her voice remained steady as she said, "Mmm. Interesting. Tempting. And in the improbable event I lose?"

"I want to hear you say I was right, that my methods work."

The silence lasted longer this time. Cassie's mind raced wildly. It was a ridiculous proposition. Surely there was a zinger in there somewhere; she just couldn't see it right off. Then she remembered his background. He had grown up in a business known for its gamblers. She had heard of flashy oilmen who settled million-dollar deals with a flip of the coin. "That's it?"

"That's it." Once again his fingers began creasing the crown of his hat.

"A rather one-sided bet, wouldn't you say?"

"Not really. You want the Horseshoe, and I want to hear you say that my methods work. Sounds like a good bet to me."

Cassie tried to think of all the loopholes, and a couple of things occurred to her. The first was money. He might plan on asking such an outrageous sum for the property that she couldn't possibly afford it. "What about the Horseshoe's price tag?"

"Fair market value. I'll even let you get the appraisal, and I don't care if your best friend is in real estate."

"And your year-end profit will come solely from the ranch, right? No salting it with oil money or anything like that?"

"I'll present you with the tidiest little set of books you ever saw, all verified by my accountant. Or your accountant, if that's the way you want it. Every dollar I spend on the ranch and every dollar I make off it. Nothing else."

"You're serious about this?" she asked, still disbelieving.

"Completely."

Cassie didn't think the bet was a fair one, at least not to Scott, and she did have some scruples. But, after all, he was the one who'd proposed it. She couldn't see what she had to lose. A chance to buy the Horseshoe versus having to eat a little crow. And how ironic if the land that was lost as the result of a bet should be regained as the result of a bet. It was just too good to pass up. Straightening, she slid her right arm across the desk and held out her hand. "It's a bet," she said.

Grinning, Scott leaned forward and clasped her hand warmly. "Want anything in writing?"

"No. I'd rather have a handshake from a friend than a contract from a lawyer."

"Are we friends?" His voice was almost seductive.

"We'd better be. I don't bet with my enemies."

For a moment their eyes locked. Scott's danced merrily, then sobered and began roaming over her face, as though trying to memorize its features. He did not release her hand. If anything he clasped it more tightly.

Again Cassie was assaulted by all those crazy responses that flustered her so. She tried to study him with clinical detachment and found it impossible. He **was simply** too fascinating, too attractive, too sensuous. **Was that** come-hither air an act or was it real? She didn't think she'd ever met a man who could fill up a room so effectively. She quickly withdrew her hand from his and sat back in her chair.

Scott got to his feet, stifling his disappointment. For a brief heady moment he had felt the fragile beginnings of...what? Rapport, detente? But something about him sure set her on edge. Getting to know Cassie was going to be no easy feat. "Guess I'll be going now. Once again, I apologize for the gate. Tell your men they can put away their hacksaws."

"Done."

"And you feel free to stop by the Horseshoe anytime, just to keep an eye on what's going on, you know."

"I trust you. Will you be coming to our barbecue on the Fourth?"

"Wouldn't miss it for the world. Hear it's quite a bash. Be seein' you, Cassie."

"Goodbye."

He had reached the door when she detained him with a word. "Scott?"

He turned. "Yes?"

"I'd like to ask you something, if I may. You can tell me it's none of my business."

"Ask away."

"Why ranching?"

He frowned. "I don't understand."

"Why did you, of all people, take up ranching, of all things?"

"Me of all people?"

"Who you are, where you come from, the way you dress, everything. It doesn't add up."

Scott thought about that. Was she saying she liked the way he dressed? Had she inquired about his background, or had someone told her and she'd remembered? Either way, he was curiously pleased. "Oh...I was just looking for something to do." He smiled again and, hat in hand, left the room.

Something to do, Cassie thought with a shake of her head. *Must be nice to be able to buy a ranch just because you need something to do.* She heard the front door open and close, then the sound of tires crunching along the gravel path that led down to the main road. Just something to do.

Well, she guessed he wasn't all that bad. Really kind of nice, in fact. It was difficult not to like a man whose eyes twinkled the way Scott's did. They might never reach a meeting of the minds, but she was glad there had been a thaw in their private cold war. It was always nicer to get along with one's neighbors.

Rubbing the nape of her neck, Cassie smiled secretively. She was going to get the Horseshoe back, she just knew it! She'd better start figuring that into this year's equation. It would mean a big outlay of money, but it would be worth it. And when the transfer of ownership finally took place, the first thing she was going to do was tear down those damned fences.

She was still seated at her desk, deep in thought, when J.B. walked into the room. "Was that Scott Maitland I just saw driving away?"

"Yes."

"What did he want?"

Cassie decided not to say anything about the bet, even though her dad would probably get a kick out of it. It would be just between her and Scott, and she was pretty sure he wouldn't mention it to anybody. "Another locked gate episode, but it's been taken care of." Propping her elbows on the desk, she clasped her hands and rested her chin on them while making a critical survey of the office. "You know, Dad, it's been ages since we've done anything to this house. It's beginning to get a little shabby."

J.B. looked at her in surprise, then glanced around in the manner of someone who had never seen the room before. "Looks okay to me. What brought this on?"

Cassie shrugged. "Oh...nothing in particular. Just seems like it's time to do some sprucing up."

"Do whatever you want, hon. Just don't spruce it up so much that it's not comfortable to live in." With that, he turned on his heel and left the room.

Cassie remained seated for a few more minutes, then absently stood and wandered out into the hall, across the foyer and into the living room. It was a big room with a stone fireplace and well-worn upholstered furniture that invited sitting. Odd tables, lamps, throw pillows and knick-knacks followed no distinct decor-

ating scheme. On the mantel were family photographs in assorted frames—her parents, Rob at
various stages from infancy on, Cassie and Robert on
their wedding day. The room was a study in imperfec-
tion, full of scuffs, scratches, wear and tear, but
somehow everything came together to exude a welcoming comfort.

To hell with it, Cassie thought. The room was fine
the way it was. It was home, a place where a million
memories lingered. She realized it was Scott's quietly
elegant surroundings that had prompted this, and she
wasn't going to try to keep up with the Joneses. Turning, she crossed to the front door and went outside.

CHAPTER FOUR

PREPARATIONS FOR THE DO's annual barbecue began weeks in advance when a steer was chosen for slaughter, and on the morning of the festivities, everyone on the ranch was up with the sun. Even as she dressed before going in to breakfast, Cassie could hear the commotion in the side yard as the hired hands went about their chores, setting up long tables and erecting an enormous tent. The beef had been put in stone-lined pits the night before, and already the smell of mesquite smoke permeated the entire area. The ranch house kitchen was a beehive of activity. A few of the cowboys were married, and their wives always turned out to make huge pots of beans and tubs of every kind of salad imaginable. Cora, the Ferenbachs' cook, had been baking bread for two days. And everyone hoped that for this one day of the year the cattle could take care of themselves. No one wanted to miss the party.

Laurie was the first arrival. After greeting J.B., she went to Cassie's room. Tapping on the door, she opened it and found her friend seated at her dressing table, wrapped in a robe and drying her hair.

"Hi," Cassie said, "come on in. I'm running a little late. God, you look terrific!" Laurie did look wonderful. She was wearing a fringed denim skirt, crisp white shirt and designer boots.

"Do you like the skirt? I bought it especially for the occasion."

It never occurred to Cassie to wear anything but jeans to the barbecue, but seeing Laurie's stunning outfit made her have second thoughts. She turned off the blow-dryer and fluffed her hair with her fingers. "Maybe I can rummage around in my closet and come up with something besides jeans for a change."

"Let me help you." Laurie crossed the room and went into Cassie's walk-in closet. She knew Cassie was no clothes horse, but what she did buy was usually the best. Laurie browsed through the long rack of jeans, slacks and blouses, then thumbed through a small collection of dresses. Nothing struck her fancy until she spied a white Mexican-style dress with bright embroidery at the neck and hem hanging in a clear plastic bag. "This!" she announced triumphantly. "This will be perfect."

"Do you really think so?"

"I know so."

"Dad bought that for me when he was in Monterrey last year. I've never had it on."

"Wear it today. It will be smashing on you. In fact, just put yourself in my hands. I'm going to make up your eyes. They're so beautiful, Cassie. You really should play them up more."

Cassie shrugged. "I never know what to do. A little liner, a touch of mascara and that's about it."

"Well, I'm going to fix you up."

"Don't make me look like a painted doll. I'll feel silly."

"Stop worrying."

Laurie supervised the entire operation, and when Cassie, from force of habit, began twisting her hair into a chignon, Laurie shook her head. "Don't do that. Wear it down. It's great."

"Are you sure?"

"Of course I'm sure. Trust me. Better still, trust yourself. Look in the mirror."

Cassie had to admit that she looked pretty good. Different, at least. "Maybe I ought to let you give me some lessons. You're always so well put together. I don't think you're going to have any trouble making George notice you today."

Laurie scoffed. "Short of setting myself on fire, I can't think of anything I could do that would make George notice me. I wonder what it is with cowboys, anyway. They all act like they're scared of women."

"Oh, they aren't all like that. Just most of them. And it's not women they're afraid of as what we represent."

"Oh? What do we represent?"

"Settling down, houses, families. That seems to scare the bejeebers out of the kind of men who choose to be cowboys. Yet, most of them eventually settle down." Turning, Cassie spoke to her friend earnestly. "And George will, too, someday. It's up to you to make him sit up and take notice."

Laurie seemed doubtful. "If only he weren't so shy. Getting him to talk is like pulling teeth. Once George says, 'Hello, Laurie, nice to see you,' he goes mute."

"Instinct will guide you."

"I'll feel silly."

"Better to feel silly than to be ignored."

"Since when did you get so knowledgeable where men are concerned?" Laurie teased.

"Ah, some things we're just born knowing." Cassie took a final look at the stranger in the mirror, then stood and walked to the window. A steady procession of vehicles was approaching the ranch from the main road. "The party's about to start. Let's go outside and have ourselves a wonderful time. Remember, take the initiative. You do look marvelous, Laurie. George would have to be blind not to notice you today."

"Or just plain disinterested."

SCOTT WAITED until a sizable crowd had gathered at the DO before putting in an appearance. He still was enough of a newcomer in the area to cause a bit of a stir wherever he went, and today he hoped he could simply fade into the background. He had one reason and one reason only for attending the barbecue: it was a chance to see Cassie again.

Not wanting to add to the parking problem, he walked to the DO, climbing the low fence by the river and scrambling up the short rise. To his relief, no one noticed his arrival. He had heard that the DO's annual barbecue was a popular event, but he hadn't expected anything like the mob scene he encountered. Several minutes passed before he saw even one familiar face, and that was J.B.'s. But Cassie's father was surrounded by people, so Scott merely roamed about, stopping when necessary to acknowledge a smile or a greeting.

Not surprisingly the largest group of guests was clustered near the kitchen door where a long table was serving as the bar. He wandered by, accepted a cold beer someone offered him, scooped up a handful of salted peanuts and began milling through the throng, ever watchful for the sight of his hostess. When he finally caught a glimpse of her, he stopped dead in his tracks, and his heart did a little dance.

She was chatting with a group of people, none of whom Scott knew. Propping a shoulder against a tree trunk, he sipped the beer and watched her. Suddenly Cassie threw back her head and laughed, pushing back an errant strand of hair at the same time. He'd never seen her with her hair down, and it was spectacular. Why on earth did she ever wear it up? He'd never seen her in a dress, either. His gaze wandered to the garment's hem and to the shapely tanned legs beneath. As he'd often suspected, Cassie could be a stunning woman when she cared to put forth some effort.

Scott waited until she excused herself to move on to another group of guests. Pushing himself away from the tree, he stepped forward into her path. "Good afternoon."

Cassie turned at the sound of his voice, aware of an abrupt acceleration of her heartbeat. He looked almost sinfully handsome. What was there about him that made him stand out from the crowd so? He wore pressed jeans and a Western shirt, and that enormous silver belt buckle gleamed at his waist. His hat—white today—was tilted back on his head slightly. The clothes weren't noticeably different from those worn by virtually every man at the gathering, but Scott managed to look like a page out of *Gentlemen's Quarterly* in them. She had wondered if he actually would come and was surprised to realize she was happy he had. She had thought about him a lot since the day of their bet, probably too much, but she couldn't say that all the thoughts had been entirely unwelcome. "Well, hello, neighbor," she said. "Glad you could make it."

"From what I've heard, an invitation to the DO's barbecue isn't to be taken lightly."

"We always manage to have a good turnout. Summer's pretty slow on a ranch, so by the Fourth everyone's looking for some activity, I guess."

He smiled at her openly and a little playfully, the picture of lazy, unstudied charm. At some time in his past, Cassie thought, Scott Maitland probably had been an outrageous flirt. Maybe he still was. She felt herself flushing under his warm regard. It was amazing that the man who could irritate her to the edge of madness could also make her feel as giddy and gauche as a teenager. She silently blessed Laurie for insisting she dress up for a change.

"There are plenty of snacks," she said unnecessarily, gesturing toward a table that was a groaning board of tidbits, "but no real food until the barbecue later."

"It doesn't appear as though anyone will go hungry."

"And there'll be dancing tonight. The band's coming from San Angelo."

"I'm not much of a dancer."

"Neither am I. Don't get enough practice. The band is mainly for the young people. How are things over at the Horseshoe?"

"Oh, everything's coming along just dandy."

"That's good. Now, I really must go speak to everyone here, so if you'll excuse me..."

"Sure. See you later."

Scott watched her walk away, noting in particular the movement of her hips beneath the soft white fabric, and his appreciative eyes remained fastened on her until he felt someone standing beside him and heard a voice saying, "Hi, Mr. Maitland."

Turning, he found himself looking at Cassie's son. "Well, hi."

"I'm Rob Tate."

"I know."

"And you're the man with the airplane."

Scott smiled. "I guess I am."

"How long you been flying?" Rob asked with interest.

"Over half my life. Since I was seventeen."

"Really? Neat! I'd give about a million dollars for a ride."

Scott laughed. "Well, I guess a ride could be arranged, but I wouldn't charge you near that much."

Rob's eyes widened, and he looked at Scott eagerly. "Are you serious? I mean, would you really take me up sometime?"

"Sure, love to. And instead of a million dollars, all I'd ask for is your mother's permission."

The bright, expectant smile on Rob's face faded slightly. "Why do you have to have that?"

"How old are you, Rob?"

"Sixteen."

"That's why I have to have that."

"Shoot! She'll just say no."

"How can you be so sure?"

Rob kicked at the ground with the toe of his boot. "'Cause Mom just says no to almost everything, at least at first."

"Yeah, well . . . moms are kinda bad about that, I guess, but you ask her anyway, and I'll see if I can't do a little arm-twisting myself."

Some of the boy's enthusiasm returned. "Would you? Okay, I'll ask her just as soon as I can get her off by herself. You won't forget?"

"Nope. I can see you're a real airplane buff."

"I'd rather learn to fly than eat!" Rob exclaimed.

"I know the feeling. I was about your age when the bug hit me. There was an airstrip not far from my grandfather's house in those days, and I used to hang around it, listening to the pilots talk and scrounging rides with anyone who would take me up. Back then people weren't as concerned with lawsuits as they are now, but when my grandmother found out about it..." Scott whistled. "I'll bet those guys still cringe when they think about the reaming out they got from that sweet little old lady. So we don't go up until your mom okays it, understand?"

"Yes, sir. Thanks a lot. I'll talk to you later."

ONCE CASSIE WAS SATISFIED that she had personally spoken to everyone present, she wandered off to the side where she could keep a watchful eye on the festivities, although a party like this one almost took care of itself. There were plenty of people preparing the food, J.B. kept the bar stocked, and the guests entertained each other.

Everyone seemed to be having a good time, even Scott, whom she'd been watching out of the corner of her eye all afternoon. He had talked to Rob for a while—about what Cassie couldn't imagine—then moved on to converse at length with the man who was president of the Cattlemen's Association. Mostly he seemed to have spent the afternoon surrounded by women, chiefly Petra Canfield. Petra, the daughter of an area rancher, was the High Country's resident femme fatale—curvaceous, blond, beautiful and young...maybe mid-twenties. She was a happy-go-lucky, vivacious woman, and since she had three older brothers to worry about the family enterprise, she went through life unhampered by the sense of duty and responsibility that had always dominated Cassie's life. At the moment Petra seemed to have become permanently attached to Scott's left hip, and he didn't appear to find the new appendage unwelcome in the least. Looking at them, Cassie felt a curious flutter in the pit of her stomach, brought on by envy or jealousy or a mixture of both.

The feeling was so unpleasant that she forced her attention elsewhere. Scanning the crowd, she caught sight of Laurie. Standing next to her, where he had been most of the afternoon, was George Whittaker. That brought a smile to Cassie's face. But even as she watched her friend and her foreman, a cowboy approached George, the two exchanged a few words, then George turned briefly to Laurie. She nodded in understanding, and the foreman touched the brim of his hat and walked away with the other man. Cassie threaded her way through the crowd until she reached Laurie.

"You two have been awfully chummy this afternoon," she whispered. "What did you talk about...or is it none of my business, I hope."

Laurie laughed derisively. "Can you imagine George saying anything that couldn't be quoted on the front page of the paper tomorrow? The man kills you with politeness."

"You mean, you've talked to him all this time, and nothing out of the ordinary happened?"

"Oh, he managed to string together some sentences. For instance, I learned he grew up on a farm in Oklahoma, and he has a sister who has twin girls. And he got me a beer a couple of times. But then a man showed up who wanted to ask him about some horses, and George went off with him. With a noticeable lack of regret, it seemed to me. Does that sound like the beginning of a wild, tempestuous love affair?"

Cassie wrinkled her nose. "At least he talked to you. At least he knows you're around. That's a beginning."

"I don't know, Cassie. George might be a hopeless case. I honestly can picture him sailing through life, blissfully alone except for his horse and a bunch of cows."

So could Cassie, but she wasn't about to tell Laurie that. "Don't give up."

"Oh, I probably won't give up, but I don't intend wasting a lot of time on him, either." Laurie smiled and patted her friend's arm. "See you around. There are a lot of people here I want to talk to."

"Sure. I'll see you, Laurie."

AN HOUR LATER the band had arrived in a huge bus, and its members immediately got busy setting up their sound equipment on the makeshift stage located near the front porch. There was a lot of hustle and bustle around the long tables under the tent as the buffet was set up. The aroma from the barbecue pit whet appetites, and the guests began drifting to the tent in anticipation of being fed. Scott was beginning to tire of Petra Canfield's company, so he felt enormously relieved when they were joined by a young man named Gary. It quickly became apparent that Gary intended fastening himself to Petra as thoroughly as she had attached herself to Scott. Mumbling something about seeing a man he wanted to speak to, Scott happily left the two young people to entertain each other. Thus free, he went in search of Cassie. When he found her, she looked at him with a frown.

"Rob tells me you offered to take him up in your plane."

Scott nodded. "Just a short spin around the local area. Are you going to let him go?"

"I ... don't think so."

"Why not?"

"Those things scare me," she said simply.

"They don't scare Rob."

"Meaning I'm not the one going up?"

"No, no, I didn't mean that. Look, I've been flying almost twenty years, and I've never had a mishap, never a close call. I'm no daredevil, I assure you. Rob really wants to go."

"I know," she said, more to herself than to him.

Scott then realized that it was Rob's wanting to go more than the actual act of flying that bothered Cassie. He touched her arm. "Kids have to get these things out of their systems sooner or later. If he's that crazy about airplanes, it's only a matter of time before someone takes him up. I promise—no one's a safer pilot than I am. I'm strapped in that machine, too, and I've grown fond of me."

Cassie wavered. He was soothingly persistent, self-confident, and somehow he managed to instill some of that confidence in her. "Well, I ... I guess it would be all right once, just around the local area. You don't do acrobatics or anything like that, do you?"

"Lord, no! I use that plane the way it was meant to be used—to get me from point A to point B as fast as possible whenever I want to go. Rob will be just fine."

Cassie studied him; Scott studied her. Then he grinned at her amiably, and she laughed. "Okay. Tell him I said it's okay."

"Come up with us. You'll love it."

"Wanna bet?" she asked.

"We've done that, remember?"

"So we have." The bet seemed foolish now, foolish and unimportant. The DO had survived without the Horseshoe for all these years. There was no question in Cassie's mind that she would win the silly wager, but...did she really want Scott to leave? The question sneaked up on her unawares. Whatever else she might say about Scott Maitland, he was an attractive man who definitely had added interest to the local scene.

Again they studied each other. It was Scott who broke the silence. "Do you have a dinner partner?"

Cassie shook her head. "No."

"Neither do I."

"Oh? It seemed as though you did."

It took him a couple of seconds to understand. "You mean Petra?"

"Uh-hmm."

So, she'd noticed, Scott thought with a pleasant jolt. That was encouraging. "Nope, she went sailing off with some young guy named Gary."

"Sorry."

"I'm not. Petra's a little young for me. Will you sit with me during dinner?"

"I usually just graze and keep an eye on things."

"Then I'll graze with you and help you keep an eye on things."

"All right, if you like."

The brass dinner bell at the back door began clanging like mad, and the stampede was on. A few stragglers still hung around the bar, but most of the guests made a beeline for the food. The amount served that day was staggering, and although chickens and Ger-

man sausages had also been barbecued, the beef was
the star attraction—dark, smoky and very spicy.

Scott stayed close to Cassie as she mixed and min-
gled, and when all the guests had settled down to the
serious business of eating, they got some food for
themselves. Scott looked out over the sea of heads
bent over dinner plates. "I don't see any vacant
places," he commented.

"Neither do I," Cassie said. "We really have a
crowd, don't we? And we won't enjoy all this good
food if we try to eat it standing up." She glanced
around, then gestured for Scott to follow her. "Come
with me. There's a table and some chairs on the back
porch. I don't think I'll be missed."

The table was a round metal one, and there were
some folding chairs propped against the house. Scott
opened two and set them at the table, just far enough
apart to give them elbow room. The porch was dimly
lit and quiet, far away from the cacophony of the
party. "Is this all right?" Cassie asked.

"Perfect," Scott said and held her chair until she
was seated. Then he sat down and tackled his own
plate. He thought he'd never eaten food that tasted so
good, but food always tasted good when eaten outdoors, even better when there was a lovely woman to
share it with. And she was lovely, a lady right down to
her fingertips in spite of living and working in a man's
world. Her hands were slender and graceful, the kind
of hands that looked as though they'd never done
anything more strenuous than play the piano.

They talked about inconsequential things—the
food, the weather, the party—while Scott longed to
talk about her. It wasn't until they had pushed their

plates to the center of the table that he began gently plying her with questions.

"How old are you, Cassie?"

"Thirty-eight."

Scott thought of Rob's age. "You married young."

"Yes, right out of college."

"What was your husband like?"

The question took Cassie by surprise. "Robert? Well, he . . ." Robert was not an easy man to describe. Not that he hadn't been a wonderful individual—he had—but only those closest to him ever thought about him much, chiefly because he'd never done anything to call attention to himself. No heads had ever turned when Robert had walked into a room. Although he had been attractive, it had been in a quiet, unspectacular way. Certainly he'd had none of Scott's polish or lazy charm or incredible good looks. Rather, he had been the kind of man people usually refer to as "the salt of the earth." He had been the best friend Cassie ever had, but dynamic he wasn't. "He was quiet, sensitive, a very caring man. Robert was . . . easy to like." She bit her lip. The description didn't seem to do her husband's memory justice. "Rob looks more like him every day, and he has an awful lot of Robert in him," she added, hoping that would give Scott a clearer picture of her late husband.

"Was he a cattleman?"

"He turned into one, but, no, he'd never been around cattle. When I met him he could barely ride a horse. He was an orphan, raised by an aunt who was a seamstress, so ranch life was entirely new to him. He loved it here. Robert had never had much family, and even though ours wasn't a large one, I'd always been surrounded by a sense of family. He would have loved to have a huge brood, but it wasn't meant to be. After Rob was born I had two miscarriages, then ran into a spate of 'female problems.' It all ended in surgery."

"What about you?" Scott asked. "Would you have liked a big family?"

Cassie's face brightened for a moment, then saddened. "I think I would have, but..." The impossibility of ever having another child was something she didn't like to talk about. "I guess you'd like to ask about Robert, what happened to him."

"Only if you feel like telling me."

Absently she drew circles on the table with her thumbnail. "It was a long time ago. Rob was only seven. Robert took winter watch in the top pasture. He liked to do that sometimes, just get away by himself. Only that time...one of the wild bulls that occasionally finds its way up there...killed him."

Scott gulped. "Good Lord, Cassie!"

"I think Robert must have been caught sleeping. He was too good an outdoorsman, too good a shot for there to be any other explanation."

"You've been alone a long time," Scott said quietly.

"I'm not really alone. I have my family, my son. I think my husband's death would have been much harder on me if I hadn't had Rob. And, too, he ensures the next generation of Ferenbachs here on the ranch."

Scott wondered if a child would have eased his own grief when Becky died, given him some sense of purpose. "I lost my wife in an accident, too—automobile—so I sympathize with you completely."

Cassie looked at him. So he had been married. "I'm sorry," she said softly. "It's a terrible thing to go through. Was it very long ago?"

"Five years. Her name was Rebecca. We met in high school but went our separate ways when college came along. It wasn't until many years later that we ran into each other again, began dating and eventually married."

"No children?"

"No. We were waiting... for God knows what." Waiting for Becky to decide she was ready for motherhood, he thought, though he'd often suspected that happy day might never have arrived. Becky had been so headstrong and fun-loving, not the hearth-and-home type at all. She had loved parties and people, dressing up and staying out until the wee hours. She had been one of those people who actually seem to gain strength and vitality as the evening wears on. The thought of motherhood had frightened her, Scott often thought, and he'd gotten impatient. They had argued about it a lot just before the sports car she'd driven like a bat out of hell jumped the center median on an expressway and hit another car head-on.

Cassie tried to think of a way to lighten the somber mood without seeming abrupt. "Have you always lived in Fort Worth?"

Scott didn't recall ever telling her where he was from. Someone else must have. He imagined he had been gossiped about a lot when he first arrived, and Cassie knew everyone for miles. "Oh, yes, always. Born and raised there, as was my sister and my dad and my mother."

"Tell me about your family," she probed.

He smiled at the question, chiefly because it was a surprise. He was accustomed to people knowing all about his family. That wouldn't be true out here in the High Country where the oil business had made no impact whatsoever, which was just one more reason the area appealed to him so. It was nice not being simply Theo Maitland's grandson for a change.

"In my family it's automatically assumed that the offspring will do whatever those who've gone before did, no questions asked."

"One hears a lot about your grandfather, but what about your parents?"

Scott frowned slightly. He was so used to his family situation that he never gave it much thought, but an outsider might find it strange. "I never was around my parents much. They've lived in Italy for years. Originally they went there to oversee Maitland Oil's Mediterranean operation, but they stayed because . . . because they liked the international scene."

"I'm surprised you and your sister weren't with them."

"Granddad wanted Judy and me to be raised in Fort Worth, for which I am eternally grateful."

Though Cassie found this unduly odd, she was careful to conceal that reaction from Scott. "Did that ever bother you?"

"No," he said truthfully, "because that's just the way it was. I never thought about it much."

"Is your sister in the family business?"

"Judy runs a home and raises children, but her husband's in the business. I can't imagine what Granddad would have said if she'd married a man who wanted to do his own thing. It was enough that he had me to handle."

"I don't understand. You've certainly followed in his footsteps."

"To a point. But I was the first Maitland who didn't go to Texas Christian. I went to A&M and studied land management. That really threw everyone. But then I got married and fell right into line. So you see, the Maitlands aren't so different from the legendary Ferenbachs."

Cassie smiled. "Had you ever heard of us before you came out here?"

"No."

"Some legend. Tell me, how does Horseshoe Ranch fit in with the family enterprise?"

"It doesn't. It's something I'm doing on my own."

"How does your grandfather feel about that?" She hoped she wasn't prying too deeply, but she truly was interested.

"Right now I guess he just figures it's something that keeps me out of pool halls and beer joints. There's not a whole lot of activity in the oil business right now."

"But later? Things are bound to pick up."

Scott shrugged. "I guess I'll worry about it later."

The same answer she would have given in his situation. People like Scott—like us, she amended—never said, "To hell with the family; I'm doing my own thing." Cassie thought it amazing that their backgrounds and family situations were so alike. Could it actually be that they, by some mysterious means, were becoming friends? A week ago she had considered him nothing but a full-blown irritant, and now she felt as though they were on their first date.

Scott, too, was struck by the similarities. "What about the future?" he asked quietly.

"Future? Rob's the future."

"That's it?"

"Of course."

She said it with an everybody-knows-that tone in her voice. And, Scott knew, that was a mistake. Kids had an uncanny knack for disappointing parents who expected too much. Cassie needed something else to base her hopes and dreams on. He decided that the "something" was a man. He further decided that he wouldn't mind being that man. Tonight had been a good beginning, much better than he would have dared hope. He was no novice with women, and he could tell she wasn't indifferent to him. She might even be more interested than she herself was yet aware of.

The band broke into their first number; the sound of the music drifted around to the back porch, drawing Cassie's attention to the big tent. Guests were stumbling out to revive themselves in the evening air. She was surprisingly reluctant to rejoin the party. Absurdly, she wished she could forget the other guests and spend the rest of the evening just getting to know Scott better. But she couldn't, and that was that. "I guess it's time to get back to my guests."

"Too bad," Scott said.

There didn't seem to be anything Cassie could say to that, so she just smiled.

"Thanks for having dinner with me. I enjoyed the food, but the company most of all."

"So did I. I'll see you later, Scott."

"Sure."

Scott waited until she had left the porch and disappeared around the side of the house before getting up and walking to the steps. Hooking his arm around a wooden pillar, he was content to stand and watch the crowd. The sun was only now low in the western sky, which meant the party probably wouldn't break up for hours. It also meant he probably wouldn't be alone with Cassie again. Scott debated just wandering home. At least the ice had been broken. He would try to arrange for their next meeting to be under less crowded circumstances.

At that moment he spied Rob strolling across the grounds. Stepping off the porch he called to the boy and headed in his direction. "I spoke to your mom."

Rob cocked his head inquisitively.

"She said okay."

The boy's mouth dropped in disbelief. "Are you serious?"

"Uh-hmm."

"Man, you are some kinda miracle worker! When can we go? Tomorrow?"

"I guess so. One o'clock or thereabouts?"

"I'll be there. Sure do thank you, Mr. Maitland."

"You're welcome. And call me Scott."

"You bet, Scott. Oh, wow! Wait'll I tell Burt Spencer. He's gonna turn pea green. I'll see you tomorrow."

Scott folded his arms across his chest, smiling as the boy hurried away at little less than a dead run. Ah, the enthusiasm of youth, he thought, then turned to survey the scene. The majority of the guests had congregated near the front porch where the dancing was taking place, but he didn't see Cassie. Glancing at his watch, he decided he had had enough of the festivities. He thought he'd like to go on home and read awhile before bedtime. He had a busy day coming up, over and above taking Rob for a spin. He'd never been much of one for staying up until all hours, not even when he was much younger, and since acquiring the Horseshoe, he'd discovered the homebody side of him had become more pronounced than ever.

Searching in vain for his hostess, he had to settle for J.B. instead. He thanked the man for his hospitality and asked him to convey the message to Cassie. Then he ambled on down the grassy rise to the post-and-rail fence that separated this part of the DO from his place. Stepping over it, he walked home in the dark, completely satisfied with the way things had progressed so far. Regardless of how Cassie felt about Rob's interest in his plane, Scott considered it a plus. Getting close to Cassie had become number one on his list of priorities, and Rob might be a good place to start.

CHAPTER FIVE

THE LAST OF THE GUESTS departed shortly before midnight. Cassie and J.B. stood on the front porch, watching until the last pair of taillights had disappeared from sight. "Good party, as usual," J.B. commented. "Record turnout I'd say."

Cassie nodded. "I can't think of anyone who didn't show."

"Even our new neighbor. I didn't get a chance to talk to Maitland much. Did you?"

"A little bit," she said evasively.

"By the way, he asked me to thank you for the nice time."

"Oh? When was this?"

"Pretty early. Seems to me it was about the time the dancing started up. He must not be much of a night owl."

Well, I'll be, Cassie thought, trying to stifle her disappointment. She'd wondered why she hadn't seen him again. Maybe she'd only imagined his appreciative looks, his interest. She would have sworn she had made some sort of impression on him, but maybe she'd been wrong. She'd honestly expected him to ask her to dance, not just steal away into the night without so much as a goodbye.

She followed her father inside the house, then closed and locked the door. All the way to her room she chided herself for her foolishness. She and Scott had engaged in conversation and exchanged a few smiles, but that hardly added up to avid interest on his part. She couldn't imagine why his early departure disappointed her, why she was giving it another thought. That was terribly untypical of her. Still, it had been such a long time since she'd talked to a man she didn't know very well, and Scott was easily likable.

That was the main problem, she decided. He'd been easier to deal with when he irritated her. Going into her bedroom, she flipped on the light switch and closed the door behind her. After turning down the bed, she undressed, went into her bathroom to wash her face and brush her teeth, then sat at her dressing table to begin what constituted her nightly beauty routine. As she uncapped a jar of cream, her eyes fell on the picture of Robert that had been sitting in the same spot for all these years.

The photograph had been taken six months before his death. She kept it close by because she never wanted to forget exactly how he looked. It was so easy for an image to dim with the passage of time. For many, many months after his death she had talked to that photograph every night before bedtime simply because he was the only person she'd ever had who she could really talk to. Setting down the jar of cream, she studied Robert's face intently, trying to recapture in her mind some of the closeness they once had shared. But it was useless. His image only smiled back at her vacantly, while the most curious thought formed in her head: *I wonder what Robert would think of Scott.*

Then, uttering a sound of self-derision, she picked up the jar and began slathering her face with cream. Scott again! He was as different from Robert as day from night, the last person on earth she should be interested in. But then, perhaps that was precisely the reason he fascinated her. Compared to the other men she had known and worked with, Scott bordered on the exotic. And to be completely honest, he probably had interested her even when he had irritated her, even when she hadn't taken him seriously.

Tonight he had seemed so different from her initial conception of him. Tonight he had been genuine, warm, and that made him even more intriguing. Still, it would do her well to remember who he was, where he'd come from and—most important of all—where he would go back to once his fling with ranching was over.

EVEN THOUGH EVERYONE SLEPT later than usual the next morning, Rob thought one o'clock would never come. He stayed as far away from his mother as possible for fear she might change her mind any minute and call off the sojourn with Scott. Once lunch was over, he made a beeline for the riverbank, where he wiled away the time, glancing at his watch every five minutes. Finally, at fifteen minutes until one, he hopped the fence and walked to Scott's house.

The boy couldn't remember ever being in the Horseshoe's main house, though he'd had a nodding acquaintance with the previous owners. It was like a palace compared to the worn comfort of his own house. "Neat place you have here, Mr. Ma...er, Scott," he said as he was ushered inside.

"Thanks. You're prompt."

"Shoot, I've been waiting on the riverbank for over half an hour."

"Why?"

"I didn't want to be a nuisance."

"You wouldn't have been. You should have come over." Scott smiled at the expression of eager anticipation on Rob's face. "I guess you're ready."

"Yes, sir!"

"Then let's go. We've got ourselves a nice clear day. But I'm warning you—it might be a little bumpy."

"I won't mind."

The prefab building that housed Scott's plane stood at the end of the runway he'd had constructed before he'd actually moved to the ranch. Rob was almost as impressed with the ribbon of concrete as he was with the sleek twin-engine aircraft. "Wow, how long is it?"

"Three thousand feet."

"Guess it cost a lot."

"Quite a bit, but I had to have it."

"Why don't you just keep the plane at an airport?"

"I like having it handy. It goes to the airstrip for gas and routine maintenance, and I take it to a fellow in Fort Worth for its annual, but when I want to go somewhere, I want to go right now." Scott unlocked the right-hand door and opened it. "Up you go. It'll be less noisy if you wear the headphones. Then we can talk to each other."

Rob could hardly contain his excitement. He watched every move Scott made and asked dozens of questions. "How fast does it go?"

"Depends on the direction you're headed and the wind. True airspeed is two-hundred-twenty. If you've got a twenty-mile-an-hour headwind, you'll do two hundred. If there's a twenty-mile-an-hour tailwind..."

"You'll do two-hundred forty."

"Right."

"How high will it go?"

"Well, it can go to seventeen thousand, but you wouldn't fly that high because the cabin isn't pressurized."

"How high are we now?"

Scott pointed to the altimeter. "See for yourself."

"Nine thousand?"

"Uh-hmm. That's above sea level. Some of the peaks around here are over seven thousand feet."

Scott had an air map of the entire area. Once they were airborne he spread it out and gave it to Rob, pinpointing their location. A lot of people never got the hang of reading an air map, but Rob had no trouble at all. "There's Alpine and Fort Davis and... Gosh, look at the observatory from up here!"

"Now I'm going to give you a bird's eye view of the DO. We'll fly over the house so you can get your bearings."

Rob was enthralled. "You think it's so big, but it doesn't look like a heckuva lot from up here. There's a bunch of stragglers in the top pasture. Wonder if George knows about 'em. The guys will spend days trying to find them, and you can see them plain as day from up here."

They flew around the area for perhaps half an hour before Scott turned back toward the Horseshoe and began his descent. The boy hated to see the flight end, but he was smart enough to know that Scott was burning a lot of gas giving him the joyride. When the plane had landed and was taxiing toward the little hangar, Scott reached across the passenger seat and flipped open the window, then his own. Rob removed his headset and sighed. "Sure was fun, Scott. Thanks."

"Don't mention it. I enjoyed it, too."

A minute or so later they were walking toward the house. "It'd be so neat if we had a plane on the DO."

"Maybe you will one day."

"Not there, not ever, not as long as Mom and Granddad are running the show. Shoot, it's only been since I was born that they started using Jeeps and trucks out in the pastures. It's just horses, horses and more horses, 'cause that's the way it's always been done."

"Your mom and your granddad won't always be in charge," Scott reminded him. "When it's time for you to take over the DO, you can suddenly decide the ranch needs a plane."

Rob shoved his hands in his pockets and said nothing for a moment. Then he looked up at Scott, squinting in the bright sunlight. "If I tell you something, can I trust you not to tell my mom?"

"Sure, Rob. I wouldn't betray a confidence. Come on inside. We'll get something cold to drink and have us a talk."

In the kitchen Scott removed two cans of root beer from the refrigerator, and he and Rob sat on the stools at the work island. "What's on your mind?" he asked with interest.

"This afternoon was great, really great, and I sure do thank you for taking me up, but ... That's not the kind of flying I want to do."

"Oh?"

"I've applied for admission to the Air Force Academy. Last February. That's the way you have to do it, after January 31st of your junior year. And I've written to my congressman requesting an appointment. I want to go on to flight training. I mean, it's fun to go up and tool around in one of these little machines, but I want to really fly. Be a fighter pilot. You know, the whole *Top Gun* thing.''

Scott's breath escaped in a low whistle. "And, of course, your mom doesn't know anything about it.''

Rob shook his head. "She'd have a fit. She knows I'm nuts about airplanes, but she thinks it's just kid stuff, something I'll get over. She's wrong! This is what I've been thinking about for years and years.''

Scott smiled. When one was sixteen, "years and years'' probably meant two, three at the most. "And if that appointment came through, you'd really leave the DO?''

"So fast you wouldn't see anything but heels and elbows!''

"I wonder. Dreams and reality have a way of colliding. Do you think that when push came to shove, you actually could turn your back on what you have here?''

Rob's gaze faltered, but only for a second. "I'd have to, wouldn't I?''

"That might be easier to say than to actually do.''

Impatient with negative thinking, the boy leaned forward and spoke earnestly. "I've been working toward this a long time. Track, for instance. Being good at sports helps 'cause you have to be in great physical shape. And being on the Student Council and class president. All those things count. It's not only grades. I'm not worried about those. I'll probably be valedictorian next year.''

Scott couldn't help being impressed by the boy's sincerity and willingness to lay the groundwork. "Sounds as though you've prepared yourself well."

"Yeah." Rob's face clouded. "But I haven't prepared Mom."

"You ought to, and soon. If you're really determined to pursue this, she'll have to know."

Rob averted his eyes. "I'd rather wait until something's actually happened."

"What you mean is, you want to wait until things have gone so far there won't be anything she can do about it, right?"

"That's about the size of it."

Scott frowned thoughtfully. "I wouldn't if I were you, Rob."

"I . . . uh, don't suppose you know her well enough to sort of pave the way for me."

"Hardly. I'm not sure I'd do it even if I did."

"Why not?"

"Letting someone else do your dirty work for you doesn't sound like an officer and a gentleman to me."

Rob sighed. Adults could be so sensible. That's why dealing with them was so frustrating. "Okay. I'll tell her just as soon as I . . . get the chance."

"Promise?"

"Yeah, I promise. And thanks again for the ride. It was neat."

"We'll do it again soon."

"That'd be great."

"You'd better get on home and let your mom see you're all in one piece."

When Rob had left, Scott reflected on the irony of it all. There were legions of young boys Rob's age who would have envied him his life, who considered cowboying as romantic as playing professional ball or piloting a spacecraft. Yet, to Rob, it was commonplace and uninteresting. Therefore, he'd never be any good at it. He only hoped Cassie would come around one of these days, for her sake as well as Rob's. No one could turn a person into something he or she wasn't.

Then he thought of his grandfather. Theo would have a fit if he knew how important Horseshoe Ranch had become to his grandson. So Scott could sympathize with Rob far more than the boy realized. He was not looking forward to the day when he would have to tell Theo that he didn't want to return to Fort Worth permanently, that he'd found something else. To his grandfather it would be heresy, open rebellion, a slap in the face. Forget that buying and operating a High Country ranch would hardly qualify as rebellion in the minds of most people. Scott wouldn't be dealing with most people. He'd be dealing with Theo Maitland, and to Theo, the future wasn't left up to choice.

And Cassie had so much of that mind-set in her. He shook his head in wonder. How strange that he was drawn to a woman who was like his grandfather, of all people!

CASSIE HAD PROMISED herself she wouldn't anxiously scan the sky looking for Scott's plane while he was taking Rob for a ride. She would just go about her business and try to forget where her son was and what he was doing. It didn't work. She found herself encamped at a spot where she had an unrestricted view of the runway, watching in fear as the seemingly flimsy machine took off, circled the immediate area, then disappeared over the hills. The sickening revolutions in her stomach didn't subside until the plane landed safely some twenty-five minutes later. Only then could she return to the house and wait for her son to come home and give her a breathless account of the afternoon's adventure.

She fervently wished that the "spin" in Scott's plane would satisfy Rob's curiosity and interest, but she suspected it would only whet both, and she was right. For days afterward the boy talked about little else but aviation in general and Scott Maitland in particular.

"He's really a nice guy, Mom. You'd never know he's from one of the richest families in the state. He just seems so... ordinary."

Ordinary? That wasn't a word Cassie would have associated with Scott, not under any circumstances. "Well, he isn't," she heard herself saying. "And he's not one of us, either."

"Huh?"

"Chances are good he'll be gone from here before long, back to his... real life. The Horseshoe's just something for him to play around with." She said that as much for her own benefit as for Rob's.

"Must be nice, huh?"

"I guess so."

"That's a keen plane he has. I think a new one like it costs over a hundred thousand dollars."

Cassie frowned. "How do you know that?"

"I know a lot about planes and flying," Rob admitted. "Scott says he'll take me up again. Maybe even give me a lesson or two."

"Why on earth would you want to learn to fly one of those silly things? I don't see any sense in wasting time like that. If you look around, I'm sure you'll find plenty that needs to be done here."

But, Rob was quick to note, his mother hadn't forbidden him to take Scott up on the offer, so he dropped the subject quickly before she had time to think and do just that. Cassie went on about her business, and he went to his room.

He knew Scott was right; he had to tell his mother he was doing everything he could to get an appointment to the academy. He also knew that when he did, holy hell was going to break loose. Naturally, his grandfather would get in on it. Rob shuddered at the thought. The one soul on earth who could intimidate him down to his toes was J.B. Ferenbach. His grandfather could strike more fear into him with a stony glance over the rim of his reading glasses than someone else could have with a bullwhip.

It was funny, Rob thought. His mother and grandfather were always talking about family, heritage, destiny and things like that. The ancestor who had moved to Texas from Ohio was a superhero in their eyes, but Rob had often wondered what that man's family had thought of the move. After all, the High Country in those days had been the last outpost of civilization, just a way station on the Butterfield Stage Line, and the Commanches hadn't entirely been routed yet. But the man had come anyway. Rob guessed that the same hankering for adventure was in his blood, too—a regressive gene or something.

But just try telling his mother that his genes were responsible for his wanting a different challenge. There wasn't much chance that the courage to confront Cassie was going to appear out of the blue, so Rob figured it would be easier if she found out on her own. He took all the literature he had collected regarding the academy and spread it out on the desk in his room. His mother would find it sooner or later, and when she asked him about it, he would tell her. That was the best he could do.

CASSIE DISCOVERED the literature the following morning when she carried some freshly laundered clothes to Rob's room. She always experienced a vague feeling of uneasiness when she entered that room, as if she somehow had stumbled into a stranger's house. Instead of the blue ribbons from state fairs and rodeos that had adorned her own teenage haven, the walls of Rob's room were hung with pictures of airplanes and some autographed photographs of astronauts he had acquired on a school trip to the Johnson Space Center in Houston. On his desk sat several trophies he had won at track meets around the state. And there were two books on his bedside table. One was a well-read copy of Charles Lindbergh's *The Spirit of St. Louis*; the other was Chuck Yaeger's autobiography. Fantasy things, dreams without substance, she told herself, but the uneasiness was there, nevertheless.

She had turned to leave the room when she spied the literature, and once she'd scanned it, she went straight to her son for an explanation. Rob did his best to answer her in an offhanded way. "Oh, some of the guys at school had that stuff, and it sounded interesting, so I wrote off for it. Not only is it a great education, it's free."

"Nothing's free, Rob. If you graduate from a service academy, you have to pay them back with X number of years of your life."

"Even so, I'd still be young, and you'll be around forever."

Cassie just smiled. "I'd like to think so, but maybe, maybe not. I'm glad you're interested in getting a good education, but it'll be best if you get it where the Ferenbach men traditionally do. The DO can't do without you all those years." As far as she was concerned, that was the end of the matter. Blissfully unaware of her son's intentions, she gave no more thought to the conversation.

Rob dropped the subject, too, even though little had been accomplished. He conveniently told himself that he had tried; it wasn't his fault that his mother had brushed the matter aside as being of no importance. If he did happen to get the appointment, went his sixteen-year-old reasoning, Cassie couldn't say she hadn't had warning.

That afternoon, as soon as he could slip away from the DO, Rob hurried over to the Horseshoe, drawn by the desire just to be around Scott, who was to his young mind far more interesting than anyone at the DO.

"You busy?" the boy asked.

"Not too busy to visit. Come on in. I'm packing."

"Packing?"

"I've got to go to Fort Worth for a couple of days. A duty call. My grandmother's slightly unhappy because I haven't been back in a spell. Things are kinda quiet, so I'd best go soothe her feelings."

"Sure wouldn't have thought someone your age would have to worry about things like that," Rob said seriously.

Scott smiled. "You shouldn't ever forget family obligations, Rob. Remember that. Doesn't matter how old you are. Your mom's always going to expect you to come to see her periodically. And speaking of your mom, did you talk to her?''

"Sorta," Rob hedged.

"Now, what does that mean?"

Rob explained. "She just kinda blew it off, you know. She doesn't think I'm serious."

"Then I guess it's up to you to make her see that you are, right?"

"Yeah, I guess so," Rob said grudgingly.

"And while we're on the subject of your mom, I want you to do a favor for me. Tell her I've gone to Fort Worth, will you?"

The boy looked faintly puzzled. "Sure. Why?"

"Just tell her, okay? Tell her I'll get in touch when I get back."

It was a good thing Rob relayed the message when he wandered back to the DO later that afternoon. Otherwise, Cassie would have wondered at Scott's silence. She had thought about him incessantly since the day of the barbecue. While being a little disturbed over Rob's fascination with the man, she found herself daydreaming about Scott in a distressingly romantic way. Still, she thought, there was a world of difference between a woman finding Scott an attractive man and her son adopting him as a role model. "Scott says" had become a permanent part of Rob's conversation, and she knew too well what an ingratiating man he could be. Just what it was she feared she didn't know for sure, but she was overcome by the need to dilute Scott's influence over Rob before it went too far. She firmly believed that all young people needed heroes, but they had to be the right kind. In desperation, Cassie went in search of her foreman.

"George, I want you to do a favor for me."

"Sure, boss, anything. You know that."

"It's about Rob.... I know this is above and beyond the call of duty, and I probably have my nerve even asking it of you, but...I'd like you to keep a tight rein on him. I want him under your wing most of the time. I'm not telling you anything new when I say there are plenty of things he should know that he doesn't. I can't think of anyone better than you to teach him, and I mean that."

George shifted uneasily, wondering what the uncustomary flattery was leading up to, half afraid to find out. "Well, thanks."

"I want you to become...his hero. And...oh, Lord, this is going to sound dumb, but you get extra points if you can manage to do it without Rob's realizing you are...if you get my drift."

The foreman got it. He kept his expression impassive, but he couldn't have been more dismayed. Please, anything but that, he thought. He had spent a lot of time with Rob that summer, and if there was one thing he'd bet a month's pay on, it was that the Ferenbach heir would never make a good rancher, or even a fair-to-middlin' cowboy. The reason was simple: lack of interest.

George would have liked to tell Cassie that. He wanted to tell her that her son danced to a different tune, that she should loosen up and accept the inevitable. He also could have mentioned all the potential disasters that could befall an operation the size of the DO if it was left in the hands of a disinterested and unknowledgeable manager. He sometimes wondered if he was doing Cassie a disservice by not telling her those things.

However, the foreman was guided by a complicated set of principles, chief of which was absolute
loyalty to his boss. He would no more have questioned Cassie's actions or motives than he would cheat
at cards or insult a woman, nor would he presume to
make suggestions unless she asked for them. So what
he actually said was, "Sure, boss, I'll do everything I
can."

CHAPTER SIX

"THANKS FOR STOPPING BY, Cassie," Laurie said as the two women walked out onto the front porch of the Tyler house.

It was a bright, hot afternoon. Cassie slipped on her sunglasses. "You're more than welcome. I enjoyed the coffee and the gossip. I'm sorry I missed Jill. Give her my love."

"I'll do that. I was so thrilled when she wanted to go into town with her friends for a change. She's done nothing but mope around this house all summer. It's about to drive me nuts."

Cassie smiled in sympathy. "I can imagine. How's her long-distance romance doing?"

"Oh, churning along, hot and heavy," Laurie said with a sigh. "I expected it to wither on the vine long before now, but apparently it's more serious than I thought. The young man calls four or five times a week, and they talk for half an hour. I'd hate to be responsible for his phone bills. Oops, be careful of that top step. I've got to get the thing fixed before someone breaks a leg.

That's not all that needs to be fixed, Cassie thought sadly as she got in her pickup and drove away. Laurie's property was in sorry condition, and that was putting it mildly. If ever a place needed a man's strong hands and back it was the Tyler ranch. Not that one man could do a lot, but he would be more help than Laurie had now.

It was a shame, really. The ranch had possibilities, but turning it into a profitable operation would require Laurie's undivided attention and some hired men. Neither was possible as long as her friend had herself and Jill to support, and no one was more aware of the dilemma than Laurie. All during the visit Cassie had sensed the woman's frustration, and it disturbed her. One concrete offer was probably all it would take for Laurie to sell out and start packing her bags. There ought to be something she could do to help her.

Cassie drove the truck onto the main road and headed for home, her thoughts all on her friend's problem. Suddenly it occurred to her that George might be able to give Laurie a hand. The late-summer months were fairly slow on a ranch. The DO wouldn't fold if its foreman spent a couple of days a week at the Tyler ranch, and Cassie knew that George would do anything she asked of him. Of course she also knew that she had probably asked far too much of him already, but she consoled herself with the knowledge that George was amply rewarded. Not in money exactly, but in prestige and the freedom to pursue the life he loved. He wouldn't bat an eye if she asked him to help Laurie.

And he was far, far too naive to suspect there might be an ulterior motive behind the request. George's mind simply wouldn't work that way. A sly smile curved Cassie's mouth. Maybe she could help her friend in more ways than one. George might be shy and standoffish when it came to women, but he was a man and he wasn't blind. Cassie had to assume that his male instincts were in good working order.

Her mind preoccupied with Laurie, she almost didn't see the dilapidated pickup pull out onto the road right in her path. Braking sharply, she uttered a mild curse. "Damned fool! You didn't even look in my direction!" Then she noticed that the truck's bed was piled high with bales of hay. Only then did she see the sign at the side of the road. Hay For Sale. The arrow below pointed directly to Horseshoe Ranch.

Cassie frowned. Hay? Oh, surely that crazy Scott wasn't . . .

But the thought had no more formed than she caught sight of the big tractor lumbering across a distant pasture. She couldn't believe it. Baling hay, much less selling it, was as foreign to the DO's operation as raising exotic animals or hothouse orchids would have been. Was that the sort of thing Scott intended doing with the Horseshoe? She seemed to recall that the terms of the bet had involved the amount of money he would make ranching. As far as she was concerned, baling hay wasn't ranching.

Impulsively, she turned right, driving through the Horseshoe's main gate and up the road to Scott's ranch. He wouldn't be there. To her knowledge he was in Fort Worth, but she wanted to get a better look at this latest innovation of his and maybe question one of the men who worked for him. Of course she knew that whatever Scott chose to do with his property was none of her business. Of course she knew she was overstepping the bounds of neighborliness and probably a few other things, but that hadn't stopped her before, and it didn't stop her now. She couldn't help it; she felt a certain proprietary sense toward the

Horseshoe, even though no Ferenbach had owned it in a century.

Scott was in the outbuilding that served as a workshop when he heard the truck rumbling up the road. Assuming it was someone else coming to purchase hay, he stepped out into the bright sunshine. Recognizing the vehicle, he was aware of a dramatic acceleration in his heartbeat. He hadn't seen Cassie since the night of the barbecue, though he'd thought about her all the time he was in Fort Worth and had telephoned her earlier, only to be told she wasn't at home. Now she was here, looking fresh and energetic, and he marveled at the voltage she generated in him.

Opening the door, Cassie stepped out of the truck, then spotted Scott strolling toward her. She disliked admitting just how good he looked to her. Every time she had seen him before, he'd looked bandbox fresh, but this afternoon he was more untidy. His well-worn shirt and faded jeans followed the contours of his body in an enticing manner, and he sported a hint of a five o'clock shadow. He pulled a handkerchief out of his back pocket and began wiping his hands. The smile on his face was as delightfully mischievous as always. Her first thought was that she'd missed him; then she reminded herself that it was impossible to miss someone you'd seen maybe half a dozen times in your entire life. "I thought you were still in Fort Worth."

Then why was she here, Scott wondered. "Got back just before sundown last night. I called you earlier, but you weren't at home."

"No, I was visiting Laurie Tyler." Cassie closed the door, propped her rump against it and folded her arms. "Scott, what in the devil are you doing?"

He stopped and looked at her, faintly puzzled. "Doing?"

"This hay business."

"Oh, that. The grass is growing like a weed. It had to be cut. I might get two hay crops this year. Maybe three."

"Ranchers don't bale hay."

His grin broadened. "Really?"

"Yes, really. Bailing hay isn't ranching."

"Well, now, Cassie, I figure anything you do on a ranch is ranching." He took a few more steps, coming to a halt within arm's reach of her.

"I thought when we made that bet we were talking about raising livestock, that sort of thing."

"Then perhaps we should have had a contract drawn up after all. I only remember saying that my year-end profit would reflect what I had spent on the ranch and what I had made out of it, nothing else."

Cassie grudgingly had to admit that was exactly what he had said. So she was out of line—again. She gave him a rather sheepish smile.

Scott accepted no further protest as a concession on her part. *Chalk up one for my side,* he thought happily. "Glad you stopped by, even if it was to complain about the way I run my operation. Can I persuade you to join me for a glass of tea? I'm parched."

Cassie knew it was getting late and there probably were half a dozen people at the DO wondering where the devil she was. She didn't care. "Sure," she said. "It is a little on the warm side, isn't it?"

When they stepped through the front door of Scott's house, a welcome rush of cool air greeted them. The place was in absolutely immaculate condition, as though no one actually lived in it. Cassie's head swiveled this way and that as she followed him down the tiled hallway. "You must have help," she commented.

"Help?"

"A housekeeper."

He stood aside and allowed her to precede him into the kitchen. "Yeah, I finally hired one last week. She's a whiz. Comes in twice a week and goes through this place like a whirlwind. It just got to be too much for me. Have a seat, and I'll get that tea."

"How was your trip?"

"Uneventful."

"I guess it was good being back home."

"It was good to see my grandparents, if that's what you mean."

It occurred to Scott that Cassie's unexpected visit was exactly the opportunity he had been looking for, that he'd be a fool not to turn it to his advantage. With that in mind, he poured two tall glasses of iced tea and handed one to Cassie. He took several long swallows of his, then began rummaging around in the refrigerator. "I'm hungry for something really good for dinner. I grew up in a house where dinner was a production. Now I find myself shoving stuff in the microwave. One of the dangers of living alone is getting lazy about meals."

"I guess so," Cassie said idly. "I've never done much cooking. There's always been someone else around to do it." She watched him for a minute. He moved around the kitchen with the same economy of movement that Cora used, like he knew what he was doing. "How come you learned to cook?"

"My wife hated to cook, and I liked to eat."

That made sense. Cassie watched him a few more minutes as he peeled tiny boiling onions. Then he dampened a paper towel and carefully wiped off some giant mushrooms. "What are you fixing?"

"Coq au vin."

"You're kidding. Do you really know how to cook like that?"

"I really know how to cook like that."

"And you go to all that trouble just for yourself?"

"On occasion. As I mentioned, I like to eat."

"Ranchers aren't supposed to like chicken."

"Well, you persist in reminding me that I'm no rancher." Grinning, he dried his hands. "Besides, too much beef is bad for you."

Cassie rolled her eyes in mock horror. "You'd better not let anyone else hear you talk such heresy. You'll be the star attraction at a lynching. Beef is our business."

"Tell you what... If you'll have dinner with me tonight, I promise not to tell anyone what we ate."

The invitation was issued with such casualness that it took Cassie a second or two to realize he actually was asking her to dinner. Her pulse quickened. "I don't see how I can turn that down. I'm dying to find out just how good you are."

He turned to her, the picture of lazy charm. "I'm the best. You'll see."

Cassie was aware of her quick intake of breath, and she smiled. Face it—he's fun, he's exciting, he's sexy. He also might be as phony as a three-dollar bill, but she didn't think so. If he turned out to be a womanizing flirt without a redeeming thought in his head, she was going to be the most surprised and disappointed soul on earth.

"What time are you serving?" she asked.

"Let's make it for seven, okay? Then we'll have time for a drink or two before we eat."

Cassie got to her feet. "I'll see you at seven."

THE AFTERNOON had turned into a scorcher, and the several hundred head of cattle milling and fuming in the pens near the branding chute kicked up clouds of dust as they waited their turn with the hot iron. Rob felt terrible. Cows were stupid animals, dirty and smelly, too. He hated branding, hated it. Usually it was a springtime chore, accomplished when he was in school and could escape it altogether, but these stock cattle had been purchased from a ranch in Kansas and had to be marked with the DO brand. Something about the combination of heat, dust and the smell of singed animal hair made him sick to his stomach. When he was sure no one was watching, he slipped away and found a shady spot under a tree where he sat and tried to get his queasy stomach under control.

His hasty departure did not go entirely unnoticed, however. One of the men handling the irons sidled up to George, who was overseeing the entire operation. "That boy's about as useless as a one-legged man at an ass-kicking contest. Why don't his mama keep him at home and outa the way?"

"His mama is this outfit's boss," George said sharply. "Best not forget that. If you want to go tell her you think her son's worthless, be my guest." And the man, properly chastised, walked away.

George watched Rob for a minute. The boy looked positively green. He gave Rob a few minutes of peace, then ambled over to the tree to squat down beside him. "Nasty work," the foreman commented idly. "I remember my first branding. I had to miss supper that night."

Rob snorted derisively. "Nice try, George."

"I'm not fibbin' to you, Rob. I was so sick I thought I was gonna die."

"Yeah. Well, you got over it, but I never will. I hate cowboying, and of all the jobs around here, I guess I hate branding the most."

"Not everybody likes it."

"I'm trying to figure out why anyone does."

George couldn't suppress a chuckle. "Tell you what, Rob. We're about through here. Why don't you just mosey along?"

Rob cocked a quizzical eye in the man's direction. He hadn't entirely figured out the foreman yet. George seemed like an all right guy, a lot nicer than some of the foremen they'd had, but Rob wasn't sure how much he could trust him. There was no question that George's loyalty to Cassie was fierce, and that made him suspect. "You gonna tell Mom I couldn't hack it?"

"Not on your life, son."

"What about the other guys?"

"None of them speaks to your mom unless she speaks first, and she saves her questions for me. That's protocol."

"Would you ever lie to her?"

George pushed his big hat farther back on his head and grinned. "Never, but I'm not one for saying more than needs to be said, either."

Rob digested that and accepted it. He guessed he could trust George after all. The foreman had been hovering over him like a mother hen all summer—at his mother's urging, he was sure—but apparently

George didn't carry tales. So at least he had one friend on the DO. Jumping to his feet, Rob shot George a grateful smile. "Thanks."

"Don't mention it."

"See you later."

"Sure."

Rob's stomach made a miraculous recovery. He hurried away from the branding area as fast as he could, heading not for the house but for the river-bank and the low fence that separated the DO and the Horseshoe. He had been itching for just this chance all day. The boy knew Scott was back from Fort Worth since Scott had called the house earlier, asking for Cassie. That had been a surprise, since Rob hadn't thought his mother knew Scott very well.

He cleared the fence in a jump, scampered up an embankment, then stopped when he spotted one of the DO's trucks parked in front of Scott's house. He knew for a fact that the only person who was away from the ranch that afternoon was his mother, and she was the last person he wanted to see. Damn, what was she doing at Scott's place? *I just hope it doesn't have anything to do with me,* he thought grimly. He was never completely free of the worry that his mother would somehow put a stop to his friendship with their neighbor. Rob was completely aware that Cassie was less than thrilled over his interest in aviation and his recent friendship with Scott. Resigned, he found a spot where he wouldn't be seen, but which afforded him a clear view of the house, and he impatiently waited for his mother to leave.

She did, finally, and when he was sure she'd had time to reach the main road, Rob continued on, climbed the steps of the rear deck and knocked on the

back door. Scott opened it a second later. He smiled
when he saw the boy. "Hi. Come on in. Help yourself to a Coke."

"Thanks." Rob opened the refrigerator door and
removed a can while Scott resumed his work at the
sink. "When'd you get back?"

"Last night."

"I saw Mom leaving. What did she want?"

"She was just visiting."

"Really? I thought she went over to Laurie Tyler's."

"I think she said she was there earlier, but on her
way home she decided to pay a neighborly call on me."

"Oh?" Rob wasn't sure how he felt about that. He
had an adolescent's inherent distrust of alliances between adults. Besides, he liked having Scott as his
friend. He wasn't too keen about having the man get
chummy with his mother. "What'd you talk about?"

"Cooking."

"Huh?"

"Among other things."

"Like what?"

A knowing smile crossed Scott's face. "Relax, Rob.
We didn't talk about anything that would interest you.
Your mother's a bit unhappy that I'm baling hay, for
one thing."

"Yeah, that sounds like Mom. Granddad, too. You
don't listen to her, I hope."

"I intend to keep right on baling hay, selling it, too,
if that's what you mean."

"Good. Mom and Granddad and everybody else
over at the DO act like it's a crime to do anything that
hasn't been done for a hundred years."

Rob had taken a seat on a stool at the work island. Scott went to sit on another next to him. "So, fill me in on what you've been up to. I haven't seen you in a few days."

"Yeah, but even if you'd been here, I probably wouldn't have seen much of you. Between Mom and George, they can always think of something I should be doing. Course, I don't blame George. I know Mom's sicced him on me. He's really a nice guy."

"Seems to be." Scott wasn't well acquainted with any of the DO cowboys, only enough to exchange greetings if he encountered one of them on the street. He knew they all thought him some kind of flake, but even at that, Whittaker had always been decent to him.

"We spent today branding," Rob went on, grimacing. "I hate it."

"Have you gotten around to talking to your mom about the academy some more?" Scott asked, though he figured he knew the answer was no.

Rob shook his head. "I told you I left all that stuff out where she'd find it. She just doesn't take it seriously."

Scott nodded thoughtfully. "People have a way of seeing what they want to see, hearing what they want to hear. You know, Rob, it's occurred to me that you and I have a lot in common."

"Yeah?"

"Yeah. I've got myself a problem coming up, just like you. Any day now I figure that phone's going to ring, and my granddad's going to tell me to come home for good. In fact, I half expected him to mention it while I was there this time. Trouble is, I want to stay here as badly as you want to leave."

"You like it here?" Rob sounded incredulous.

"Yes, I do."

The boy gave that some thought. "Well, you're not into that 'git along little doggie' business like my family is. You do some neat things around here."

"I have some ideas I want to give a try, but the main reason I like it here so much is because I'm doing something that no one else in my family has ever done. You see, our families are a lot alike. My granddad just assumed I would go into the oil business. I don't ever recall being asked if that's what I wanted to do. But it was fine for a while. I even liked it. Now I've found something else. And I don't think Granddad will accept that any more than your mom accepts what you want to do."

Rob was alive with interest. It was nice to find an adult with family problems. "What are you going to do? When the phone call comes, I mean."

"I'll have to tell Granddad how I feel. Just like you're going to have to tell your mom about your plans."

"I was afraid you were going to say that. I haven't gotten the appointment yet."

"You ought to tell her before you get it." Scott propped his elbow on the counter and looked at his young guest thoughtfully. "I'm glad you stopped by. There's something I want to talk to you about. While I was home I ran into an old high school buddy who graduated from the academy. I told him about you, and he did a little reminiscing. Are you sure you know what you'd be getting into?"

"I . . . think so. Yeah, sure I do."

"It won't be like going to an ordinary college."

"I know that."

"You can't have a car. You can't even wear civilian clothes the first year. Your days are structured from the time you get up in the morning until you go to bed at night."

"I know all that, Scott."

"You have to get used to a bunch of guys who are only a couple of years older than you are, telling you what to do. There aren't any frat parties and beer busts. You study, train and study some more, and the pressure to excel is tremendous."

"What's the matter? Do I look like some kind of wimp to you?"

Scott laughed. "Not at all. I just wondered if you knew it's no romp. And once you get out of the academy, you have to go on to pilot training, which is no picnic."

"Shoot, I'll ace that."

"What if you don't?"

"I will."

Scott had to give the boy credit; he had self-confidence in abundance. "What are you going to do if the appointment doesn't come through?"

"I don't know. Just go to college and..." Rob shrugged. "I don't know, but for sure it won't be cowpunching."

"If you want to fly, you could try the airlines."

"The airlines? Heck, I'd about as soon drive a bus."

Scott reached out and gave the boy's shoulder a companionable pat. "Okay, so I'm convinced you're serious. Now I'll tell you something else my friend mentioned. You stand a better chance of getting an appointment if you apply to all four service academies, instead of just one."

"I know, and I've given some thought to the Navy, because of the flying, but . . . I'm not too crazy about ships and the sea and all that. And, too, I like the idea of Colorado, and . . . Well, I guess I'll just take my chances with the Air Force."

"Okay. So we're back to the beginning. You'd better tell your mom. Sure, it'll be rough. It's never easy to disappoint people, especially parents, but once she gets over the initial shock and realizes how serious you are, she might even help you." It was so easy to give someone else advice, Scott thought.

Rob just looked at him. "You don't know Mom. She gets so choked up about the ranch and the family and all that. If you ask her, she can tell you about every dadblamed Ferenbach all the way back to some guy who left Germany to keep from being hung. Tradition! I've had that pounded in my head ever since I can remember. Mom should have been born about two hundred years ago."

Scott smiled. How nice that she wasn't. And thinking about Cassie reminded him of how much he still had to do before his dinner guest arrived at seven. He got to his feet. "I'm having company for dinner, so I'd better get busy. Just sit there and talk to me while I work."

Rob shook his head and slid off the stool. "Nope. I'd better hightail it home or I'll have more problems than I already do. I don't want anybody to start looking for me. If you want to know the truth, I'm sorta playing hooky. Nobody but George knows that, though, and I don't think he'll tell. Thanks a bunch for the Coke."

"You're welcome. Come back anytime. I enjoy the company."

J.B.'S EYES raked his daughter from head to foot. She
was wearing a coral-and-white-print dress with a lacy
collar that he was sure he'd never seen before, and her
white shoes looked new, too. But, then, Cassie owned
a lot of nice clothes she seldom wore. It was always
something of a shock for J.B. to see her dressed fit to
kill, looking so feminine and pretty, since she did it so
rarely. He sometimes forgot just what an attractive
woman his daughter was. For perhaps the dozenth
time in his life he thought what a shame it was that she
hadn't married again. A waste of womanhood, in his
estimation. But, of course, a solid man like Robert
Tate didn't come along every day of the week, and
Cassie wouldn't have had much truck with a man who
wasn't solid.

"Something going on I don't know about?" he
asked. "What are you all gussied up for?"

"I'm going out to dinner," Cassie said nonchalantly. She was glad her father didn't know how long
she had spent getting ready that night. She, who normally spent maybe five minutes on her makeup and
hair, had taken the lion's share of an hour getting
dressed. And she was certainly glad J.B. didn't know
how nervous she was.

"Oh? Who with?"

"Scott Maitland."

A second or two of silence passed while J.B. thought
about that. "Do tell. Business or pleasure?"

Cassie shrugged. "He invited me, and I accepted.
Seemed like the neighborly thing to do."

"Hmm." Her father pulled on his chin thoughtfully. "I didn't know you knew him that well."

"I don't. Guess this will be a chance to get acquainted."

"He's kind of a weird one. Not much like folks around here."

"Oh, I don't know. He seems nice enough. Just different."

"Where're the two of you going?"

"To his house. He's cooking dinner. He claims to be something of a gourmet, so I'm expecting a real treat."

J.B. just looked at her, thinking that this was the strangest development he could imagine. The last he'd heard, Cassie considered Maitland a first class nuisance and that she wanted him gone. Now she was having dinner at his house, and J.B. didn't think a desire for being neighborly had a thing to do with it. Certainly not on Maitland's part.

He glanced at his daughter again. She was one good-looking woman, and Maitland appeared to be a real man. Not much surprised J.B. when it came to human behavior, but this did. It wasn't only that Cassie was having dinner with Maitland; J.B.'s surprise stemmed mostly from his daughter having dinner with a man to begin with. "Well, have a good time."

"Thanks."

"Reckon you'll be out late?"

Cassie cocked her head and turned to her father quizzically. "I don't have any idea. Why? You thinking about waiting up for me?"

"The thought occurred to me."

Cassie just laughed.

CHAPTER SEVEN

Scott never fussed unduly over a dinner. He was too sure of himself in the kitchen for that. When the doorbell rang at seven o'clock, the coq au vin was in the oven, a salad waited in the refrigerator, the potatoes were ready to cook, and the man of the house sat lounging in an easy chair engrossed in a magazine. Closing it, he got to his feet and went to the door to welcome his dinner guest.

The sight of Cassie always seemed to do odd things to his equilibrium, and at that moment her effect on him was more pronounced than ever. She was even lovelier than she had been the night of the barbecue, if that was possible. Tonight she looked like a woman all dressed up for an important occasion, which pleased Scott enormously. A dozen heady sensations spun through him, not the least of which was the delight of knowing they would be alone together for the first time. Tonight was the night to make an impression on her.

"Good evening, Cassie."

"Hello, Scott."

"You look wonderful."

"Thank you." She would have liked to tell him how nice he looked, too, but would have felt hopelessly foolish doing so. It was the first time she had seen him in anything but Western garb. He was dressed simply

in dark tailored slacks and a pale blue sport shirt. Both
were obviously expensive, and he wore them well. She
decided he probably felt more natural in such clothes
and only used Western wear to help him blend in with
the local scenery.

Scott stepped back and motioned her inside.
"Please, come in."

"Hmm," she said, sniffing the air appreciatively.
"If dinner tastes half as good as it smells, I'm in for a
treat."

"It will. I promise." Placing his hands on the small
of her back, he walked with her into the living room.
"Have a seat, and I'll get us a drink. What'll you
have?"

"Something tall with vodka."

"Tonic all right?"

"Fine."

He disappeared in the direction of the kitchen. Instead of sitting down, Cassie strolled around the
beautiful room, studying the various objects of art
displayed here and there. She knew very little about
art, but even in her ignorance she somehow knew that
Scott had surrounded himself with things of value. She
herself couldn't imagine living with such exquisite
objects. She stopped to admire a porcelain rose
perched atop a mahogany base. The rose was so life-
like she couldn't resist touching it with a fingertip to
make sure it wasn't real.

"Pretty, huh?" Scott's voice came to her from behind.

"It's beautiful," Cassie said, turning.

He handed her a glass. "It's a music box. Half of
the things you see sitting around are music boxes.
They belonged to my wife."

"And you keep them with you. I think that's wonderful."

"The collection is quite valuable. I'll leave it to my niece someday. It's highly unlikely I'll ever have a daughter, not at this late date."

As she lifted her glass to take sip of her drink, Cassie thought of something that hadn't occurred to her before but should have. Scott's house was so beautifully furnished, right down to the ashtrays and magazine racks. Certainly it in no way looked like anyone's temporary quarters. When he had moved in, he had moved in to stay awhile, confident of success from the beginning. She wondered if his grandfather knew that. Probably not.

"You shouldn't say that. Parenthood will be possible for you for years and years yet. By the way, how old are you?"

"Thirty-five."

"Good grief, I'm older than you are!"

"So?"

"So..." She shrugged. "It just surprises me, that's all."

Scott grinned. "You don't look your age."

"So I've been told."

They sipped their drinks in silence for a moment before Scott asked, "Would you like to see Trendsetter?"

"Ah, the famous bull. I can hardly wait. I'm not sure I've even seen a picture of a half-million-dollar bull."

Scott led Cassie through sliding doors to the deck and down toward one of the outbuildings. Trendsetter was a pampered prince with his own quarters and a hired hand assigned the sole task of taking care of him. He was a magnificent animal, but the minute Cassie set eyes on the bull, she turned to Scott in horror.

"He's a Brangus!"

"Right."

"This is Hereford country."

"So it is. But after checking around, I discovered that keeping the highlands 'Hereford country' is based more on tradition than good, sound reasoning. And I happen to prefer Brangus."

"Don't you ever conform to anything?"

"Not if I can help it."

Cassie shook her head and cast another glance in Trendsetter's direction. A little stab of envy shot through her. Certainly the DO had never owned such a bull. But the envy was quickly replaced by practicality when she recalled the bull's price tag. No animal, not even a superb specimen like Trendsetter, was worth half a million dollars, something she was quick to tell Scott.

He only smiled. "You don't know that for a fact, Cassie."

"I know for a fact that spending that much money for a bull is foolhardy. An animal can't begin to return that kind of money. You're in the red before you even begin."

"My problem, I suppose."

"I feel terribly guilty about that bet of ours. I'm dealing with a novice. And an optimistic one, at that. The worst kind."

His smile broadened. "Please don't waste feelings of guilt on me. And the bet stands."

As they walked back to the house, Cassie thought of the bet. It had become an embarrassment to her.

She didn't want Scott to leave, and she was gradually owning up to it. She wondered what she would do when the end of the year came, and she had to face the matter head-on. He would say, "All right, Cassie, you win the bet. I'll sell you the Horseshoe." And she would say...what? She couldn't very well tell him she'd changed her mind about wanting it. He'd see through that, and she had a feeling he was too proud not to see a deal through. She supposed she would use money as an excuse, plead lack of funds. Anyone would understand that, and she would be off the hook.

That made her feel much better.

WHETHER IT WAS BUYING and housing an expensive animal or setting a table for dinner, Scott did everything with a flair, Cassie noticed. He took no halfway measures. The dining table had been set with blue linen, dazzling white china and sparkling crystal. His wife's possessions, she had to think, but he used them. Most men wouldn't. The fine things would simply have been stashed in a cupboard somewhere and left for a future generation to enjoy. There even were candles and fresh flowers on the table. She was a bit overwhelmed. The coq au vin was superb, as promised, and the wine made her lightheaded. J.B., George and everyone else over at the DO would have scoffed at the elegant ambiance and the "sissified" food, but Cassie was enchanted. For the first time she realized a certain gentility had been missing from her life that she'd only barely realized existed. But then, the linens, crystal and china would have been as out of place at the DO as...as a plow. Scott's world was entirely different from hers.

They ate unhurriedly, talking about nothing of importance, but to Cassie's ears the conversation fairly sparkled. Then they lingered over coffee and dessert. Being alone with Scott in his house and sharing a superb dinner over the lovely table invited warmth and confidentiality. "You're very different from what I thought you'd be," she confessed.

"Oh? What did you think I'd be?"

"I'm afraid you'll find it very stereotyped."

"Ah," he said with a smile and a nod. "Let me see if I can guess. Flamboyant? Featherheaded? Braggart? Throws money around and in general makes an ass of himself?"

She giggled. "That's pretty close. But you're not like that at all."

"I think I've just received a compliment. Cassie, you have me confused with my dad's generation."

"I don't understand."

"You see, Granddad and his contemporaries were pioneers. They made their fortunes by sheer hard work. There's no harder work in the world than what you can find in the oil patch. The people of Dad's generation spent all their time playing golf, hanging around the Petroleum Club and watching their real estate appreciate. The third generation, my bunch—well, we have money, there's nothing we can do about that, but we try to do something with it. If we don't go into another line of work, we do 'good works.' I couldn't lead the meaningless existence my parents do, not in a million years."

Cassie looked at him, savoring a feeling of closeness and camaraderie. She liked Scott Maitland, really liked him. He was something else.

They stayed at the table over an hour. Yet, when Scott finally rose and extinguished the candles, it seemed to her that the meal had passed in a flash. On the tip of her tongue was an offer to help him clean up, but just in time she decided that would spoil the mood he had orchestrated so splendidly. Instead, she simply said, "Thank you, Scott. That might go on record as the finest meal I've ever eaten."

"Good. I enjoy cooking for an appreciative audience."

"Anytime you feel you need one, give me a call, will you?"

"You bet. Oh, I forgot, we've done that."

They looked at each other and smiled. Cassie had always believed she could put great faith in her first impressions, but Scott had effectively put that belief to rest forever. "I must say it amazes me that a man like you can cook at all, much less superbly."

"A man like me? You said that once before, if I remember correctly. What do you mean, a man like me?"

"I imagined you had grown up surrounded by servants?"

"Wrong. When I was growing up I spent most of my time with my grandparents, and they're the most unassuming people on earth."

"No cooks and servants?"

"Nope. A twice-a-week cleaning woman was it. My grandmother did all the cooking. You see, Cassie, you have some preconceived notions about me that are way off the mark."

"I guess so."

Having those preconceived notions proven wrong made Cassie considerably more curious about his grandfather, so later, when they were seated in the living room, sipping a sweet liqueur, she quizzed him.

"Granddad? He's as hard as Grandma is soft, if that tells you anything. They met and married in a little town in Oklahoma in the 1920s. The town was supposed to be undergoing a boom, but the railroad passed it by, and it turned to dust. So Granddad lit out for Texas, just happened to land in East Texas at the time of the big oil strike and just happened to get in on it. Probably pure blind luck to begin with, but he's worked his tail off ever since."

"But before that? What's the Maitland family history?"

"Lord, who knows? Granddad's daddy went to Oklahoma as a boy with his family. From Alabama, I think, but it might have been Georgia. That was right after the Civil War. Since most folks who left the South after the war were running from something, usually the law or creditors, maybe it's just as well the family history is a little fuzzy."

"How did your grandparents end up in Fort Worth?"

"It was the place to be in those days. The oilmen just congregated there, the way the cattle barons had forty years earlier." Scott was tired of talking about his family. He wanted to know more about Cassie. "What about the Ferenbachs? That's a rather unusual name. German?"

She nodded. "With some Dutch thrown in. Oh, I could tell you about the Ferenbachs all the way back to the French Revolution, but I think I'll spare you." Glancing at her watch, she set her glass on the coffee table and got to her feet. "I'd better be going. We rise and shine awfully early over at the DO."

Scott stood also. He wanted to ask her to stay awhile longer, but it probably was time for the evening to end. They were, he hoped, embarking on a courtship, so it was wise to let it build gradually. "I hate to see the evening end. I've enjoyed it."

"So have I."

Outside, the night air was wonderfully soft and warm. Scott walked her to her car, a late-model Buick, he noticed. He'd never seen her driving anything but a truck or the four-wheel drive. "How many vehicles do you people keep over there?"

She smiled. "Three trucks, the four-wheel and this, that's all. There's always something around to drive. I guess that's why Rob's never hounded us for a car, but it seems strange that a sixteen-year-old boy doesn't long for a fancy XL something-or-other."

"Yeah." Scott genuinely felt sorry for Cassie, knowing the shock her son had in store for her. Opening the car door, he slipped his hand under her elbow. She turned, tilting her face slightly. "Good night, Scott. Thanks for a lovely evening."

"We'll have to do it again soon."

Cassie had no idea how she knew she was going to be kissed, but she did. Realizing that, she tensed. Most women her age would have accepted a kiss as the logical conclusion to an evening like this, but she was a babe in the woods where men were concerned. Just knowing she was going to be kissed sent her pulse racing. She stood rigidly and watched his head bend toward hers.

Scott meant the good-night kiss to be quick and friendly. He simply put his hands lightly on her shoulders and bent his head to capture her mouth with his own. But her lips were soft and warm, almost virginal, and while she didn't exactly respond to the kiss, he felt the little involuntary shudder that raced through her body. He lifted his head and looked at her. From the expression on her face, one would think she had never been kissed before, that it was the last thing she had expected now. The temptation was too great. His hands slipped to her waist, he pulled her closer and kissed her again more insistently, and this time, he noticed with pleasure, those soft lips moved slightly under his. It would have been so easy and natural to hold her longer, to kiss her until . . .

Enough, his mind cautioned him. *You've made your point. The lady knows you're more than a little interested. Don't pounce.* Reluctantly, he broke the kiss and stepped back.

"Good night, Cassie."

"G-good night," she said in a voice that was almost a whisper. She slid behind the steering wheel like a woman diving for safe cover.

Cassie drove home in a bemused state, one moment basking in the warm feeling Scott's kiss had inspired, the next chiding herself for handling the good-night so badly. He must think her a complete klutz. A thirty-eight-year-old woman should have more poise and sophistication. For sure she shouldn't have reacted to a simple good-night kiss as though it was the most profound thing that had ever happened to her.

Unfortunately, that came close to being the case. She hadn't been kissed in a very long time, and Scott's nearness had completely unnerved her—a good reason to exercise extreme caution. He had no emotional ties to the High Country. His roots lay elsewhere. He wouldn't be around over the long haul.

Even so, tonight had been fun, and she couldn't remember the last time she could have said that. She suspected she and Scott would be seeing a lot of each other while he lived at the Horseshoe, and she knew she wouldn't do a thing to discourage that.

CASSIE WAS IN THE FARM-and-ranch supply store the following morning, talking to Ace Ellis, the owner of the store, and waiting for him to tally her bill. She heard the tinkle of the bell over the door, heralding the arrival of another customer. Absently glancing over her shoulder, she saw Scott coming through the door. Her heart gave an involuntary leap. With only partial success, she tried to wipe away her silly grin before he spied her.

Scott made no such effort. The moment she saw Cassie standing at the counter, his face broke into a broad smile, and he did nothing to hide it. Threading his way through the kegs of nails that stood on the floor, he walked up to her.

"Good morning," Cassie said.

"Hi, neighbor. Sleep well?"

"As a matter of fact, I did. You?"

"Like a baby. Morning, Ace."

The proprietor glanced up. "Morning, Scott. How're things going."

"I can't complain. I just stopped in to see if that fencing you ordered for me has come in."

Ace nodded. "That it has. I was going to call you today. We can deliver it out to your place this afternoon, if that's all right."

"Fine. If I'm not there, someone will be around who can tell the driver where to unload it."

"Good. Good. Say, Scott, I heard what you did for ol' Miguel Torres. That was awful nice of you. Awful nice."

Cassie thought Scott looked uncomfortable or embarrassed or both. He mumbled something under his breath, and then he turned to her. "Got time for a cup of coffee at Annie's?"

"I think my incredibly busy schedule just might permit that."

She scooped up her bulky package, but Scott quickly relieved her of it. "I'll put this in your car for you. Then we can walk."

"Thanks." Once they were outside the store she asked. "What did you do for Miguel?"

Scott shrugged. "I guess Ace was talking about my giving him a job."

"Oh, Scott, how nice. Miguel used to be quite a cowhand, but that hip of his has pretty well put him out to pasture, and he's lost without work."

"He's a good man." Scott had noticed as he drove into town that the High Country seemed unusually busy that morning. All sorts of campers and other vehicles thronged the streets and the roads winding through the mountains. "What's the occasion?" he asked. "Why all the people?"

"Rock hounds," Cassie explained. "Some club is holding a get-together here to do whatever it is that rock hounds do. They descend on us periodically. Then the hunters will come, and the gliders to take advantage of updrafts or something. We've gotten pretty used to tourists. Some of them come just for the altitude and clean air."

Their destination, Annie's Cafe, was the kind of place that usually was filled with regulars, but that morning it was crowded with the geology enthusiasts. However, they left en masse soon after Cassie and Scott arrived. Taking a back booth, they were greeted by Ruthie Holden, a pretty young waitress.

"Hi, Cassie," Ruthie said as she cleared the table. Then she turned to Scott and lavished him with a smile that rivaled a burst of sunshine. "Hi, Scott. Haven't seen you in a while."

"Been busy, Ruthie. You're looking mighty pretty this fine morning."

Cassie thought that Ruthie might faint from happiness. "Thanks," she simpered. "What'll you all be having?"

"Coffee for me," Scott said. "Cassie?"

"Coffee's all I want, too."

Ruthie returned with the coffee in a minute. Once she'd set the cups in front of them, she turned to Scott again. "I heard what you did for Miguel, Scott, and I think it's just about the nicest thing anyone ever did for anybody."

Cassie frowned in puzzlement. Of course it was nice that Scott had given Miguel a job, but everyone was going a trifle overboard over it. "I didn't realize that Miguel's state of employment was so important to everyone."

"Employment?" It was Ruthie's turn to frown. "You mean you haven't heard? Miguel's told everyone he's seen. He's so excited. Scott's paying for him to have a hip operation. It's going to be done in San Angelo next week." With that she walked away.

Cassie stared at Scott in amazement. "I think that's probably the most wonderful, the most generous thing I've ever heard of."

Again he looked embarrassed. "Aw, the poor guy says he's been suffering for years, and he doesn't have a dime's worth of insurance. It doesn't make sense for him to have to live with that hip when it can be fixed. I told him not to tell anyone."

"You can't keep a secret around here. That's something you'll discover with time. Besides, why would you want to?"

"I guess that's a lesson I learned at my granddad's knee. He and Grandma have paid for entire wings on hospitals, but no one's ever heard a word about it. Granddad won't even allow a plaque with his name on it to be hung on a wall. He calls such gestures 'grandstanding,' and he places grandstanding in the same category with government regulations, windfall profits tax and OPEC."

Cassie smiled at him over the rim of her coffee cup, thinking what a truly astonishing man he was. He clung to old values for no other reason than he thought them right. "You realize, I hope, that you might lose good help. Miguel likes being a cowboy. Once that hip mends, he might look for work on a more...er, conventional ranch."

Scott grinned. "You're probably right."

"Still you do it?"

"Still I do it. I'm going to be pleased as punch to see that guy hopping around like a kid."

Ruthie stopped by their booth, checked their cups and poured more coffee into Scott's. She flashed another dazzling smile before moving on.

"She's pretty, isn't she?" Cassie commented.

"Who?"

"Ruthie, of course."

Scott pretended to seriously study the waitress's retreating figure. "Mmm, I guess so. She sure fills out those jeans. You just have to wonder how the devil she manages to get into them." He settled back and gave Cassie the same once-over. "Speaking of pretty, you look like about a million and a half dollars this morning, Cassie."

"Thanks. You're a real gent." Lord, she hoped she wasn't blushing. He was flirting, and she loved it. But she knew she didn't look so great. She'd just tied back her hair and put on a swipe of lipstick before leaving the house. That scarce attention to her looks was going to stop as of now, Cassie decided. From this minute on she was going to borrow a page out of Laurie's book. No one ever caught Laurie out of the house without blush and eye makeup.

Cassie and Scott finished their coffee, and when they left the cafe, he walked her to her car.

During the drive back to the DO, she marveled again at the effect Scott had on her. And once she'd delivered the supplies to George, she went straight to her office and called the beauty shop she normally patronized only when she needed a haircut.

"GOOD LORD, CASSIE!" Laurie exclaimed. "What have you done to yourself?"

"Like it?" Cassie patted her new hairdo.

"I love it. When did you have it done?"

"Yesterday."

Laurie scrutinized her carefully. "You look so... I don't know... different."

Good, Cassie thought. She was glad that the rather exorbitant amount of money she'd spent at Marie's Salon had produced results. She hadn't gone to the shop with the idea of a make-over, but Marie had had other ideas. "Really, Cassie, isn't it time to do away with the flowing locks? Why not let me cut it a tad shorter and give you a perm? Just a body wave. You'll love it."

And by the time she'd left the shop, Cassie had had a cut and perm, her hair had been highlighted, her eyebrows waxed, and her nails manicured. She told herself she'd just needed a change, a lift, but she knew better. There was only one thing on earth that could make a woman suddenly start taking an uncommon interest in her appearance and that was a new man in her life.

Of course, it probably was stretching a point to say that Scott was "in her life" at this point. What had passed between them was nothing more than his flirting with her and her fantasizing about him. Harmless stuff. But she'd never known a man as sexy or appealing as Scott Maitland.

"Different, huh? I guess that's a compliment."

"Definitely."

"Then thanks." Cassie folded her arms on her desk and smiled at her friend. "I hope it was all right to ask George to give you a hand. It occurred to me that I should have talked to you about it first."

Laurie's cheeks flushed slightly. "Of course it was all right, but I almost fainted when I opened the door yesterday and saw him standing on the porch. I really don't think he'll be of much help, though. There's simply too much that needs doing."

Precisely what George had said when he returned from the Tyler ranch the day before. "I don't know, boss. That place needs a heap of TLC. Laurie might be better off just selling it and doing something else."

Cassie had just looked at him, thinking how incredibly dense he was and wondering if perhaps his male responses weren't in such good working order after all.

"Besides," Laurie went on, "the school year starts in a little over a month. After that I'll only have the weekends." She made a helpless gesture with her hands. "You can't get much accomplished that way."

"Keep the good thought, Laurie," Cassie said inadequately.

"I'll do my best." Laurie's expression was pensive. "Tell me, did you and George...er, talk or anything?"

"George is all business. He spent most of the day walking around the ranch and making tsk-tsking sounds. He did fix that front step, though."

Cassie picked up a pencil and began twirling it through her fingers like a baton, lost in thought for a minute. Then she said, "Why don't you come to Sunday dinner? You haven't in such a long time. Bring Jill. We'd love having you."

"Do you still have those huge feasts with all the hired hands?"

Cassie nodded. "They look forward to it. Cora goes all out."

"And I suppose George is always there."

"Oh, yes, always."

Laurie smiled. "Cassie, you're about as subtle as a meat ax. But, thanks. I'd love to come. I don't know about Jill, but I'll definitely be here." She got to her feet. "Guess I'd better be on my way. There's plenty I should be doing at the house."

"I'm glad you stopped by. Here, let me walk you to your car. I've been inside the house all day, and I'm ready for some fresh air."

"It's not too fresh this afternoon, I'm afraid."

The heat was a momentary shock after the air-conditioned comfort of the house. As they strolled to the car, Laurie instinctively glanced in the direction of the corral. "That man talking to George," she muttered, squinting into the distance. "Isn't that Scott Maitland?"

Cassie's heart tripped. She stopped and looked in the same direction. "I...think it is. I wonder what he wants." Surely Scott had come to see her. What else would bring him to the DO?

As the two women watched, the foreman touched the brim of his hat, stepped back and walked away. Scott turned, obviously on his way to the house, but when he saw Cassie and Laurie, he stopped, smiled and waved. "Hi," he called.

"Hi," Cassie called back, and he headed in her direction.

Laurie touched her on the arm. "I don't dare get involved in more conversation or I'll never get home. I'll be talking to you in a few days."

"Sure, Laurie. Goodbye."

Laurie's car drove off just as Scott approached. "Did I scare her off?" he asked.

"Hardly. She had to get home. What brings you over here?"

"I came to tell George there's a big gap in the fence that's all but hidden by brush. Some livestock might find it, though."

"That was neighborly of you." Cassie masked her disappointment at discovering he hadn't come to see her.

"I thought so, too." He grinned his disarming grin, his eyes raking her. Something was different about her, although in his masculine way he couldn't put his finger on just what it was for a minute. Then it came to him: she'd changed her hair. It was shorter, lighter, curlier. Would a new hairdo make that much difference? It didn't seem likely. And he wouldn't have thought it was possible for her to look better than she had the last time he'd seen her, but she did. He seemed to be standing there, grinning at her like an ape, but he couldn't take his eyes off her.

A woman would have had to be incredibly naive not to see the approval in his expression, and like any woman, Cassie was enormously pleased. She prayed she wasn't blushing, but she felt very warm, and it had nothing to do with the weather. Lowering her gaze, she tried to collect herself. "I'm glad you stopped by. I was going to call you later." That was a lie; not until this instant had she given the slightest thought to also inviting Scott to the DO on Sunday. But she did owe him a return invitation, didn't she?

"Oh?"

"I . . . wanted to invite you to Sunday dinner. We usually have a big gathering. It won't be anything as elegant as you served me the other night, but . . ."

"Thanks. I'd love to come."

"We give everyone time to get out of church. About one o'clock?"

"I'll be here."

Cassie gestured toward the house. "Would you like to come in for a glass of tea or something?"

Scott glanced at his watch, then lifted his shoulders apologetically. "I wish I could, but I have a group of extension agents from all over the state coming in to look at my pastures. They'll be here a couple of days, so I guess I'll be tied up with them." It was his way of explaining why he wouldn't see her until Sunday.

Extension agents? Cassie knew they were charged with the task of keeping ranchers and farmers informed on the newest methods of raising livestock and crops. "You're spreading the word," she said, and there was a hint of disapproval in her voice that Scott didn't miss.

"The feeling among them is that if my grasses do half as well as I claim, they might save the Western range. Love to have you join us for the tour."

He was a true proselyte, Cassie thought, out to convert the world. She might be interested in Scott himself, but she wasn't in the least interested in his unorthodox methods of ranching. "I don't think so."

"Then I guess I'd better be going. See you Sunday."

"Yes, Sunday."

They looked at each other a moment longer, then Scott reluctantly took his leave. Cassie stood watching him as he made his way down the rise. Then she turned and went back to the house, meeting her father as he came out the front door.

"Laurie's coming for dinner Sunday," she said. "Scott Maitland, too."

A barely perceptible lift of his eyebrows and a quick nod were J.B.'s acknowledgement.

"Be nice to him, Dad."

J.B. scowled. "What in thunder else do you think I'd be?"

SUNDAY DINNER, though pleasant, proved to be unsatisfactory for Cassie. For one thing, there simply were too many people present. Although an invita-

tion to Sunday dinner at the main house was open to
everyone on the ranch, only a hard core of a half
dozen normally showed up. That afternoon there were
nine, and one man brought his wife. Along with Scott
and Laurie and one of J.B.'s old friends, it made for
a large, noisy gathering. Cassie didn't really mind, but
she had no chance to visit with Scott, although several times they exchanged pointed looks over the
mounds of fried chicken.

Talk around the table, as always, centered on the
weather and livestock, but it was less animated than
usual, probably because Scott was there. None of the
men who worked on the DO could figure out the
newcomer who claimed to be a rancher but seemed
more interested in growing grass than in raising cattle. Collectively, they thought him weird, but if Scott
was aware of that, he gave no sign. He seemed as at
ease as he would have been with a roomful of oil field
roustabouts. Cassie admired his lack of pretense.

Once the meal was over, the hired hands wandered
outside for a game of horseshoes, George among
them, which dashed Cassie's hopes that the foreman
might spend some time with Laurie. J.B. and his old
chum went out on the front porch for a game of dom-
inoes, and Rob immediately fastened himself to Scott's
side. Cassie and Laurie found themselves in the
kitchen helping Cora clean up. ''Has the word 'wall-
flower' suddenly taken on a whole new meaning for
you?'' Laurie asked wryly, and Cassie laughed in an
attempt to mitigate her peevishness. The day was very
like hundreds of other summer Sundays at the ranch,
so her feeling of disappointment was downright silly.

It wasn't until late afternoon, when the crowd finally began dispersing, that she found herself alone

with Scott. Good manners, it seemed to Scott, dictated that he, too, take his leave of the Ferenbachs, who doubtlessly had had their fill of company. Cassie walked with him as far as the post-and-rail fence.

"How was your visit with the extension agents?" she asked.

"They're impressed." He disliked discussing ranching methods with her, since he was fully aware that she disapproved of the majority of the things he said. "I enjoyed this afternoon, Cassie. Very much."

"Did you? I'm glad. I didn't expect quite so many people. Cora always manages to cope. I thought we might have to call a halt to these Sunday dinners, for her sake, but she wouldn't hear of it. She said they're—"

"Tradition?" Scott interrupted.

She smiled. "Yes."

They walked side by side until they reached the fence. There Scott paused and casually placed his hands on her shoulders. "Are you busy tomorrow?"

"Tomorrow? Not especially."

"I've been invited to an auction at a ranch up near Fort Stockton. It's run by a fellow I knew at A&M. Attendance is by invitation only, but I can bring a guest. I'd like you to come with me."

"That wouldn't be Olin Tucker's auction, would it?"

"Uh-hmm. You ever been to it?"

"No, but I've heard plenty about it. Sounds as though it's more of a circus than a cattle auction."

"Oh, I don't know. You might find it . . . er, interesting. He's done a lot with embryo transfers. It'll further your education."

Cassie sighed with exasperation. "Scott, have you ever momentarily considered just trusting the willy-nilly ways of bulls and cows out in the pasture and forgetting all this other stuff?"

He grinned. "Not really. Like you said, it's willy-nilly. But introducing you to embryo transfers isn't why I asked you to come along."

Some nuance in his voice compelled her to look squarely into his eyes. She couldn't tell if his expression was teasing... or caressing. Possibly it was a mixture of both. "I think I'd... enjoy it."

"Good. I'll pick you up around nine. How's that?"

Cassie wondered if she was ready to have everyone on the ranch know she was spending the day with Scott. Maybe it was absurd, but she decided she wasn't. "Tell you what, I'll be at your house at nine. Okay?"

There was a pause before Scott said, "If that's the way you prefer it, that's fine with me." He reached out and fingered a strand of her hair. "I like it this way. It's becoming."

"Th-thanks." She'd wondered if he'd noticed.

"I'm enjoying the hell out of this truce between two old adversaries."

"Adversaries? I thought we were friends."

"Friends?" He chuckled. "For now I guess that'll do." Then he bent his head and brushed her lips lightly with his. "See you in the morning." Stepping back, he agilely cleared the fence and walked off. Cassie's heart felt as light as butterflies on the wing.

CHAPTER EIGHT

THE ROAD FROM THE RANCH to the historic town of Fort Stockton passed through breathtakingly scenic but lonely country. Not a single community of any size broke the monotony of the sixty-mile trip, and since Scott had the convertible's top down, conversation was all but impossible. Once they reached town, it wasn't difficult to find the Tucker ranch; they just followed the crowd. The fifteen miles of dirt road running from the highway to ranch headquarters were clogged with cars, trucks and campers.

Tucker was a pioneer in embryonic transfer, a process by which the eggs of a so-called supercow were transplanted into a common recipient cow, enabling a supercow to produce thirty or forty calves each year. Since offspring of the process often sold for over forty thousand dollars each, one did not have to be a great mathematician to understand that owning a supercow could be profitable indeed.

Scott figured that by having a supercow and a bull like Trendsetter, he could assure himself of breeding top-dollar cattle that were raised on vitamin-packed hybrid grasses. However, he had mentioned none of these grand plans to Cassie. He was sure he knew what she would think of them.

Cassie would no more have owned a supercow or bought the eggs of one than she would pay half a million dollars for a bull, but the sideshow that the Tucker auction turned out to be was worth the trip. The event had the air of a county fair. When Scott drove his sleek Mercedes through the ranch's main gate, he was stopped by a pair of stern security guards who checked his invitation and took down his license number before waving him on. The area that had been set aside for a parking lot was clogged with vehicles, some of them bearing license plates from as far away as Utah and Missouri.

"Get your bearings and try to remember where the car is," Scott said, taking Cassie by the arm. "In case we get separated. This is a madhouse."

Cassie agreed. She had been to cattle auctions, plenty of them, but this was a carnival. Everywhere she looked, affluent cattlemen and their elegantly coiffed, jeweled wives milled around, seeing and being seen. Booths had been set up here and there to dispense tacos, burritos and frozen margaritas. A Dixieland jazz band filled the air with music. There were displays of alfalfa hay, hybrid grass seed and roping supplies, and in the distance, a striped auction tent next to some cattle pens reminded everyone of the main reason for the event. Cassie and Scott eventually made their way to the pens.

There were no stock cattle for sale at the Tucker auction. These were ultraspecial, prizewinning animals who commanded top dollar. Each lot of calves had its sire's name displayed prominently on the pen. "Like the Westminster Dog Show," Cassie commented.

"Or the Kentucky Derby," Scott said.

"You know, there's not a thing in the world wrong with upgrading a herd, but this is ridiculous. People pay these enormous sums for prize cows, forgetting that they can get sick or hurt or fail to reproduce, just like ordinary ones.''

Scott looked at her in mock horror. "Perish the thought.''

"You aren't considering actually buying one of these animals, are you?''

"Not one. Some. Olin sells them by lots. This lot, for instance." He read the information posted on the pen gate. "These are recipient cows due to calve in a few months. They're the ones I want.''

"You've already sunk a small fortune in a bull, and now you want to spend another few hundred thousand on cows. Scott, there's no way you can make back all that money.''

"I can and will.''

Cassie shook her head, half in amusement, half in exasperation. "What am I going to do with you?''

Scott's expression altered in a subtle way. For a split second his laughing eyes turned sober. "I have a few suggestions," he said, and even his voice changed. Cassie's smile faded, too, and for what seemed like minutes but could only have been seconds, they stood looking at each other, their eyes searching. Then his hand moved as though he was going to reach for her.

At that moment a booming masculine voice could be heard above the general cacophony. "Hot damn! Scott, you old son of a gun, there you are!''

Cassie turned to see the burly figure of a man dressed in a flashy white Western suit with maroon boots, hat and string tie. He was a bull of a man who would have stood out in any crowd, even without the rather startling clothes. He was waving his arms and grinning from ear to ear. She somehow knew he was their host. Though she'd never met Olin Tucker, she had heard of the flamboyant businessman turned rancher who had purchased a sorry, overused ranch near Fort Stockton, irrigated it and set about turning it into a showplace of modern ingenuity.

When he reached Scott, Olin Tucker promptly enveloped him in a bear hug, knocking Scott's hat askew and crushing his face to his massive chest. "How the hell are you, kid?"

Scott disentangled himself, righted his hat and assured Olin he was fine, thanks. "I want you to meet a friend of mine. Olin, this is Cassie Tate."

"How do you do, Mr. Tucker."

Olin made a courtly little bow, and his hat came off with a flourish, revealing an unruly shock of sand-colored hair. "Pleased to meet you, ma'am. You from around here?"

"Cassie has the ranch next to mine," Scott explained. "We're neighbors."

Colin frowned in thought. "The DO?"

"Yes," Cassie said.

"You related to the Ferenbachs?"

"J.B. Ferenbach is my father."

"Do tell! Son of a gun!" Olin pulled on his chin. "Glad you could make it. Maybe you'll go back home and tell all those folks in the mountains that I'm not near as crazy as they think I am."

"I wouldn't count on that, Olin," Scott said with a grin. "They don't approve of me, either."

Cassie shot him a chastising look before smiling at Olin. "All of this is very interesting, Mr. Tucker. I wouldn't have missed it."

"Lord, don't call me Mr. Tucker. I'm Olin to everybody." He returned his attention to Scott. "How d'ya like ranching so far?"

"Some of my neighbors will tell you that what I'm doing isn't ranching."

"Yeah, well I wouldn't lose any sleep over that. Some of my neighbors have been saying the same thing about my little ol' operation for years, but I figure I'll make a couple of million here this afternoon. Not bad for a day's work."

Cassie blanched. He couldn't be serious. She had heard that Olin Tucker was more of a flashy huckster than anything. Maybe he was exaggerating for Scott's benefit.

But if he was joking, he was a good actor. He seemed to be perfectly serious, and Scott obviously took him seriously. "That's good for you, Olin, but not so good for those of us who are going to shell out all of those big bucks."

"Yeah. I'll be making the money today, but you just get yourself some of this high-dollar livestock, and one of these days you'll be holding an auction and raking in the dough. That's what we call brother-in-lawing." Olin winked and gave Scott a hearty slap on the back. "Y'all just browse around and have a good time. I gotta go keep an eye on things. Pleased as punch to have met you, Cassie. Tell ol' J.B. I said hello."

"I'll do that."

Watching the man walk away, Scott chuckled. "Olin's as full of it as ever."

"I was expecting an old classmate of yours," Cassie commented, "but he's quite a bit older than you are."

"Not really. He just looks a lot older."

"Then why does he call you 'kid?'"

"Sort of a private joke. I guess I looked awfully young when I was a freshman. Olin thought so, at any rate. I've been 'kid' ever since."

"Did he have anything to do with your decision to take up...ranching?"

Scott smiled to himself. Why didn't she just go on and add, "Not that what you do is ranching," since that's what she meant? "No, I'm not that close to Olin. Probably haven't seen him half a dozen times since college. The fact that we both ended up in this part of the world is more coincidence than anything. I don't even know for sure how he found out I was here. I just got a phone call from him one day, and we shot the sh...er, breeze for a while. Then the invitation arrived."

Cassie looked out over a sea of people. "Lord, it's hard to believe that supposedly intelligent people would pay such ridiculous sums for livestock."

"They're all just hoping for the equivalent of a Derby winner someday."

"Do you suppose anyone here is really in the cattle business."

"Oh, I imagine some are."

"But not many, right? The trouble with people in the West is, once they make money doing something else, they want to buy a ranch. So they raise thirteen cows and screw up the market for those of us who are seriously trying to make a living in the cattle business." The minute the words were out, she regretted them. "Present company excluded, of course."

The corners of Scott's mouth quirked...in amusement, she hoped. "Oh, I doubt I'm really excluded from that rather testy observation. Come on, let's go

get us some food and see what else is going on. The
auction isn't until two.''

ONE THING CASSIE COULD SAY for the day at the
Tucker ranch: it was an experience. The sideshow had
nothing to do with what she thought of as a "serious" cattle auction. When the bidding got underway,
Olin Tucker took center stage, jumping around and
encouraging the well-heeled guests like an overzeal-
ous cheerleader, sometimes drowning out the professional auctioneer with his antics. Cassie had to admit
it was fascinating.

When the lot of cows Scott was interested in came
on the block, the bidding opened at twenty thousand.
Scott sat beside her, writing figures on a small notepad he'd pulled out of his pocket, raising the pencil
periodically to signal the auctioneer. When the bidding reached thirty-five thousand, and he was still a
player, Cassie was gasping. She couldn't believe he was
serious. On and on the bidding went, until Scott and
a man at the rear of the tent were the only bidders left.

"Thirty-six-five," the auctioneer intoned. "Do I
hear thirty-seven? Thirty-seven?"

Scott raised the pencil.

"Thirty-seven. Do I hear thirty-seven-five? Thirty-
seven-five? I have thirty-seven-five. Do I hear thirty-
eight?"

Scott closed the notepad and stuffed it back into his
pocket.

"That's it?" Cassie asked.

"That's it. My limit was thirty-seven." He shrugged
off the loss good-naturedly and joined Cassie in simply enjoying Olin's spectacle.

Once the last of the livestock had been sold, the jovial host announced that a big-name country music star would be arriving any minute to do a show, and there would be fireworks after dark, so would everyone please hang around for more eating, drinking and music. Then—and Cassie wouldn't have believed this if she hadn't heard it with her own ears—he led the crowd in a lusty, if slightly off-key rendition of "The Eyes of Texas." That done, the business part of the day's activities was over.

"I must say, this is the wildest thing I've ever seen," Cassie said, laughing, as she and Scott left the tent.

"One thing about Olin—he isn't dull."

"But none of this—" she made a sweeping gesture to indicate their surroundings "—has a thing in the world to do with the real cattle business.

Scott took her by the arm. "No, it doesn't, I'll grant you that. I doubt that Olin intends for it to. Looks like the party's just starting. Do you want to stay, go, or what?"

She shrugged. "I'll leave that up to you."

"Is there any reason you want to be home by a certain time?"

"No."

Scott thought a minute. "Well, to tell you the truth, I've had just about all I can stand of this hilarity. Why don't we go back to my house and rustle up something for dinner?"

Warning bells started clanging in Cassie's head. There was no good reason for her to be so drawn to Scott. They had nothing in common. Their ideals and values were totally different. They didn't even think alike. So why did she prefer his company to that of anyone else she knew? It was at odds with her usually sensible nature. Why was the prospect of going to his house and having dinner with him so damned appealing? Was it because they would be very alone? Was she hoping he would make a pass at her?

She didn't know, but it definitely was appealing. The warning bells were conveniently ignored. "That sounds like fun," she said brightly. "I'm sure no one expects me home for dinner."

"Good. Let's go find Olin and tell him goodbye."

AN HOUR AND A HALF LATER they were in Scott's kitchen, and he was chopping and slicing away at the work island. "See what I have in the way of fresh vegetables, will you, Cassie?"

"Why don't you just open up a can of something?"

"I never used canned if anything fresh is available."

She opened the refrigerator and pulled out the vegetable crisper. "There's some squash here. No, correction. There's a lot of squash here."

"Yeah, I got that at a roadside stand, but they wouldn't sell me just a little. Okay, get out three or four of them. I hate to see it go to waste. I think I'll grow my own next year."

"Why didn't you buy a farm?" she asked wryly. "You certainly seem bent that way." Placing the squash on the counter, she watched him for a minute. "Lord, that smells good. What's it going to be?"

"The Monday Night Special. I'm improvising with hamburger and whatever else occurs to me. But I'll make Grandma's squash casserole, too, just in case this is a flop."

She watched a few more minutes. "You're going to make some woman a wonderful husband. You not only can cook, you seem to enjoy it. I envy you. I'm afraid I belong to the Shake 'n Bake crowd."

Chuckling, Scott gave the contents of the pot a quick stir and put the lid in place. "I admit that if I had a house to clean and three kids underfoot, I probably wouldn't think this was fun. But doing it for myself and guests, just for pleasure . . . it's a great way to unwind."

"Maybe I'll take it up someday, when I have to turn over the reins of the ranch to Rob."

Scott turned to look at her but said nothing.

"I'll have to do something," Cassie went on. "I've always had a lot of responsibility. I can't imagine being idle. I'll have to adjust."

"Your dad must have gone through the same thing at one time."

"Yes, but there are differences. He serves on the board at the bank and does a lot of civic things. I could do that sort of thing, too, but it only interests me up to a point. And Dad can always go out and hang around with the ranch hands. I couldn't, of course."

"Why not?"

"The men wouldn't like it."

"But you're the boss."

"True. And they accept me as such, but the reason they do is because I know where to draw the line. I don't try to be one of the boys. They wouldn't put up with that for a minute. When the time comes, I'm sure I'll find something to do."

"Maybe get married again?"

The question surprised Cassie. Sliding onto one of the stools, she propped an elbow on the counter and placed her chin in her hand. "Oh, I...it doesn't seem likely, does it? After all this time, I mean."

"You never can tell, Cassie. Life throws us curves sometimes."

"What about you? Do you suppose you'll ever marry again?"

"I don't know. There was a time when I would have said no, but now...I don't know."

She was tempted to ask what had happened to change his mind but decided against it. "I think it's odd that a young man would even momentarily consider living alone the rest of his life. Why did you?"

"Laziness, for one thing."

"I don't understand."

"It takes a lot of time to get to know a woman well enough to be sure you want to marry her...and even more time learning how to live with her."

Cassie agreed. Love, real love, did not assault you out of the blue.

"I guess I never was willing to give it so much attention," Scott went on. "Now I'm older and, I hope, wiser. I know I'm more patient. Now I dislike saying 'never' about anything."

Cassie nodded. "You're still young enough to have a family. That's something a man who was interested in me would have to take into consideration. No more children." She wondered why she had felt compelled to say that.

Scott looked at her with an expression she couldn't define. "Well, I suppose there was a time when I wanted a family, but it's been years since I've even thought of that."

"I'll bet your grandfather has."

"I'll bet you're right, but what made you say that?"

"I just know how patriarchs are. It's a shame that Dad didn't have a son. As it is, he's the last of the Ferenbachs, and I guess you're the last of the Maitlands."

"I have an uncle in Louisiana, my dad's brother, and he has a house full of kids of both sexes."

"Then you aren't the sole heir apparent."

"Yeah I am." He grinned his disarming grin. "'Cause I'm Granddad's favorite."

Cassie thought it strange that his candor didn't sound the least conceited. He simply was stating a fact. And reality overcame her. "That means you won't be staying at the Horseshoe long," she said.

Scott frowned. "Oh? What makes you think I won't?"

"Simple. If you're his favorite, he'll want you home. And a man like you could never turn his back on his . . . destiny, or whatever you want to call it."

Scott opened the refrigerator and withdrew a bottle of white wine. While he uncorked it he said, "You persist in saying 'a man like you.' You really don't know what I'm like."

"No, that's true. I only know what you've told me."

He filled two long-stemmed glasses and handed one to her. "There's a lot more to me than what I've told you, Cassie."

She couldn't understand why the name she had always considered so ordinary sounded feminine and lovely when Scott said it. She reached for the glass, their fingers touched, and their gazes locked. Cassie felt a catch in her throat as his head unmistakably bent toward hers. The shrill ringing of the telephone was a jarring intrusion. Yet the second ring sounded before the spell between them was effectively broken. Utter-

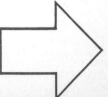

NO COST! NO OBLIGATION TO BUY! NO PURCHASE NECESSARY!

PLAY "LUCKY 7"
AND GET AS MANY AS SIX FREE GIFTS...

HOW TO PLAY:

1. With a coin, carefully scratch off the silver box at the right. This makes you eligible to receive one or more free books, and possibly other gifts, depending on what is revealed beneath the scatch-off area.

2. You'll receive brand-new Superromance® novels. When you return this card, we'll send you the books and gifts you qualify for absolutely free!

3. Unless you tell us otherwise, every month we'll send you 4 additional novels to read and enjoy. If you decide to keep them, you'll pay only $2.74 per book*, a savings of 21¢ per book. There is no extra charge for postage and handling. There are no hidden extras.

4. When you join Harlequin Reader Service, we'll send you additional free gifts from time to time, as well as our newsletter.

5. You must be completely satisfied. You may cancel at any time just by dropping us a line or returning a shipment of books at our cost.

* Terms and prices subject to change.

FREE! ACRYLIC DIGITAL CLOCK/CALENDAR

You'll love this acrylic digital quartz clock! The changeable month-at-a-glance calendar pops out and may be replaced with a favorite photograph. This stylish clock/calendar can be yours when you play our Lucky 7 game!

PLAY "LUCKY 7"

Just scratch off the silver box with a coin.
Then check below to see which gifts you get.

YES! I have scratched off the silver box. Please send me all the gifts for which I qualify. I understand I am under no obligation to purchase any books. If I choose to continue in the Reader Service, I'll pay the low members-only price. I can cancel at any time by dropping you a line or returning a shipment at your cost.　134 CIH KA5U

NAME

ADDRESS　APT

CITY　STATE　ZIP

 WORTH FOUR FREE BOOKS. FREE DIGITAL CLOCK/CALENDAR AND FREE SURPRISE GIFT

 WORTH FOUR FREE BOOKS AND FREE DIGITAL CLOCK/CALENDAR

 WORTH FOUR FREE BOOKS

WORTH TWO FREE BOOKS

Terms and prices subject to change.
Offer limited to one per household and not valid to current Superromance subscribers.

PRINTED IN U.S.A.

ing a heartfelt "Dammit," Scott reached for the instrument.

"Hello," he all but barked, then softened his tone immediately. "Yes, Granddad...yes, sure...okay, wait a minute, will you?" He handed the receiver to Cassie. "I'll take this in my office. Will you hang up when I get in there?"

"Sure."

"I'll try to make this short." His heart hammered with trepidation. This, he feared, was the call he had dreaded but had known was coming. His grandfather sounded all business, so Scott knew he'd damn well better be all business, too.

WHEN HE RETURNED to the kitchen some ten minutes later, Scott was deep in thought. Theo hadn't said much, but he had summoned his grandson home, which could only mean one thing. Maitland Oil was going to start drilling again. Scott wondered what in hell he was going to do. He had absolutely no desire to return to Fort Worth. The Horseshoe was barely off the ground; his relationship with Cassie had just begun. He didn't want to go back to doing the same old thing, seeing the same old people. He'd had a taste of freedom, of being out from under the family umbrella, and he loved it. Here in the High Country his name meant nothing, and that, he'd discovered, was liberating.

But Cassie had been half right in her assessment earlier. It wouldn't be easy to turn his back on his destiny. It might even prove to be impossible.

Cassie had been intently studying his troubled expression. "Problems?" she asked softly.

"What? Oh, no, not really. Just family business. You know how that goes."

"Yes, I know."

"I'm going to have to go to Fort Worth, probably this coming weekend."

Cassie studied a fingernail. One of these days he would just stay. Precisely what she had predicted would happen from the beginning. So why was she sitting here, enjoying his company, grabbing at every opportunity to be with him? He wouldn't be around long, and they weren't well suited, anyway. Her attraction to Scott made no sense at all.

Maybe I could look on this simply as a lark, something not meant to be taken too seriously, she thought. But with the thought came the realization that she would never be able to embark on a fling with Scott Maitland. She had a feeling he would become the very core of a woman's life.

"Guess I'd better get the squash going, or we'll never eat," Scott said distractedly, his mind still on the phone call and the problems it elicited.

"Please, can't I lend a hand?" Cassie asked. "I'm not entirely helpless in a kitchen...almost but not entirely."

"Think you can peel and slice an onion?"

"That sounds like a job I just might be able to handle."

They both managed to stay busy until the food was ready, exchanging small talk about nothing in particular, but Cassie could tell that Scott was preoccupied, and she had to assume the phone call was behind it. She found herself trying to envision his grandparents and the sort of life he had led prior to coming to the Horseshoe. Nothing much came to her since she im-

agined it had been as far removed from her own life as
was possible. And she wondered about his wife, what
kind of person she had been. Cassie conjured up a
picture of a beautiful woman, also born to the purple
and skilled in all the social graces, someone perfectly
dressed at all times who drank champagne from crystal glasses. Someone totally unlike me, she thought
dispiritedly.

They ate in the kitchen, and the food, as before, was
delicious. Cassie never had found it necessary to be the
one to keep the conversation going, but she did that
night. She felt like she was chattering, and about the
most insignificant things into the bargain, but anything was better than dead silence. She was grateful
when the meal ended; then she could insist on helping
Scott clean up. Whatever was wrong with him showed
no signs of getting better, so she intended leaving as
soon as she decently could. She also intended giving
serious thought to ending the relationship with Scott
before it went any further. There wasn't much point in
becoming close to a man who would be going away.

Then, as Cassie was drying her hands on a towel,
Scott did a startling thing. Turning to her abruptly, he
placed his hands on her shoulders and said, "Come
with me, Cassie."

"Wh-what?"

"To Fort Worth this weekend. Come with me." The
idea had occurred to him midway through the meal.
Cassie would be his inspiration, his constant re-
minder of why he wasn't ready to return to Fort
Worth, of all he had here in the highlands. Of course,
he didn't actually have her, but someday he might.

As for Cassie, the invitation couldn't have come as
more of a surprise. "But . . . what for?"

"To meet my grandparents, for one thing, and to have them meet you. I'd like to show you where I grew up. And I'd like the company. We could fly up Friday afternoon and come back before dark Sunday."

"Fly?" There was more than a trace of panic in her voice. "In your plane?"

"You'll be safe, I promise."

"Well, I . . ."

"Please don't tell me the DO can't do without you for forty-eight hours. How long has it been since you got away for a couple of days?"

She could have said "Never" and been telling the truth. She couldn't remember ever being away more than a few hours. "A long time," she said.

"I thought so. Look, Granddad has some business he wants to discuss with me, but that won't take more than an hour or so. The rest of the time we'll have to ourselves. We'll do the town. It's the best way I know to show you what my life was like."

"We'd be staying with your grandparents?"

"Yes, so your sense of propriety won't be offended. That is, it won't unless you decide you want it to be."

Cassie hesitated, not because she didn't want to go, but because she was trying to caution herself against this strange attachment to a man she shouldn't have liked at all. Yet within her there existed a compulsion, a need to do something, just once, that wasn't particularly smart, that was even a bit rash and dangerous, something that wasn't the least rooted in rational thought.

Her mind raced. If Scott had simply asked her to accompany him to Fort Worth, she probably would have declined without hesitation. But he had asked her to visit his grandparents, to stay in their house, and that made all the difference in the world. At least she convinced herself it did. The resolve to end the relationship crumbled like clay. "Well, thank you, Scott. I think I'd like that."

He smiled, reached out and let his fingers brush lightly across her hair. "Good," he said. "We'll have a great time. I think my grandparents will surprise you."

Scott's grandparents were the last thing on Cassie's mind at that moment, for the minute he said the words, he moved closer to her, so close that the heat from his body warmed her. Bending his head, he let his mouth toy with hers before capturing it in a long, drugging kiss. At the same time his arms wound around her, holding her so tightly she couldn't breathe. Cassie thought her bones had melted. Slowly she raised her arms and locked them behind his neck, not at all hesitant about returning the kiss. It had been a very long time since she'd been kissed, but the mechanics easily came back to her. This kiss wasn't in the least like the others they had shared. This one had . . . substance.

A muffled little sigh escaped her lips. She felt as if Scott's entire body had enclosed hers, and the feeling was warm and comfortable. She reveled in it. The dizzy sensations whirling through her mind and body were instinctive and demanding, perhaps unpreventable. It occurred to her that a weekend with Scott, away from everything familiar, might intensify her desire, but she didn't want to think about that or whether it was right or wrong. The moment was too nice.

Scott let one hand slip to her waist. He liked the way she felt, soft and solid all at the same time. Her response to the kiss prompted a feeling of sheer pleasure in him that was all out of proportion. A man usually expected a woman to like being kissed. Had he thought Cassie would be any different?

When they broke apart, Scott looked at her and saw that her eyes were shining, and the color in her face had heightened. She seemed unsteady. She even teetered slightly, and there was wonder in her expression. He wanted to laugh and hug her ferociously, but he did neither. He simply gazed at her with smoldering eyes that weren't entirely free of wonder themselves. It had really been incredible for him, too.

"Thanks for today," she said. Her voice had taken on a peculiar, quavering quality. "It was . . . fun."

"Yes, I thought so, too."

"I'd better be going. It's been a long day, and . . ." She let the sentence trail off. She didn't dare say anything because what she wanted to say would have been all wrong. She wanted to ask him to hold her again and kiss her again and press himself insistently against her again so that she could feel his hardness. Just knowing she wanted all those things made her mind reel and stumble. It was too soon to want all those things from this man, much too soon. Therefore, she ought to go home.

Scott didn't want her to go. He wanted her to stay so that he could hold her and kiss her, get closer to her. Every minute he was with her he was aware that something wonderful was building. He had known for some time that he wanted to make love to her, wanted it more than he'd ever wanted anything. He found the thought of making love to her invading his imagination at the oddest times.

But things were progressing so nicely that perhaps it would be best to take it slow and easy. Instinctively, he knew that Cassie would require special handling. He liked kissing her, and the thought of making love to her was unbelievably exciting, but when—he refused to consider "if"—they finally were intimate, he wanted it to be the most real, the most honest thing that had ever happened to her. Never once had he imagined having a brief, wild fling with her.

Ever since he had been old enough to think about such things, Scott had honestly believed it took a long time for a relationship between a man and a woman to build, and this attraction to her seemed to have happened awfully fast. From the moment he had first seen her, that night at the cattlemen's meeting, Scott had wanted to get to know her better, and that wasn't like him. He wondered if he could trust what he was feeling. It didn't seem possible that all the crazy sensations she inspired—the unsteady heartbeat, the loss of rational thought—should assault him like a thunderbolt. Spontaneous emotion was new to him.

He stepped back. "All nice things must end. It's back to work for me tomorrow, too." He slid his hand beneath her elbow and walked her to the front door, where they shared another kiss, this one quick and light. Scott stood in the doorway and watched her walk to her car. She opened the door, then turned to look at him.

"I forgot to tell you I'm sorry you missed out on your test-tube babies."

Scott laughed and wagged an admonishing finger at her. "No you're not. Don't fib to me, Cassie."

"I still think the willy-nilly ways are best. You're running a ranch here, not a laboratory." With a little wave, she slid behind the steering wheel and drove off.

Thankfully, everyone had gone to bed when she got home. She turned off the one light that had been left on and walked soundlessly down the hall to her bedroom, praying all the while that no one would hear her and open a door. She simply wasn't up to confronting her father or son at this moment. She was sure she looked different; she certainly felt different. She felt so warm all over and out of breath. And once she was safely in her room behind a locked door, she looked in her dressing table mirror. Her eyes were too bright and her cheeks too rosy. Otherwise, the same old Cassie stared back at her.

Undressing, she crawled into bed, too keyed-up to sleep. On her bedside table was a paperback novel, a fat one, over six-hundred pages. Laurie had given it to her and said, "If this one doesn't fog up your glasses, you're shockproof."

It was a racy book about a woman with lusty appetites who had met a man with similar . . . er, desires. It was full of glitz and glamour and sex. The last chapter Cassie had read included a twelve-page love scene that had incorporated language and anatomical descriptions that would make a sailor blush. She remembered thinking that the book surely had been written by a man under a feminine pseudonym. She hadn't been able to imagine a woman conjuring up such uninhibited behavior.

Now she wasn't so sure. In Scott's arms she had experienced some pretty romantic thoughts herself. Picking up the book, she thumbed back through it and reread the scene before turning in. And that night she had her first erotic dream in years. Waking, she felt both startled and pleased. It was good to be thinking like a woman again. She had been sexless too long.

THE NEXT MORNING Cassie dawdled over breakfast. Normally she ate in a hurry and went straight to her office. This morning, however, she waited until everyone but J.B. had left the table. Her father always lingered over a second cup of coffee, and then, if nothing pressing demanded his attention he would drive to Fort Davis and wile away a few hours in the boarding house, drinking more coffee with his cronies. Cassie wanted to talk to him before he got away. He had to know about her weekend plans. It wouldn't have occurred to her to lie to him, or even to hedge on the truth slightly.

"I'll be gone this weekend, Dad."

"Oh?" J.B. said, scarcely glancing at her.

"Uh-hmm. I'm going to Fort Worth with Scott."

That brought her father's head around with a start. "You're what?"

The announcement had seemed harmless enough until she actually got the words out. But J.B.'s expression had her feeling guilty, and that was ridiculous. "You heard me. Scott's asked me to go to Fort Worth with him."

J.B. couldn't have been more stunned if she had kicked him. "Cassie...honey...what is all this?"

"I'm going to meet his grandparents."

"What in hell for?"

"Because he invited me."

A moment of heavy silence hung over the room before J.B. said, "You know, I've never questioned any of your decisions or actions, and I've always hoped you might meet some man who interested you. But this sudden...er, friendship with Maitland bothers me."

Cassie felt uncomfortable. She and her father rarely discussed personal matters. But then, she thought ruefully, she'd had no personal life to discuss with him. "Please, Dad, we're just going to his grandparents' house for a couple of days."

"This family of his—they can't be anything like the folks you're used to."

"Scott says they'll surprise me. He says they're very unpretentious people."

Her father looked pained. "Are you sure you know what you're doing?"

"Not really, not yet. How could I? I barely know him," she said truthfully, with a nervous little laugh. "But when I find out, you'll be the first to hear about it."

CHAPTER NINE

"OH, LORD!" Cassie exclaimed, simultaneously closing her eyes and placing a hand over her racing heart. The little plane lifted off the ground and left her stomach behind. She kept her eyes squeezed tightly shut until she felt a tap on her arm. Opening them, she saw Scott smiling at her, half in amusement, half in sympathy.

"We're airborne. You don't intend keeping your eyes closed all the way to Fort Worth, I hope."

She let out a fluttery little laugh. "I'm sorry, but the sensation of leaving the ground took my breath away."

"It may take a few minutes, but you'll get used to it. And it's a great way to travel."

She nodded uncertainly.

Actually, once she settled down and convinced herself the plane wasn't going to drop to the ground at any second, Cassie rather enjoyed the flight. And for saving time, it couldn't be beat. To make the trip by car would have eaten up over seven hours, but they made it in just under two. The weather was good, the plane was comfortable, and with Scott to talk to, the two hours passed in a flash.

When they landed, and he flipped open the windows, however, the humid heat assaulted Cassie's senses. It was oppressive after the high, dry air she was accustomed to. She felt she would melt in the khaki jumpsuit she had worn for comfort on the trip. She hated meeting Scott's grandparents for the first time looking limp and bedraggled.

They discovered there was a company car and driver waiting for them. "Hmm," Cassie said, impressed. "Rank does have its privileges."

"My main privilege is being related to Granddad." Scott turned to their driver. "Take the scenic route home, Clarence."

The man laughed and said, "Yes, sir."

The "scenic route" meant avoiding the freeways that crisscrossed the city. Instead, their route took them past the museums and parks and gardens, the broad boulevards and smart shops that Cassie wouldn't normally have associated with Fort Worth, which still was "Cowtown" in her imagination. To the east she caught a glimpse of the downtown skyline. "Funny. I didn't think it would be such a . . . city."

"You've never been here before?" Scott asked incredulously.

"No. I've never been much of anywhere, I guess. San Antonio several times and El Paso twice. Mexico City once. That's about it. Cities make me feel all closed in." For some reason, the admission had her feeling every inch the country bumpkin. "I guess you've been everywhere."

"Everywhere, no. Lots of places, though."

"For instance."

"For instance, New York for a year. Italy to spend six months with my parents. All up and down California when we had interests there."

To Cassie, he might as well have said he'd been to the moon and back. "Did you ever consider settling down in one of those places?"

"Nope, never did."

"Because of your grandfather?"

"Partly."

"Yet you bought the Horseshoe. How come he didn't raise cain over that?"

Scott looked at her in all seriousness. "That's a question I'd like to know the answer to myself. I expected a lot of static, believe me." He shifted his attention to the scene outside the car window. "Look around. This is where I grew up."

The neighborhoods where the oil-rich of Fort Worth lived lay in an arc to the west of the city and reflected the changing styles of each succeeding generation. The old neighborhood, where Scott's grandparents lived, was dense with ancient magnolias. The streets swept along the edge of the nearby country club's golf course, and the houses that flanked them were large, but more comfortable than ostentatious, built by people who still thought of themselves as pioneers and who clung to Puritanical ideals. Most, like the Maitland house, were of a vaguely English style, dark brick and half-timbered, completely traditional. Solid and permanent. It was, Cassie thought, a neighborhood that just as easily could have been a suburb in Connecticut or Virginia. The luxurious palaces and villas built by the second and third generations, who were not motivated by any pioneer spirit, were nowhere to be seen on those quiet streets.

But no one ever would have taken it for a middle-class neighborhood. It screamed of affluency. "What was it like growing up here?" Cassie asked.

There was only a moment's hesitation before Scott said, "Easy. I always had to work, of course— Granddad never could stand seeing anyone just sitting around—but it wasn't the salt mines. I always knew I had it pretty easy.''

Theo was not at home. Nor were any servants in evidence. Cassie and Scott were greeted instead by the woman to whom Theo had been married for fifty-nine years, Norma Maitland. She was small, sweet-faced and silver-haired. She greeted Scott warmly, and it was obvious she adored him. But Cassie received the bulk of the elderly woman's attention. After all, this was the first time since Becky's death that her grandson had brought a woman home. What devoted grandmother wouldn't read plenty into that?

Norma approved of what she saw. Cassie wasn't flashy, for which the elderly woman could only thank the heavens, and she didn't appear to be at all like Becky, whom Norma had sometimes thought to be flighty. Of course, this woman was older. A widow with a son, Scott had told them. She looked, Norma decided on the spot, sensible, an adjective she saved for high praise. If there was one thing Norma heartily disapproved of, it was Scott's parents and their jet-set life-style. Cassie looked like the kind of woman who would be good for Scott. It remained to be seen if she behaved like it, too. There was only one thing wrong: she wasn't a Fort Worth girl.

''Welcome to our home, my dear. We are delighted to have you here.''

''Thank you, Mrs. Maitland.''

''Please call me Norma. Everyone does. Scott, put Cassie in the front bedroom upstairs, then call your grandfather at the office. He wanted to know the minute you got home. Come on in the kitchen with me, Cassie. I'm baking.''

The kitchen was huge, a room meant for serious cooking. Although Norma cooked simple, old-fashioned food, she always prepared enormous quantities of it so that she could give the surplus to the domestic help and some of her husband's employees. The minute she and Cassie entered the room she went straight to the oven and took out two pies, then placed two more inside and set the timer. "There won't be any leftovers tonight," she said with a smile. "Not with Theo, Scott and my son-in-law for dinner, to say nothing of the children. Everyone's anxious to meet you, dear."

The door swung open, and Scott came into the kitchen. "Did you call Theo?" Norma asked.

"Yes, and he wants me to come on down to the office." Scott cast an apologetic glance at Cassie. "Do you mind? I won't be gone long."

"Of course I don't mind."

"Run along," Norma said, as if she was speaking to a small child. "This will give Cassie and me a chance to get acquainted before you men show up and monopolize the conversation."

"I guess there's something around for me to drive."

"Take my car." Norma reached in a drawer, withdrew a set of keys and tossed them at him.

"I'll see you ladies in a bit," he said and left by way of the back door.

Norma giggled. "Wait until he sees my new car. The dealer called the color 'desert beige,' but I'm telling you, it's almost pink. Theo wouldn't be caught dead in it." She looked at Cassie with a measure of seriousness. "I wasn't joking when I said the men would dominate the conversation tonight. They always do.

They operate in a man's world. I hope you won't take offense."

"I won't," Cassie assured her. "I'm accustomed to a so-called 'man's world.' "

"Scott tells me you manage your family's ranch. Really manage it."

"Yes."

"Odd. In my day, land was given to the oldest male relative, no matter how distant, even if there were a dozen daughters living on the place. I came from Oklahoma farmers. My family settled there during the Land Run in 1889. What with various uncles and nephews staking their claims adjacent to ours, we ended up owning a sizable piece of property. I had three sisters and one brother, and the brother inherited the land."

"How unfair!" Cassie exclaimed.

"Yes, I suppose it was, but I never gave it a moment's thought. That's just the way things were. I wonder what Theo would have done if we'd had two daughters instead of two sons." She giggled again. "That might have been very interesting, Theo as the father of two daughters. I think he would have been rather helpless at times. As for myself, I would have loved having a daughter. Scott's sister has been such a joy to me." Norma glanced at the timer on the stove. "There's time before the pies are done for me to check the camellias. Would you like to come with me?"

"I'd love to."

Norma's greenhouse was a riot of blooms. There were azaleas, camellias, gardenias, African violets, some spectacular ferns, along with more prosaic plants like patio tomatoes and hothouse cucumbers. The temperature and humidity gauges were checked, then each pot and tub came under Norma's knowledgeable inspection. "Oh, dear, mealybugs," she said. "I have my work cut out for me tomorrow." One particularly sad-looking plant was given the death sentence. "I've done all I can, but the poor thing is terminally ill." As she plucked the victim from its pot, she said, "I'd better go check the pies, and I really need to get started on the ice cream. Scott might never forgive me if I didn't have homemade ice cream."

The two women left the greenhouse. While Norma disposed of the plant, Cassie's eyes swept over the beautifully manicured lawn and the stately old house. "This is such a lovely place, Norma. You must love it."

"Oh, yes. We built it in 1936, after the big East Texas oil boom. The day we moved in was a milestone in our lives." She laughed. "For weeks afterward I would just wander through the rooms, thinking how incredible it was that such a grand house belonged to us. We certainly never expected wealth. At least, I didn't. You see, when Theo and I left Oklahoma and came to Texas during the Depression, we literally had nothing but each other. I mean, we owned nothing. But you know, I was just as happy then as I am now, because I wanted that man from the minute I first laid eyes on him."

Cassie couldn't remember ever being more touched. Scott had been right; his grandparents surprised her, and his background was vastly different from the one she had imagined. Many times during the past week, Cassie had had misgivings about making this trip. Her father's dismay over it was only one of the reasons. Mainly she had feared she would find herself com-

pletely out of her element. But now she was glad she
had come. She wouldn't have missed it for the world.

THE THREE-STORY white brick Maitland Building in
downtown Fort Worth was impressive in a modern,
anonymous way. Its reception room was adorned with
tropical plants and expensive paintings, all chosen by
Norma. The tables were strewn with copies of the *Oil
and Gas Journal.* In Theo's office the walls were hung
with inscribed photographs of presidents and movie
stars. Scott sat amid the familiar surroundings,
vaguely remembering his first visit when he was a
child, and listened while his grandfather talked on the
phone with a friend who had won an oil lease in a
national lottery. As usual, the deal was being con-
summated over the phone. No lawyers would be con-
sulted; no contracts would be written. This was
between two old friends who trusted each other far
more than they trusted legalities.

So, as Scott had suspected, activity was starting up
again. His stomach churned with uneasiness. Today
might not bring on the final confrontation he had been
dreading, but today the subject of his return to Fort
Worth would be brought up. Scott prayed he would
handle it well and not knuckle under.

He studied his grandfather intently, as he had done
countless times in his life. Theo's bearing was imper-
ial and folksy all at once, and he possessed directness
and utter simplicity, along with the wiliness of a riv-
erboat gambler. At eighty, he still stood tall and
straight, and he still came to the office every day and
stayed until five, unless the weather was particularly
nice. In that case he took off early for a round of golf.

He seemed impervious to age, but Scott knew his grandfather was acutely aware of the passage of time.

Theo hung up the phone. "So, how're things goin'?"

"Pretty good, Granddad."

"Makin' any money?"

"No, but I'm sure spending some."

Theo chuckled. "Gotta spend it to make it. That was John Copeland on the phone."

"I gathered," Scott said.

"We're going to drill a well for him."

"I gathered that, too."

"Things are looking up, son. You about ready to get back in the thick of things?"

Scott deliberately looked thoughtful. "Well, you kinda got me at a bad time, Granddad. You see, that property I bought needs a lot of work."

"Hire someone."

"It's not that simple." Scott began explaining the things he was doing at the Horseshoe. Theo listened patiently for a time, but then he silenced his grandson with a raised hand.

"Spare me. None of that means a damned thing to me. This wouldn't have anything to do with the lady you brought home, would it?"

"Cassie's my neighbor."

"That didn't answer my question."

"We're just friends. That's all we could be. We haven't known each other very long."

"What's she like?"

"She's . . . she's a nice lady. I don't know how to describe her, Granddad. You'll just have to meet her."

"Is she pretty?"

"Very."

"Hmm." Theo gazed over his spectacles with the cunning of a fox. "Just don't go fallin' for some little filly in the hinterlands, son. Your future is right here. Now..." Slapping his knee, he got to his feet. "We'd best be gettin' home."

Scott stood and followed his grandfather out of the building. He hadn't accomplished one thing, and he knew for a fact there would be yet another talk with Theo before the weekend was over. Scott hadn't jumped at the chance to come back home, and though nothing had been said, it was apparent that the elderly man was feeling uneasy.

CASSIE HAD SPENT the afternoon watching Norma prepare more food than it seemed one household could possibly consume. By the time the men arrived at the house, both women had managed a few minutes to change clothes and freshen up, and they were seated on the sun porch off the dining room.

Theo stopped in the foyer to sift through the day's mail. Hearing Cassie laugh, Scott followed the sound, stopping for a minute on the sun room's threshold, unseen by the women. He simply stood and studied Cassie for a minute. She had changed clothes and now wore a blue sundress that showed off smooth, tanned shoulders and arms. She and Norma were talking animatedly, oblivious to his presence. Cassie looked wonderful, and Scott was surprised to realize he was proud of her. *She isn't mine to be proud of,* he thought.

Then his grandfather brushed past him and burst into the room to interrupt the women and plant a kiss on Norma's cheek. Cassie's eyes searched for Scott, found him, and they exchanged a smile before she turned to meet his grandfather.

She was impressed on the spot. She belonged to a world where strong, powerful men were admired and appreciated, and one had only to look at Theo Maitland to know he was strong and powerful. He also was impeccably groomed, had courtly manners in the presence of ladies, and his inquisitive eyes missed nothing. They thoroughly inspected Cassie without a trace of rudeness.

"I'm so happy to meet you, Mr. Maitland," she said, extending her hand. As with Norma earlier, she immediately felt comfortable with this man.

Theo didn't shake her hand; rather, he took it and held it between both of his. "My, my, you are a pretty one."

"Thank you."

"If you don't mind, I'll just sit here, and we'll get acquainted. Scott, reckon you could get an old man a bourbon and water?"

"Coming up." Scott moved to the bar at the end of the room. While he mixed the drink he watched Cassie and his grandfather. Theo was asking her the predictable questions: where did you grow up, where did you go to school, do you have brothers or sisters, how did your parents meet? This kind of "kitchen table" talk was the way Theo sized up strangers, and it never failed to draw them out. Not that Cassie needed to be drawn out. Scott could tell she was perfectly at ease. She had poise and breeding that belied her background, the life she currently led and her lack of worldliness. He knew plenty of women of class and privilege, products of exclusive finishing schools and world travelers, who could take lessons from Cassie.

He carried the drink to his grandfather, then took a seat on the other side of Cassie. At that moment everyone's attention was captured by some commotion in the front of the house. Scott's sister, Judy, her husband, Roger, and their three children—two boys, one girl—had arrived for dinner. Judy was a bubbly woman with a tumble of dark hair, like Scott's, and a captivating smile, also like Scott's. It would have been impossible for the two of them to deny their kinship. From then on the evening was filled with noise and laughter and the warm camaraderie of family. Cassie had a wonderful time.

DINNER WAS A SUMPTUOUS FEAST of roast beef, mashed potatoes, green beans, tomatoes from the greenhouse and homemade biscuits, all followed by the pie and ice cream. It was the only kind of fare that Theo considered "real food." Scott's penchant for gourmet cooking appalled his grandfather. Cassie noticed that Norma had been right about there being few leftovers. Theo, Scott, Roger and the two young boys could have held their own with any group of hungry cowhands.

And, as Norma had warned, the men dominated the conversation. back at the DO, talk around the dinner table centered on weather and cattle; in the Maitland dining room that night the chief topic of interest was a big well that had come in in southern Oklahoma, leading to the speculation that "the Arbuckle has been tapped," whatever that was. Seated next to Scott, Cassie found it strange to hear him converse intelligently about spudding in and setting pipe and pay zones. She had to forcibly remind herself that it was the oil business, not ranching, he had known all his life, that this was his rightful milieu. The thought was somewhat sobering. He even looked different in his sharply creased slacks and expensive polo shirt. She missed the jeans and boots and the Stetson he set so rakishly on his head. When he was dressed like that, she could almost believe that he really did belong in her world, crazy ideas and all.

She felt him touch her arm, snapping her out of her reverie. Theo and Roger seemed to be arguing good-naturedly, and Judy and Norma were giggling over some local gossip. Cassie then realized that Scott was talking to her. "Oh, I'm sorry... did you say something?"

"I asked if you wanted more potatoes?"

She shook her head. "No, thanks."

He lowered his voice even though no one was paying attention to them. "You looked like you were a million miles away."

"Not a million."

"A few hundred, then?"

She smiled sheepishly. "I guess so."

"You're not homesick, are you?"

"Don't be silly!"

"Are you glad you came?"

"Yes, I am."

"Good." He touched her hand before returning his attention to the others at the table.

It was after eleven when Judy and her brood left. Theo and Norma said good-night and went off to bed, leaving Scott and Cassie alone for the first time since they'd arrived. "Oh, Scott, Your grandparents are adorable!" she enthused. "And amazing. So full of energy. Norma told me that she gets up at seven every morning, and if today was normal, she doesn't stop."

"I know. The old pioneer blood. Down deep in Granddad's heart lies the notion that work is the only reason for being alive, and Grandma's not about to let him outdo her. I apologize for all that shop talk at dinner. Were you bored?"

"Bored? Not at all. I thought it was interesting, even though I didn't understand most of it. What's the Arbuckle?"

"It's a formation in southern Oklahoma that geologists think is very rich in oil, but no one's been able to hit it big yet." Scott had just about had all the oil-patch talk he wanted, and he was sure Cassie was tired of it, so he changed the subject. "Would you like a coffee or a nightcap?"

"Not a thing, thanks."

"Tired?"

"No."

They had returned to the sun room, and Scott had turned off all the lights but one small lamp. Cassie had taken a seat on the white wicker love seat with the bright flowered cushions. Now Scott sat down beside her; they filled the love seat snugly. "Did you and your grandfather get your business taken care of?" she asked, grabbing at the first topic that came to mind.

"We . . . er, touched on it." A second or two of silence passed. "I know what he wants. He wants me to come home."

Cassie's heart tripped. "Are you going to?"

Another few seconds passed. "Nope," he finally said. "Not now."

But maybe someday? Cassie wondered, even as a wave of relief swept through her at his announcement. She, who only a few months ago had hoped he'd leave the High Country as quickly as possible, now experienced a sense of loss at the thought of his doing just that. "Did you tell him that?"

"More or less. I told him this wasn't a good time for me." Scott looked at her fully and smiled his lazy smile. "The old devil's first thought was that you had something to do with that."

"M-me?"

His eyes weren't smiling. "Uh-hmm."

"I hope you set him straight. I don't want him to resent me." She felt his arm slide around her shoulders. A tiny shiver raced along her spine, something she was sure Scott couldn't avoid noticing. He had the most unfortunate knack for making her feel graceless and inexperienced in relationships, which, truthfully, she guessed she was. In thirty-eight years she had known only one serious involvement. "You should have told him about Trendsetter and all that dumb grass and..."

"I tried, but it didn't mean anything to him."

"Seriously, Scott...what are you going to do?"

"Take it a day at a time, I guess." He curled a strand of her hair around his index finger. "Wait and see if I win our bet. I might *have* to come back."

Cassie expelled a labored breath. "About that bet. It seems rather foolish now, doesn't it? We could call if off, and..."

"Not on your life." Scott's hand moved to the nape of her neck, and with gentle pressure, he brought her face closer to his. She looked at him, wide-eyed and uncertain. He bent his head to kiss her slightly parted lips and found them warm and pliant. His other hand went to her waist as he gently pulled her into the circle of his arms, noting with pleasure the way she melted into the embrace, her ardor as she returned the kiss. When he lifted his head he saw her eyes, luminous and dark, and he knew then, with certainly, that he had the power to move her. Nothing in the recallable past had filled him with such satisfaction. "That's better. There were times when I thought you were afraid of me."

"No, it's not you I'm afraid of."

"Yourself, then?"

"Hmm," she murmured obscurely.

"Cassie..." His voice throbbed with intensity. "I think I'm falling for you."

"I...don't see how you can possibly know that. We haven't known each other very long."

"How long does it take?"

Her breath came out on a suspended sigh. "We're so different."

"I hope so."

"I mean, in ways we should be alike, we're...different."

"Well, if we were very much alike, what could we possibly learn from each other?" And he bent his head again. Her arms slid up, and her hands locked behind his neck.

Certain impressions came to Cassie. The texture of his cheek as it pressed against hers, the firmness of his shoulders, the coarseness of his hair at the nape. One arm held her tightly; his other hand rested at the side of her breast. Strangely, that didn't seem the least improper.

Only a few weeks ago, had anyone asked her if she'd ever been lonely, she would have said no. Now, as the heat of Scott's body transferred to hers, as his tongue made its first tentative entry between her lips, she admitted that she probably had been the loneliest per-

son on earth. Once she had thought that romance was
something she didn't need. Silly girl! Now she wanted
it more than she'd ever wanted anything. Once her life
had been a smooth, open road, as straight and obsta-
cle-free as a West Texas highway. Now it was full of
bumps and dips and unexpected curves, and the odd
thing was that she welcomed them. It was as if she had
been given a good kick, and her feminine psyche had
started working again.

The transformation seemed to have happened in an
instant, but it might have begun last spring at the
rancher's meeting when she'd first noticed his good
looks. Scott's early attempts at fitting in with ranching life had been laughable, and there still weren't
many of her neighbors who took him very seriously,
but everybody liked him. In spite of what she'd
thought in the beginning, he was every inch a gentleman, completely free of conceit. It was all but impossible to recall the man she had thought of as a
nuisance. He might have some odd ideas, and she
might never agree with them, but he could make her
insides boil like molten lava. No man had ever done
that, not even Robert.

This relationship was going to change into something more meaningful, of that she was certain. She
wasn't prepared to say whether she and Scott were
drifting into a courtship or a seduction, a short-lived
affair or a lifetime commitment, and she wasn't sure
if she even cared which it was. That more than anything told her that the changes in herself were dramatic.

Scott broke the kiss, and a strange, garbled noise
sounded deep in his throat. "Damn," he said, "I wish
we were somewhere else."

So did Cassie. But they weren't. They were here, in his grandparents' house, where kisses were all they could share. Shifting in his embrace, she straightened. "I guess ... I'll call it a day now."

Owning up to the reality of the moment, Scott released his hold on her. Sighing, he buried his face in her hair and kissed her temple. "Yeah. Me, too." They sat in companionable silence for a few seconds longer; then, regretfully, he struggled to his feet and pulled her with him. "Give me a minute to turn out the lights."

He kept his hand at her waist as they climbed the stairs, and at the door to her room, he pulled her close for another melting kiss. When their mouths parted, Cassie allowed her lips to trail down to the hollow at the base of Scott's throat, to linger there for a moment before she slipped out of his arms and backed into the room. "Good-night," she said.

Scott simply stood, as if in shock, and waited for her to begin closing the door. "Good night, Cassie. Tomorrow, all of it is ours." He walked off in the direction of his own room.

When the door was firmly shut, Cassie placed a hand to her racing heart, and a small smile touched her lips. No, she really didn't care if Scott only had seduction in mind. She'd be a willing participant.

Walking to the room's lone mirror, she stared at her reflection in wonder, touching her very warm face, noticing the high rise of color in her cheeks. She ran her hands down her body, imagining they were Scott's hands. Her very nerve ends seemed to tingle. How quickly life could change! All it took was for one special person to enter it, and nothing was ever the same again. She wouldn't have thought it possible, yet never in her life had she felt so alive.

CHAPTER TEN

FROM FORCE OF HABIT, Cassie awoke with the sun the following morning. Raising on her elbows, she listened. The house was totally quiet, but no doubt Norma would be stirring soon. She sat up, pulled her knees to her chest and hugged them, then studied the room closely. Yesterday afternoon she had given it only a cursory glance as she'd changed clothes, and last night she had been so mesmerized by Scott's kisses that she'd undressed quickly and climbed into bed, hoping she would dream about him. She hadn't. She had fallen into a deep sleep almost immediately.

The big bedroom was wonderfully cozy and time-worn, probably still furnished the way it had been when the house was built. The bed she slept in was a mahogany four-poster with a patchwork quilt for a spread, and the percale sheets were so soft that Cassie imagined they had been through a thousand launderings. A lowboy and mirror stood against one wall, a rose-colored settee against another, and there were lace Austrian shades on the windows. The room had, for want of a more descriptive word, charm.

Yawning, she laid her head on her raised knees and thought about Scott. Briefly last night as she was undressing, she had wondered if the bright light of day would bring any change in her fascination with him. She was somewhat surprised to find it hadn't. If she took a few minutes to actually do it, she probably could have come up with at least two dozen reasons why he was the wrong man to fall for, but she had no intention of doing that. She didn't want to sort and analyze this. She just wanted to enjoy it. And she could hardly wait to spend today with him. So when she heard the first footsteps going along the hall and down the stairs, she bounded out of bed and began getting dressed.

Cassie was in the breakfast room a full twenty minutes before Scott put in an appearance. She chatted with Norma and Theo over a bacon omelet and toast and was enjoying a second cup of the best coffee she had ever tasted when he sauntered into the room, looking as bandbox fresh as always. Well rested, too. He slept well, she thought. *I wonder if he dreamed of me.*

"Good morning, everybody," Scott said brightly, but it was Cassie's shoulder he touched as he made his way to the coffee pot on the sideboard, and it was Cassie's eyes he caught and held as he sat down across from her. "How is everyone this fine Saturday morning?"

Theo looked up from his newspaper and made a scoffing sound. "It's going to be two degrees cooler than Hades today."

"Oppressive," Norma commented. "We must be due for a storm."

"I hope you're wrong," Scott said with a slight frown. "At least I hope it waits until Cassie and I are on our way south. What does the paper say, Granddad?"

"Partly cloudy. High near a hundred. Thirty percent chance of afternoon thunderstorms. Same thing it's said every day for weeks."

"Golf?" Scott asked.

Theo shook his head. "Too hot for me. I'm off to the mill."

Norma looked up. "Oh, Theo, it's Saturday!"

"So?"

"So, I don't see any reason to open the office on Saturday."

"Pray what else would I do?"

Norma shrugged. "I guess I can't change those workaholic ways after all these years. But don't get tied up. Remember, we're having dinner with Dave and Marge tonight." She cast an apologetic glance toward Scott, then Cassie. "I hope you two don't mind, but this engagement was made weeks ago. We really should go."

"Don't give it a thought, Grandma. I'm going to take Cassie out to dinner tonight."

Theo folded the paper and got to his feet. "Want to come with me?" he asked Scott.

"Not this morning. I thought I'd show Cassie our fair city."

"It's gonna be pretty hot for sightseeing," Theo said but didn't press the issue. He simply left the room, went out the front door, and a minute later the others heard his car start. Before meeting Scott's grandfather, Cassie would have bet that a man of his stature had a chauffeur. Now that she knew Theo, however, the idea seemed ludicrous.

"Do you need your car today, Grandma?" Scott asked Norma. "I'll be glad to rent one."

"No take it. I have a mealybug problem in the greenhouse, so I'll have to wash all the leaves of the infected plants with rubbing alcohol. Tedious, but I despise using pesticides on my dear plants."

Despite the heat, Cassie and Scott managed to put in a full day doing touristy things. At noon they stopped for Mexican food, then spent two hours in the old historic stockyards district, sopping up the Old West atmosphere, something Cassie thoroughly enjoyed. But by late afternoon, thunderheads had built up to the point that they were in for a real storm. They beat a retreat back to the house, arriving just before it opened up. While the wind blew and the thunder crashed and the rain came down in silvery sheets, they listened as Norma told them about her relentless assault on the mealybugs. The cocktail hour arrived at about the same time Theo did. Scott mixed a drink for his grandfather, poured a glass of wine for both Cassie and his grandmother and opened a beer for himself. After another convivial half hour or so, everyone went upstairs to dress for their dinner dates. Scott had made reservations at the country club for seven-thirty.

Forty-five minutes later, the storm had blown itself out. Scott waited downstairs, dressed to the teeth in a dark business suit. It had been a long time since he'd worn one, and he couldn't say he felt comfortable. If he'd had his way, he would have put on his High Country garb and taken Cassie to his favorite barbecue-and-beer joint. But he thought she might like to go somewhere really nice.

One by one everyone else drifted down. Cassie was last, and when she appeared at the threshold of the room, Scott thought she was so beautiful that for a moment he actually could not breathe. She was wear-

ing a dress in some kind of flowing material that was
the color of ripe peaches, and by some mysterious al-
chemy, the same color seemed to suffuse her cheeks.
She walked into the room, smiling sweetly, and he
wanted her so badly he couldn't speak.

Cassie had paused at the threshold because once she
got a look at Scott, she hadn't been able to move.
Never having seen him in anything but casual clothes,
she had to take a minute to come to grips with the as-
tonishingly handsome picture he presented. He was so
distinguished, like an unusually young chairman of the
board. The strangest feeling overtook her. She realized she didn't like seeing him that way, that it only
served to underscore the differences in their lives. She
wanted him back in jeans and boots, expounding all
those absurd theories of his, just looking... familiar.

But then he turned and saw her, and all her doubts
vanished. A woman would have to be incredibly naive not to read the message in his eyes. They filled with
wonder and not just a little lust, and he smiled. Walking up to her, he spoke in a voice barely above a whisper. "Words fail me, Cassie. I think you might be the
most beautiful sight I've ever seen."

"Th—thanks. That's nice to hear."

He took her by the hand, and they joined his
grandparents. As Cassie sat down, she chanced to notice the expression on Theo's face. Having seen Scott's
reaction to her, he frowned slightly. Her heart sank.
He doesn't approve, she thought.

Well, of course he doesn't approve, her sensible inner voice said. *You didn't expect him to, did you? It's
the same as with your dad. Nothing personal. It simply isn't what they had in mind.*

Then Theo's frown subsided, and he smiled. "How nice you look, my dear."

"Thank you, Mr. Maitland."

"You really do look wonderful, Cassie," Norma chimed in. "Such a gorgeous color! You know, I have a new rose that's almost exactly the same shade. Exquisite. Come on, Theo, we must be on our way. I dislike keeping anyone waiting. Scott, darling, be sure to lock the front door when you leave. You still have a key, I hope."

"Sure do. You guys have a good time."

Every muscle in Scott's body tensed when the front door closed behind his grandparents. The house was absolutely quiet except for the drumming of his own heartbeat. He and Cassie were alone, completely alone, with no one but themselves to answer to. The thought was so enticing that it sent his pulses racing. Without being conscious of doing so, he glanced at his watch. It was five after seven. How would she feel if he simply called the club and cancelled their reservations? It was a little late for that, but... With deliberation, he walked to the bar at the far end of the room. "Would..." He was forced to clear his throat before continuing. "Would you like a drink?"

"Do we have time?"

"For a quick one."

"I think I'll pass and have something before dinner."

Scott reached for the handle of the bar's refrigerator, noticed the unsteadiness of his hand and changed his mind. He didn't want a beer. Turning, he looked across the room at Cassie and found her staring at him with the strangest expression. Currents of electricity seemed to sizzle back and forth between them. He thought he was going to explode. What would she think if he suggested they just not go? He honestly didn't know, couldn't begin to guess. That expression on her face was undecipherable. He didn't know that much about Cassie, not yet, and that was why he wouldn't suggest it. They were on the brink of something wonderful, and he could botch it quickly with a thoughtless move. Steady, he cautioned himself. Not too eager, not too lustful. Try not to think about making love for a couple of hours. He didn't know how he was going to stand it.

One thing he did know: if he so much as touched her right now, he would be on the phone in an instant.

"Are you ready?" he asked.

"Yes," she said, still staring at him.

"Then I guess we'd better go."

THE COUNTRY CLUB was one of the city's oldest, a quietly elegant bastion of exclusiveness. In the dining room the tables were set with starched linens and sterling silver, and a squadron of white-coated waiters moved about unobtrusively, tending to the diners' slightest whim. Cassie was a bit awed by its opulence. "Doesn't look much like Annie's Cafe, does it?" she murmured.

"No, and the food's not as good, either," Scott said with a smile.

"Oh, come on."

"No, I'm kidding. The food is excellent. At least, it always was before."

And it still was. Cassie took great delight in ordering things she had never eaten before, dishes like sweet potato bisque and grilled quail with red pepper sauce. There wasn't one familiar taste, and she ate with rel-

ish. Scott ate, too, but he might as well have ordered
a bowl of soup for all the attention he paid his food.
Mostly he sat watching Cassie in the soft glow of can-
dlelight, enjoying her delight and thinking about
kissing her.

He sipped from his wineglass, and over its rim, he
let his gaze settle on her mouth as she bit into a piece
of meat. Then it roamed down the gentle curve of her
throat to her breasts, and he was no longer thinking
about merely kissing her. Good God, what was wrong
with him? He felt like he had at seventeen when he
thought about sex all the time.

Cassie felt his eyes upon her, looked up and was
startled by what she read in them. Scott had been in
such an unusual mood all evening. Gone was the lazy
charm, the teasing banter. She couldn't even say he
looked thoughtful or serious or preoccupied. He
looked as though someone had kicked him in the
stomach. Apparently he had finished eating, since his
plate had been pushed away. He hadn't eaten much,
while she had all but cleaned her own plate. "Didn't
you like your food?" she inquired solicitously.

"Yes, it was good. Yours?"

"Oh, it was delicious, just...wonderful." Dab-
bing at her lips with a napkin one last time, she pushed
her plate away, too. Their ever-alert waiter scooped it
up immediately, along with Scott's.

"Shall I bring the desert cart, sir?"

Scott glanced at Cassie, but she shook her head.
"No, thanks. I couldn't eat another bite."

"Coffee?"

She shook her head again. Scott turned to the
waiter. "That'll be all, thanks."

The man nodded obsequiously and hurried away. Scott took a drink of water, set down the glass, and his pained expression returned.

"Scott, is something wrong?"

He started to say no, then changed his mind. "Yes, there is."

"What is it?"

"Don't you know?"

Cassie's breath seemed to catch in her throat. She looked at him fully and honestly and saw exactly what was wrong, what he had been thinking about all evening, just as clearly as if he had voiced it. Now she was thinking about it, too. For a minute they might have been the only two people in the room. They were gloriously oblivious to anything but each other. One of her hands rested on the table. Her eyes lowered, and she stared at it. She didn't have the faintest idea what to say.

Scott reached across the table and covered her hand with his. "It's still early. I doubt the folks will be home anytime soon."

Cassie was sure she was strangling. She didn't know just how long she sat there rigidly, simply looking at him, unable to speak and wondering what, if anything, was registering on her face. He might as well have said, "Let's go to bed before my grandparents get home." That's what he meant. She could feel her face grow warm and hated that. "Scott, I..."

"Just say no, if that's what you want."

"That's the trouble. I'm...not sure...that's what I want."

Scott's throat grew tight. With the lift of a finger he summoned their waiter, who appeared with their dinner check on a little tray. Scott signed it, adding the man's tip to the amount. Cassie picked up her handbag, and like two robots, they stood and left the dining room.

When Scott pulled in to the driveway of the stately house where he had spent the better part of his life, he couldn't remember getting there. He didn't think Cassie had spoken so much as a word since leaving the club. Did she regret this? He'd know. As soon as they got inside where there was privacy and he could talk to her, he'd know. She had to want to make love as badly as he did, or it wouldn't happen. It was as simple as that, but ... dear God, he hoped she did. His stomach muscles were so tight they hurt.

It was odd, Cassie thought, that she hadn't had misgivings until she stepped into the foyer of the house. Then she tensed. It didn't seem they should be there, thinking what they were thinking, and she couldn't have said why. It just didn't seem right.

She felt Scott standing behind her, then his hands at her waist. With the gentlest pressure, he turned her to face him. Studying her intently, he tried to give a name to what he saw in her eyes. Uncertainty? Probably. He could hardly blame her since he felt a little uncertain himself. Not about wanting her—he had never been more sure about anything—but about this being the right time and place. He hadn't been confused back at the club, but he was now. He bent his head and kissed her tenderly, with the barest touch of passion, and when he raised his head he smiled. Standing so close, he could feel the tenseness leave her body. She smiled back. So he kissed her again, and this time he put his heart into it. He was rewarded by the feel of her arms slipping around him and her hands rubbing his back. When they parted, she smiled again.

Scott was faced with man's ever-present problem—the inability to do any serious courting while standing up, and it certainly was not yet time to sweep her into his arms and carry her upstairs. Instead, he merely took her by the hand and led her through the dining room and into the sun room where one small lamp had been left on. While Cassie sat down on the love seat, he removed his suit coat and his tie, undid the collar of his shirt, then sat down next to her, comfortably close.

Cassie relaxed in the warm curve his arm made and laid a hand on his knee. It came across as more of a companionable gesture than a sensuous one. She felt him nuzzle her hair. An involuntary sigh escaped her lips. It amazed her that Scott had sensed her need for a quiet interlude like this before they progressed to the inevitable.

Lord, it's been such a long time, she thought. *I wonder if I'll remember how to behave.* Then Scott moved his mouth to her ear. The warm feeling that raced through her was soon replaced by a sharp, sweet sense of need, and she knew she would do all right. He made her feel so wonderful, so womanly, so desirable. She turned her face so that he could kiss her mouth.

"Oh, Cassie...sweet... I wish I knew how to tell you..." Warm and moist, his mouth opened to claim hers. He felt her nestle closer to him, and the hand on his knee moved upward. He reached for the hem of her dress, raised the filmy material, and he stroked her stocking-clad thigh. He kissed and stroked her until she was intoxicated, drunk with courage.

That was when they heard the car door slam—one, then another. Lifting his head, Scott looked at his watch, frowning. "It can't be," he muttered almost inaudibly. "It's not even nine-thirty." But a moment later they heard the front door open, and he knew it could be. His body sagged. His grandparents were home. Looking down, he saw Cassie's upturned face, her parted lips and half-closed eyes, and he actually wanted to cry.

When Theo and Norma walked into the room they found Cassie seated and Scott flipping the channels on the television set. He turned and smiled. "Well, you two are home pretty early."

Theo grumbled. "After we ate, Dave and I just sat there getting sleepy, so I said the heck with it. How was your dinner?"

"It was fantastic," Cassie said, still struggling with a heartbeat that was faster than normal.

"Yeah, the club puts on a pretty good spread. Anything worth watching on the tube? I seem to have gotten my second wind. I'm not near as sleepy as I was at Dave's. I probably was just bored by Marge's incessant chatter."

"Be kind, dear. Poor Marge's problem is the lack of any real interests," Norma said. "If you aren't sleepy, I am, so I'm going to toddle off to bed." Acknowledging a chorus of good-nights, she left the room.

Absently, Scott turned to the sports channel. There was a baseball game on. Theo settled into his favorite chair, folded his hands across his middle and began watching. Scott looked at Cassie; Cassie looked at Scott. She read such disappointment in his eyes, then resignation. There was nothing to do but go through the pretense of watching TV, at least for a while. He sat back down beside her and slid his arm along the back of the love seat. His fingertips fell lightly on her shoulders, and they sat vacantly staring at the screen. Theo made some comment about the game, and Scott responded with a grunt. Cassie thought she could actually feel the tension in the air, like a tangible thing, but possibly it was only within herself. Theo didn't appear to notice anything amiss.

At ten o'clock the elderly man switched channels to the news. With some difficulty, Cassie got to her feet. "I think I'll go to bed now. If you'll excuse me..."

"Of course, dear," Theo said. "Good night."

Scott got to his feet and gently placed a hand on her arm. She tried to look at him, discovered she couldn't and dipped her lashes. "Good night," she said softly.

"Good night, Cassie." He watched her leave the room, a longing inside him that was like a knife twisting his stomach. He would have liked to follow her but decided against it. What good would it do? With a definite sag to his shoulders, he sat back down and stared at the TV once more.

A few minutes passed; then his grandfather turned to him. "Son, I've been to four goat ropin's and a couple'a county fairs."

The hint of a smile touched the corners of Scott's mouth. That was his grandfather's favorite way of saying "I've been around, and nothing much gets by me." Scott nodded but said nothing.

"You look at that little gal like you're starving to death and she's a ham sandwich. Better be careful. After talkin' to her yesterday I got the impression wild horses couldn't drag her off 'a that ranch of hers. You just better be careful."

Scott clasped his hands and stared at them. "Yeah," he said obscurely.

"Now, I know what it's like to itch. I panted after your grandma for a year before she'd let me touch her, so I know. But there are plenty of gals around who can scratch an itch."

This is probably the perfect time to tell him, Scott thought. Just tell him the way I feel about the Horseshoe, about Cassie. Tell him I itch, all right, but there's only one woman who can scratch it. Instead, he continued staring at his hands and said nothing.

"When you first came up with this ranchin' stuff, I thought it'd give you somethin' to do till business picked up. Now, if you want to keep the ranch in the family, well and good. We'll hire some tenants to take care of it, and you can go play with it every once in a while. But you'd better not go gettin' too attached to that little gal. I got some things in mind, and they include you." Theo then set his chin determinedly, which meant he had said all he intended saying. He gave his attention to the TV again. "Looks like we got some weather headin' our way. That gonna do anything to your plans tomorrow?"

UPSTAIRS, CASSIE had finished getting ready for bed and was reaching for the bedside lamp switch when there was a knock at the door.

"Yes?" she called.

"It's Scott."

She cinched her robe around her waist and went to open the door. "Hi."

"Hi." Reaching out, he touched the side of her face. "Seems like there's some stormy weather due in here tomorrow afternoon. Nothing in our part of the world, though. I'm thinking maybe we ought to leave here early in the morning. That okay with you?"

"Of course. You're the captain."

"I'd like to leave before nine."

"Fine. I'll be ready."

His eyes telegraphed a yearning that made her heart leap. She leaned toward him and placed a melting kiss on his mouth. "Good night."

"There are some doors between us tonight, but they won't always be there. Good night." He hesitated, then backed away and walked down the hall to his own room.

Closing the door, Cassie leaned her head against it for a moment. Something he had said lingered in her mind. *Our part of the world. Ours!*

THEY WERE AT THE AIRPORT by eight-thirty the following morning, driven there by Theo himself, and shortly before nine, they were airborne. The trip home took longer since they were bucking the prevailing south wind the whole way. Later, Cassie couldn't remember what they had talked about during the trip or if they'd done much talking at all. It was almost eleven-thirty when Scott hangared the plane. As he got their luggage out of the hold, he said, "Let's go inside and see what we can rustle up for lunch."

"Let's," she said simply, knowing all the while that food was the last thing he was thinking about. He wanted to get her behind locked doors. She wanted it, too.

The walk from the hangar seemed like a yawning mile to Scott, but ahead was the house, a sanctuary, a place where they could shut out the rest of the world. Cassie had been so quiet during the flight, and even now she was saying nothing, just walking fast, staying abreast of him. What was she thinking? They climbed the steps of the deck, and Scott unlocked the back door. Cassie stepped into the kitchen. He had closed all the blinds before he had left. The house was dim and quiet. Behind her she heard the door close and the click of the lock.

Scott set the suitcases on the floor and walked to stand behind her. "No one expects you home until just before sundown, right?" His voice sounded husky, strained.

"Right."

He stepped closer, close enough to get a whiff of her cologne. For three days his need for her had consumed him. Now the wanting was a fire. He wanted to get inside her head, her heart, her body, to become lost in her. If she didn't want the same thing, he honestly didn't know what he would do. He was a bit old for tears. "Is there any reason for anyone to know you're back?"

She hesitated, but only for a couple of seconds. "I can't think of one."

He expelled a ragged breath. "Good Lord, we really are alone at last."

"I was thinking the same thing." She turned to him with shining eyes. "Isn't this marvelous? It seems I've been wanting this for a very long time."

CHAPTER ELEVEN

CASSIE SEEMED TO FLOAT right into his arms, and Scott reached for her as if grabbing a lifeline. His hands went around her waist and lingered a moment before one crawled up her back and the other moved lower. He held her against him so tightly she could barely breathe. They kissed, then again and again, each kiss growing more fiercely passionate. When they finally broke apart, both were visibly shaken.

"Lord, this is all I've thought about since Friday," Scott admitted. "I thought I was losing my mind. I haven't been in such bad shape since I was a teenager."

Cassie realized it was almost all she'd thought about, too. "I know."

He recalled his grandfather's words: "You look at that little gal like you're starving to death." "I was that obvious, huh?"

"I . . . I think I probably noticed because, frankly, I was thinking about it, too."

Her admission tantalized him. "I'm laying it on the line. I'm crazy about you . . . insane. I've been falling in love with you since the first time I saw you. Do you have any idea how a man hates being out of control? Several times I've thought I've read something in your eyes, and I know how you kiss me, but you've never said a word to give me a clue as to how you feel."

"I think..." She swallowed hard and tried again. "I think I love you. Oh, Scott, it must be love. A woman doesn't want like this unless she's in love." Capturing his bottom lip between her teeth, she nibbled gently. "It hurts and feels good all at once."

"I know."

"It's been a long time for me."

"For me, too."

"You just don't seem the celibate type to me."

"I mean it's been a long time since I've felt, really felt something. I had forgotten what it's like to have your nerve ends tingle, to want...well, a lot more than just sex. I guess what I'm trying to say is, I had forgotten how it feels to care."

He kissed her again, moving his mouth back and forth across the unresisting line of her lips. Her hands roamed over his back, rubbing, petting. Scott felt almost numb from wanting her; yet a vital part of him was leaping to life. Cupping her buttocks, he held her and moved his hips slightly, hoping to ease the ache, but the movement only caused the pressure to intensify.

Cassie gasped and leaned back to steady herself. Her legs felt weak and rubbery and incapable of support. She looked at him, her mouth slightly open. She saw desire blazing from his eyes, and it excited her even more. "Scott, I...I don't think I can stand up much longer."

He nodded, but a minute passed before he released her. Then, holding her hand, he walked out of the kitchen into the hall and turned right.

Cassie had never been in this part of the house. They passed two small bedrooms and a bath and entered Scott's bedroom at the far end of the hall. It was

a neat, elegant room, a completely masculine retreat.
The big bed against the wall was covered with a navy-
blue and rust spread. There was an oversized club
chair by one window, and next to it was a table laden
with books. A tall chest of drawers in burnished oak
stood against one wall. The room was very like Scott
himself. In her entire life she had not been in a man's
bedroom. She and Robert had shared her childhood
room. The drapes and blinds were closed, making the
room dark even at midday. The rest of the world
seemed far away, and that was where she wanted it to
stay.

"It's such a nice room, Scott." *Oh, Cassie, what a
dumb thing to say!*

He turned and gathered her to him. "Except for my
housekeeper, you're the only woman who's ever been
in it."

"I'm glad."

"So am I. I really am." Scott felt strangely choked
up and inarticulate. Where were all the smooth,
soothing words that a man used with a woman in a
situation like this? At some time in his dim, distant
past he had been pretty good with all those hot whispered phrases, but now he couldn't think of a damned
thing to say. He just hoped he could make it good for
her. Not only good, but perfect.

Suddenly Cassie felt awkward. She wasn't sure what
her first move should be. Should she begin undressing or wait for him to do it? He was just holding her,
not moving at all. Resting her head on his shoulder,
she flicked at the first button of his shirt, then the
second, and her hand slipped inside to feel the satis-
fying warmth of his chest. It was broad and hard and
had a small, thick thatch of coarse hair. "Oh, Scott,

you feel wonderful. Just wonderful." She heard his sharp intake of breath, and she flicked the third button out of its hole.

That simple movement of her fingers galvanized Scott into action. He looked down at her just as she looked up at him. The blood was pumping so hotly through his veins he was sure she could see it. "Cassie." It was an agonized sigh. "Cassie."

She was wearing a jumpsuit that zipped up the front, and Scott knew a woman wouldn't wear much underneath a garment like that. The thought brought his excitement to a fevered pitch. She kicked off her shoes; he fumbled for the zipper. One sweeping motion of his hand and a push off her shoulders was all that was needed to dispense with it. She stood before him in a wisp of bra and a lacy brief. Her breasts weren't large, but they were high and full, mounding slightly above the bra. Her waist was trim, and she had wonderfully long, straight legs, beautiful velvety thighs. When he reached down to stroke them, she parted them slightly.

Scott practically ripped his shirt trying to take it off. He undid his belt and whipped it off, then unzipped his jeans. He was starting to push them down his hips when Cassie stepped forward, slid her arms around his neck and pressed her breasts against his chest. "I want to feel your skin next to mine," she said, never dreaming she would ever say those words to a man.

His hands stopped what they were doing and moved upward to unfasten the clasp of her bra. He pushed the tiny straps down her arms, and the piece of lingerie fell to the floor between them. "There, that's better," he said, and he took a soft mound in each hand, teasing their tips with his thumbs. Cassie pressed her lips against the small valley at the base of his throat, murmuring a sensual litany of nonsensical words. They rubbed and petted and kissed until the molten fire in their loins had them on the edge of explosion.

Scott stepped back and impatiently pushed at his jeans, but Cassie stopped his hands with hers. "Your boots," she said. "You forgot your boots."

He almost fell on the edge of the bed and realized he had forgotten to turn down the spread, too. He was handling this as clumsily as a teenager. He lifted one leg, but it was Cassie who bent over and tugged at the boot and then at the other. She raised her head, smiling, and gently pushed him back on the bed. "Let me finish for you. You seem to be having some trouble."

Numbly, Scott complied, lifting his hips slightly to help her. When she had freed him of both his jeans and undershorts, the magnificent extent of his arousal was evident. Without taking her eyes off him, she wiggled out of her panties.

"God a'mighty, Cassie, you must be the most gorgeous woman on earth!"

Uttering a little laugh of happy triumph, she almost leaped toward the bed, landing on top of him. For a minute or two he simply lay beneath her, enjoying her kisses, the salty-sweet taste of her tongue. But when she began erotically moving her hips against him, the gentleness, the fun, gave way to the need they shared, and what ensued was a whirlwind of passion. Their arms and legs entwined. They rolled and tossed, kissed and petted. Like a hungry man, Scott tasted her breasts, the taut flesh of her stomach, the inside of her thighs. Cassie found his turgid, throbbing manhood and encased it with her fingers, urging him toward the place where his mouth was.

"Cassie, I wanted to make it last and last," he murmured.

"Don't. I can't stand it anymore, Scott. I want to feel you inside me."

"Wait, just...a...minute." His tongue continued to tantalize her until she writhed and moaned and shuddered uncontrollably. Then he moved up over her, entering, thrusting until in no time she felt the spasms begin. Heat erupted in the very core of her body; her limbs shook. Scott kissed her open mouth and closed eyelids, keeping the tempo, the rhythm, striving for endurance but losing the fight. Finally there was nothing he could do but give in to it and seek his own release. The climax seemed to go on and on and on.

Cassie lay beneath him, scarcely noticing the weight of his spent body. Her own seemed weightless. It amazed her that she felt so different—warm and content and happily sated in the aftermath. Everything about her seemed to have changed in what had only been a flash of time. Even her skin felt different, so flushed and rosy. She had loved every second of it. She reminded herself of the heroine in that novel—totally uninhibited, unashamedly reveling in a man's love-making. She honestly couldn't remember anything to equal it. Scott made her realize how barren her life had been. Where had such unbridled passion come from? It was completely new to her, but having experienced it once, she suspected she'd never want to be without it again.

With a lusty sigh, Scott rolled off her and drew her against him where he could hold her in his arms. For long wordless minutes they simply lay there, entwined. Finally he asked, "Are you cold?"

"No, I've never been warmer in my life. That was wonderful. I never wanted it to end."

"Nothing lasts forever, sweetheart, especially that. It was all I could do to make it last as long as it did."

"Mmm, you'll make me your slave."

"Good, just what I always wanted—a slave."

"It sounds super corny to say it was never like that, but I have to. It never was."

"You have my permission to sound corny. To tell you the truth, it hasn't been that good for me too many times in my life."

Cassie uttered a scoffing sound. "Come on, you're just saying that. I've heard men talk when they didn't know I was within earshot. 'Sex is like home cooking; even when it's not too good it's pretty good.'"

"That's locker room talk, and I wasn't just saying that. Today, us, was special."

"What makes it special for a man?"

"Oh..." He hugged her closer. "Wanting to do this, for one thing. Not wanting it to end. Not wanting to get up, put on my pants and go home."

She smiled against his chest. "You are home."

"I don't want you to go home. Is that better?"

"Yes." Snuggling against him, she stretched and purred like a satisfied cat. A minute or so passed, and she realized that Scott was absolutely still, his breathing shallow and his hold on her relaxed. "You're not going to sleep, are you?"

"The thought crossed my mind."

"It seems a shame to waste any of this glorious afternoon sleeping."

"You wore me out, sweetheart."

"Oh, surely not. I feel marvelous, so alive, like...like I could dance until dawn. And I haven't danced in years."

A chuckle rumbled up from his chest. "Good Lord."

Stirring, Cassie raised her head so her lips could make tiny kisses along his neck. "Your skin is so warm, and it tastes good." She kissed the hollow of his throat. "I feel your heartbeat here." She laid her lips against the hollow again. "It's getting faster."

"I'll say."

Her fingertips traced a trail of fire down his flat belly, stopping to play with the line of coarse hair before continuing their downward journey. She cupped him, held him, stroked him, while the tip of her tongue traced circles around his flat nipples. Scott allowed her the pleasure of gazing at and fondling his body, sensing that she was discovering an eroticism she had never known before. Each spot was touched and studied intently, as though she'd never seen a man's body before, so he lay as still as he could for as long as he could, letting her satisfy her curiosity.

But soon he was rising and hardening again and longing to be buried deep inside her. His temples throbbed, his heart lurched. The ache in his groin was becoming unbearable. He gave her another minute; then his hands grabbed her buttocks.

Scott lifted her effortlessly, and she sat astride his hips. She rocked slowly for a minute, savoring the feel of him. Then she lowered herself upon him and felt him fill her again. His hands held her breasts, something she discovered she loved. She could count on her fingers the times she had climaxed with Robert, and then she had had to be the one to work at it. But she and Scott immediately found the rhythm again, as perfect as before. Cassie was astonished that it could be so good. Their bodies moved together, faster, lost in a blaze of feeling, climbing to the mountain top, faster still, until they fell trembling to earth.

"Oh, God, Cassie, I love you."

"I love you, too."

"Feels good, doesn't it?"

"It feels wonderful. I've learned so much about myself this afternoon. I don't know how to tell you... You see, I never knew... I just never knew... I could cry."

"I know."

"Do you? Yes, maybe you do. That's why you're so special."

She was exhausted and exhilarated all at the same time. At last they slept.

"HOW OLD WERE YOU when you first got interested in girls?" Cassie was propped on one elbow, drawing light circles on his chest with the tip of her fingernail.

Scott smiled lazily. "Jesus, what a question! Women ask the damnedest things. What you really want to know is when I got interested in sex, right?"

"Well... I never had a brother, and this certainly isn't something I could discuss with my son."

"What about your husband?"

She looked away for a second. "I think a question like that coming from me would have embarrassed him."

Ah, Scott thought, that explained her curiosity. Her husband must have been one of those men who couldn't open up with a woman. She had missed a lot. He pursed his lips. "Fourteen, I guess. Definitely by

fifteen. I very happily lost my virginity on my six-
teenth birthday. An older guy fixed me up with someone who was 'experienced.' "

"Sixteen! No wonder you're so good. You've had
a lot of practice."

"I'm going to take that as a fantastic compliment."

She lay back down, resting her head on his shoulder. "Sixteen. Rob's age."

Scott rolled over so he could look down at her. The
last thing he wanted to talk about or even think about
was Rob. He brushed her hair away from her face and
kissed her tenderly. "Do you know what time it is?"

"No, and frankly, my dear, I don't give a damn."

"It's two o'clock, and we haven't eaten since seven.
Aren't you hungry?"

"Strange, but I haven't given food a thought."

"Well, I'm going to have to eat something. I'm
wasted."

"Spoil sport."

But Cassie had to admit that the thought of food
suddenly had appeal. They dressed quickly, and minutes later they were sitting in the kitchen munching on
sandwiches and drinking root beer. She hadn't known
how ravenous she was. Scott watched her with
amusement. "You're a woman of lusty appetites,
love."

She smiled at him sheepishly. "I guess I am."

"And you didn't realize that before today, right?"

"Yes." Raising a napkin to her lips, she dabbed
daintily. "Thanks to you, I've learned a lot about
myself I didn't know."

"For instance."

"For instance, I didn't know I was capable of un-inhibited behavior."

"Passion," he corrected.

"All right, passion. It's new to me. I wouldn't have dreamed I was capable of rushing headlong into a re-lationship I had doubts about."

"Us?"

She nodded. "I didn't think we were well suited at all. I didn't think we had anything in common. But there was an attraction right from the start, and I did nothing to discourage it. That just wasn't character-istic. I've always been such a sensible person."

Scott felt a stab of emotion he couldn't give a name to. "And loving me isn't sensible, is that what you're saying?"

Cassie looked at him and smiled wistfully. "No, I'm saying that loving you probably isn't sensible, but I don't care. That's what's so unusual. I don't care."

"Ah, Cassie." He put an arm around her shoul-ders and gave her a little hug. "I don't think love is ever sensible. That's what makes it so great, so much fun."

"And it was fun. That's what really knocked me for a loop. It was grand, glorious fun. I didn't think any-thing like this would ever happen to me, and I'm going to enjoy every second of it."

Her sandwich was laid aside, and she turned to him, smiling. "This is going to cause an awful lot of talk, you know. You'll never be able to keep it a secret, not around here."

"Secret? I don't want to keep it a secret. I'll take out an ad in the paper, if you like. Scott Maitland loves Cassie Tate, with a plus between our names, like kids carve on tree trunks."

"Did you ever do that? Carve a girl's name on a tree trunk?"

"Hell, no, and I never knew anyone else who did, either."

"For sure none of the fellows I knew when I was growing up would have been caught dead doing such a thing."

"What was it like growing up here?" Scott asked. "I gave you a glimpse of my past, but I don't know much about yours."

Cassie gave it some thought. "It was...nice. I don't mean dull. I just mean nice. This is a quiet part of the world, and I don't guess there are too many of those left. When I was a kid, you didn't make waves or do much except what you were told to do. You have to remember, I started college in 1968. All those riots and sit-ins and protests, pot smoking and easy sex. It was like it happened on another planet. There was none of that around here. I never knew anyone who was involved in that sort of thing. We went to 4-H meetings and raised livestock to show at county fairs. That's what it was like, and I loved it."

"You've never had the urge to roam, to see other places?"

"Not really. Once in college one of my professors gave an assignment—pick a place you'd like to live if you couldn't live here, then write a report on it. My friends all picked places like Paris and Rome and Hawaii. I wrote mine on the Australian Outback. Does that tell you anything about me?"

Scott laughed.

"I thought I'd like to see it, but I never thought I wanted to actually live there. I figured I'd miss the green. Of course, this country isn't always as green as it is now. The rains did wonders for it." She took a sip of root beer. "Of all the places you've lived, which did you like best?"

"Home."

"You mean Fort Worth."

"Until recently. Now I think of this as home. I like it here." He grinned at her wickedly. "I wonder why."

"I can't imagine. Must be the climate." Cassie's throat seemed to close, and relief engulfed her. He thought of this as home. He would stay. She was very quiet, savoring that knowledge.

Cassie planned to leave just before sundown, but she didn't want to go, and Scott didn't want her to. She was sure this was the first time in her life she hadn't been itching to get back to the ranch after being gone for even a short time. Later she couldn't have said what they talked about for the remainder of the afternoon. Nothing very noteworthy. They simply enjoyed the quiet time together. Mostly Scott puttered around and worked in his office, while Cassie inspected his house. She studied some family photographs and was particularly interested in the ones of his parents. They were a handsome couple who looked high society, but Cassie conceded that that conclusion might have been drawn because she knew they were.

Scott owned books, all sorts of books, more books than she had ever seen gathered in one place except a library. Many were textbooks, but she noticed that he read Westerns and spy thrillers for entertainment. That was a little tidbit of information about him she hadn't known before, and somehow it seemed important. She wondered what he would think about the rape-and-take saga that was lying on her bedside table. The thought brought a smile to her face.

At six o'clock she gathered up her things and prepared to go home, but when she went to see Scott in his office, he protested. "I don't want you to go, sweetheart."

"If I don't show up before it gets dark, Dad'll have a posse out looking for me. He doesn't trust that plane of yours any more than I do...er, did."

"Then call home, tell 'em we just got in, and you're staying for supper."

It was too irresistible to turn down. "I guess I could, couldn't I?" she said and reached for the phone on his desk.

"Well, I'm glad to hear you're back safe and sound." J.B.'s voice had a strange inflection that surprised Cassie. "Did you have a good time?"

"Wonderful."

"That's good." His tone was flat.

"Listen, Dad, I'm going to have supper over here. I'll be home soon afterward, okay?"

A split second of silence passed before J.B. answered. "Reckon so."

"See you later. 'Bye."

"Goodbye, Cassie."

She remained standing by the phone with her hand on the instrument for a minute, a small frown furrowing her brow. Scott noticed. "Something wrong?"

"What?" She turned to him. "Oh, not really. I think Dad's a little taken aback by my sudden fascination with you."

Scott thought of Theo. "Yeah."

"I don't think it's personal," she added quickly. "It's more on the order of the way your grandfather feels about me."

"You caught on to that, huh?"

"Yes. What's more, I have a sneaking hunch that Rob is going to be jealous. He's pretty well liked having you as his friend."

Scott smiled and shook his head. "For a couple of people who mean no harm, you and I suddenly seem to be making waves all over the place. Funny, to me this seems just about the most right thing that's happened in my life."

"Me, too."

Scott rubbed his chin thoughtfully. "And those Ferenbach traditions scare hell out of me sometimes."

"Scare you? That's absurd."

"Is it? What if your father asks you to stop seeing me?"

"Good Lord, Scott. I'm practically a middle-aged woman. Dad wouldn't do that."

"What if he did?"

She pretended to give it serious thought. "I guess I'd handle it the way you dealt with your grandfather. I'd be sweet and respectful, but then I'd run over here as fast as my little legs would carry me."

"Your legs aren't little. They're long and gorgeous, and you have thighs that feel like velvet."

He was lounging in his swivel chair behind the desk, grinning that disarming grin. Cassie smiled seductively and moved around the desk, sliding onto his lap. He spread his legs to accommodate her. Wrapping her arms around his neck, she forced his head back and kissed his mouth soundly, sliding her tongue between his teeth. He relaxed and enjoyed the kiss, then held her tightly and returned it. When they parted, he smiled mischievously. "I'm finding it hard to believe that this is the same woman who, only a few short months ago, marched over here to tell me, in no uncertain terms, that everything I was doing on this ranch was wrong. Her eyes flashed fire, and she called me Mr. Maitland. That can't have been this little spitfire."

Her smile matched his. "Oh, you still do some pretty goofy things when it comes to ranching, but . . . you do other things so well that I couldn't possibly quarrel with them. Ooh, I do love the way you feel, Scott. So . . . manly." Rubbing her hips against him suggestively, she kissed him again, then once more. The pressure of his embrace intensified. She moved again.

"Cassie," he gasped, "you can't possibly be considering . . . again . . ."

"Why? Is there a limit to how many times . . ."

"I'm afraid a man is limited in his ability to perform."

"Hush. Just put yourself in my capable hands." Her hands began all the sensuous maneuvers designed to excite and arouse. Some of them she had read about in that novel. She went on a rampage of kissing, nipping, licking. In no time at all his eyes had that glazed look. Oh, she felt wild, wicked and wanton and insatiable, and she was having the time of her life.

"Mmm," she murmured against his neck, "I wish I could crawl up inside you so I'd never have to be away from you, not even for a minute. I don't want you to leave out a thing, not one detail."

"Good Lord, sweetheart..."

Her hands and mouth never stopped working. By now she had his clothing in total disarray. To Scott's surprise and everlasting gratitude he felt himself rising again. The temperature of his body seemed to have heated up by several degrees. He was holding Cassie so tightly he wondered how she could breathe. The swivel chair began to sway. He clutched her hips and tried to lift her.

"Darling, I'm about to explode. Off to the bedroom."

"No," she whispered.

"No?"

"Here," she demanded.

"Here? In this chair?"

"No, it moves too much. The floor."

She slithered out of his lap and pulled him with her. Scott gave the chair a kick, and it went sliding across the floor, bumping into the wall. Levering himself over her, he looked down at her heavy-lidded eyes, her smiling mouth and reached for the jumpsuit's zipper. She reached for the top snap of his jeans. Cassie's capable hands! He'd never experienced a day like today in his entire life. He was living out every romantic fantasy he'd ever had.

CHAPTER TWELVE

CASSIE HAD NEVER been happier, and it showed. Almost everyone she knew had commented on how wonderful she looked, though only a few suspected the reason behind it. She refused to let anyone intrude on her happiness, not even J.B. or Rob, who weren't exactly thrilled over her new romance. She understood. She couldn't expect her father or her son to comprehend what loving Scott had done for her, the heady new dimension he had added to her life. Sometimes she had the oddest urge to throw up her hands and shout with glee.

Her father watched this obvious new happiness with concern, wondering just what Cassie was getting into. J.B., like Theo, simply didn't think his daughter and Scott Maitland were well suited, although he had sensed that some sort of undercurrent had existed between them from the beginning. Cassie, he now could see, had never been indifferent to Scott. The initial hostility hadn't lasted long. If there was one thing he was sure of, it was that Cassie's feelings about Scott weren't hostile. He'd never seen a woman with more stars in her eyes. A part of him wanted to protect his daughter, while a more sensible part of him was reminded that Cassie was a thirty-eight-year-old widow with a son. He doubted she would welcome his "protection."

Still, J.B. couldn't see a fellow like Scott hanging around these parts very long, and he was sure that Cassie would never leave. He feared she wouldn't be able to handle a broken heart. Despite her age, his daughter wasn't very sophisticated when it came to men. He thought about that a lot, and worried about it even more.

But he didn't discuss his uneasiness with Cassie. It was up to her to ask if she wanted his advice, and J.B. wasn't sure he'd give it even if she did ask. Giving advice was a surefire, guaranteed way of falling into a bucket of worms.

Rob's reaction to the new closeness between Cassie and Scott was just as complicated as his grandfather's, though in a different way. At first he couldn't believe there was anything serious going on between them. To the boy's way of thinking, Scott was the neatest guy around, and his mother was just ... well, just Mom. He found it all but impossible to imagine her attracting a man's attention.

But not even a sixteen-year-old could continue to ignore the obvious affection between them, and as the weeks wore on, he became increasingly miffed about it. He was jealous, pure and simple. How could he talk to Scott or have any fun with him if his mother was always hanging around?

Then a peculiar thing happened. Rob suddenly noticed that Cassie didn't hover as much as she used to. She wasn't constantly badgering him to do this or that, and with George working over at Laurie Tyler's place two days a week, Rob could count on two whole days of peace, provided he could stay out of his grandfather's way. He rarely saw Scott alone anymore, so he was also spared those lectures about telling his mother his plans, which he hadn't gotten around to doing yet. That occasionally nagged at his conscience, but he always managed to dismiss it. How could he have a talk with her when she spent half her time over at the Horseshoe?

Actually, when he thought about it, Rob had to admit that things were going pretty smoothly now. He recalled something a teacher once had told the class: anything desirable is attained only by sacrifice. He had attained a measure of freedom; the sacrifice was time with Scott. But he still couldn't figure out what a great guy like that saw in his mother.

The one person who was absolutely thrilled over Cassie's relationship with Scott was Laurie. "I think it's wonderful, super," she confided. "If only something like that would happen to me."

"Oh, Laurie, you mean...you and George...nothing?" Cassie cried in dismay.

"That's pretty much the size of it. He comes over twice a week, regular as clockwork, and he works his buns off. I give him lunch, and he tells me what he's doing and what he's going to do next time. I help him as much as I can or as much as he'll let me. At the end of the day I offer him a beer. He always accepts, and we talk about nothing in particular. Certainly he never talks about himself, no matter how hard I try to get chummy. Then he leaves, and I don't see him again until next time."

"That's a shame," Cassie said. "I think you and George would be so good for each other, even though it might mean losing the best foreman I ever had."

"You know, I've never stopped men dead in their tracks, but they aren't totally indifferent to me, either.

George has me buffaloed. You don't suppose he has a girl somewhere, do you?"

"I can't imagine where she'd be. You'd know if he was seeing someone who lived around here, everyone would know about it."

"Maybe there's a woman back home in Oklahoma."

"Come on. She'd have to be the world's most patient soul. George has been with us four years now and worked in Wyoming before that. No, I'm afraid that foreman of mine has just got a cowboy's natural fear of the ties that bind."

Laurie sighed. "Well, George isn't the first disappointment in my life, and he probably won't be the last. But sometimes when I look into those blue eyes of his, I..." She threw up her hands and laughed. "Forget it."

Cassie thought Laurie's calm acceptance of life was admirable, though her friend was a bit young to have acquired it. And she couldn't talk to Laurie without feeling a little guilty about her own happiness... for a minute or two. Life was too full to have room for negative emotions. She was thirty-eight years old and in love for only the second time in her life. Even then she had done things backward. A woman's first love should be wild, passionate, maybe a little insane. Then, sensibly, the second time around she should opt for companionship, stability, affection, respect. Robert had been her sensible love; Scott was the one who set her on fire.

SUMMER WAS DRAWING TO A CLOSE, and the new school year had begun. Rob didn't bother pretending he wasn't happy to be going back, and that would have bothered Cassie more if she hadn't been so wrapped up in Scott. She wanted to be with him all the time and begrudged the hours they had to be apart. She didn't shirk her duties. No one had cause to fault her performance, but she no longer lived and breathed the DO Ranch. Every spare minute was spent over at the Horseshoe. If Scott was busy in the fields, she walked beside him and listened to him talk to his hired hands. They discussed things she knew very little about, but that didn't matter. She couldn't ever remember being content simply to walk and talk with another human being.

At this point she wasn't prepared to say where they were heading, though she had a pretty good idea, nor did she think about it much. She was living for each day, seizing the moment, and that was something she'd never done in her life. Scott made her feel wildly exhilarated one minute, quietly peaceful the next, and he had the most wonderful knack for always making her feel beautiful and utterly feminine. Small wonder she wasted little time worrying about the reactions of others to the romance.

And what a romance it was. Unbridled passion, the kind she'd read about in novels but suspected didn't exist in real life, was brand new to her, and it was like an unexpected journey to Wonderland, with a new surprise and delight around each bend of the road. Every time she knew she was going to see Scott, she felt a little giddy with excitement, and as she cleared the fence and walked to the Horseshoe on a particularly fine afternoon in September, her step was quick, her spirits high.

Usually she could find Scott close to the house, but that day she had to look all over the place for him. She finally spotted him in one of his pastures, tromping through ankle-deep grass with some kind of tank strapped to his back. Then she saw that there was a wand attached to the tank. Obviously he was spraying the grass. Lord, what was he up to now? He did so many crazy things that she actually found herself waiting with anticipation to see what the next one would be. Perching on the fence, she watched him a minute, marveling at the pleasure she derived merely from looking at him. Then she called out.

"Hey!"

He turned and waved. "Hey, yourself."

"What in the world are you doing?"

He yelled something, but Cassie couldn't understand what it was. "What?"

"Wait a minute. I'll be right there." He turned away, unstrapped the apparatus and, carrying it, began walking toward her. When he reached the fence, he laid the tank on the ground and climbed up to sit beside her. "Hi," he said with a grin.

"Hi." She leaned into his welcoming kiss. "Mmm, you taste salty. Been working hard?"

"Like a slave."

"What are you doing?"

"Destroying the catclaw."

Nothing he did ever really surprised her anymore, so at this rather startling announcement, she merely chuckled, but if ever there was a futile chore, he had found it. "Are you serious? Good Lord, Scott, you could spray every day for twenty years and not get rid of the stuff. These mountains are alive with it."

"Ah, ye of little faith. You just wait. I've already gotten rid of maybe a quarter of the catclaw on my place, and I'll get rid of the rest of it, too, sooner or later.''

Cassie just smiled and shook her head. Catclaw was a spindly shrub with spiked claws on stems that could grow to ten feet, and it had a vicious nature. It sucked precious water out of the ground and tore open the hides of animals and, sometimes, cowboys. But it was indigenous to the area, and on the DO it was considered, along with drought, part of nature's way. The cowboys seemed to derive masochistic pleasure from doing battle with the hated plant. Certainly no one would have thought to try to eradicate it. It was just there, like the grass and the sky and the mountains.

But Scott didn't think that way. He honestly believed he could make nature do the bending, and to that end he labored long and hard every day. Cassie had learned to accept that. She guessed that all those crazy notions were part of his great charm. And looking out over his emerald pastures of lush grass, she admitted to a twinge of envy, even though she suspected that none of his new-fangled measures were destined to pay off over the long haul. Those fancy hybrid grasses would be taken over by the native ones, the catclaw would reseed, and he would have to put up with a drought someday, for drought was as inevitable as the waxing and waning of the moon. So she was convinced that the longer he ranched, the more he would adopt the tried-and-true methods that had worked for a century or more.

Yet he was forever trying to convert her to his way of thinking, so now she was going to try her hand at doing a little converting of her own. It was time Scott got a taste of real ranching life. ''I wonder if I could persuade you to give me twenty-four hours of your time," she said.

"Why, Cassie, sweetheart, you can have all of it."

"I'm serious. Specifically, tomorrow. I want you to ride up to the top pasture with me, just for the heck of it, just to get in a little time in the saddle. I haven't done much cowboying lately, and I miss it. We'd have to be gone overnight. I'd planned to take George or one of the men with me, but..."

That brought Scott's head up with a jerk. "You had thought about spending the night out there with one of the cowboys? Over my dead body!"

"Relax. I'd be as safe as if I were in a granddaddy's lap. No man who works for me would dream of making a pass. The point is, I wonder if you would like to go instead. Cook over an open fire. Sleep under the stars. Get a hefty slice of the great outdoors. And, if you'll pardon the expression, see how a real ranch is run."

He grinned endearingly but said nothing. For a minute Cassie thought he might be going to say no. "You can ride a horse, can't you?"

"Of course I can ride a horse."

"There seems to be a pitiful lack of horseflesh here on the Horseshoe, but you can ride one of ours. I'll pick out a gentle one for you."

"I don't need a gentle one, Cassie. You can give me one named El Diablo for all I care. I rode a lot when I was younger."

Her eyes sparkled. "I'm really anxious to go, but if you don't want to come with me, I'll just get someone else."

"No way! Of course I'll go with you." Scott leaned close and said seductively, "You realize, I hope, that if I go with you, you might not be as safe as if you were in your granddaddy's lap.''

"I'm counting on that."

He rumpled her hair. "Have I created a sex-crazed monster?"

"I think so."

"You smell like new-mown hay drying in the sunshine."

"I'm not familiar with that smell, but I assume that's a compliment, so I guess thanks are in order."

"Are you staying for supper?"

"Uh-hmm. It's getting to be a nice habit." Cassie had no idea what the people at the DO thought now that she seldom graced their dining table, but she really didn't care. She was enjoying life too much to care about much of anything but Scott.

He hopped down off the fence, then held out his arms to her. "Let's go in. I'm tired and dirty. I need a beer, a shower and a heavy dose of you."

They walked through the back door just as Scott's housekeeper was leaving for the day. Her name was Thelma Campbell. She had told them she was forty-five, but she looked older, possibly because she was quite overweight. She was the most pleasant woman imaginable, and she positively simpered whenever Scott was near. She came twice a week and worked all day, though Cassie couldn't imagine what she found to do. Scott's house was almost antiseptically clean. Perhaps Thelma was the reason.

"Hello, Thelma," Cassie greeted brightly. "How are you?"

"Just fine, Mrs. Tate, thanks." The housekeeper turned to Scott. "I'll be going now unless there's something else you'd like for me to do."

"Not a thing, Thelma."

The woman nodded and gathered up her handbag.
She shot Cassie the usual curious, speculative glance,
as though she was bursting to ply her with questions.
Thelma worked for three other families in the area and
was no doubt partially responsible for getting the
gossip about Cassie and Scott spread so quickly and
effectively. Oddly, being the target of gossips for the
first time in her life didn't bother Cassie a bit. She even
felt a little smug. Cassie Tate, who never had been any
great shakes as a glamour girl, had captured the heart
of the handsomest man around.

Scott opened the refrigerator door and took out a
can of beer. "Want something, sweetheart?"

"I don't think so, not now."

"Come on in and talk to me while I wash off some
of the grime."

Scott's bedroom had become as familiar to her as
her own. She stretched out on the bed and watched
him undress. He was without self-consciousness. Naked, he was a bronzed Greek god, so splendidly virile
it made her heart lurch just to look at him. She inti-
mately knew every inch of that hard, lean body, and
that knowledge sent a small shiver of delight through
her.

"How's Rob?" he asked. "It's been a spell since
I've seen him."

"He's fine, I guess. To tell you the truth, I haven't
seen much of him since school started. Unfortunately, he seems absolutely delighted to be back in the
classroom and spared ranch chores." Her voice
sounded thoroughly disgruntled. She hated that but
didn't seem able to control it. And that, she knew, was
the source of most of her irritation with her son. She

simply didn't know what to do, which put her at a disadvantage. She adamantly refused to consider that Rob might be too old to be influenced by her any longer.

"Nothing wrong with that, is there?" Scott asked. "Most parents wouldn't think so."

"I . . . I don't know. He just overdoes the school thing, I think."

Scott hesitated, neatly folding the clothes that were going to be tossed in the laundry tomorrow. He tried to keep his voice as offhand as possible. "Does he ever discuss the future?"

Cassie looked at him with a frown. "Future? What's to discuss?"

"Oh, plans. You know, the kind of things kids think about at his stage of life."

She lifted her shoulder, attempting a nonchalant shrug, but the gesture came across as an uncomfortable movement, something Scott was quick to notice. "He'll graduate from high school and then go to Sul Ross, what else?" Of course that was what was going to happen. She wouldn't let herself believe differently, wouldn't allow things to be any other way. So she couldn't understand why the uneasiness persisted whenever Rob's future came up.

"Right," Scott said. "See you in a minute." Deep in thought, he went into the bathroom and turned on the shower. He knew that Rob still hadn't told Cassie his plans; he was sure he would hear plenty about that from Cassie when the boy finally did. Rob was making a terrible mistake in allowing his mother to go on believing what she wanted to believe. On top of that, Scott disliked knowing something he had to keep from her. It seemed dishonest, and he wanted to be completely honest where Cassie was concerned. He wanted to give the boy a stern lecture.

Then he thought of his own situation with his grandfather. He hadn't been able to bring himself to tell Theo he was staying at the Horseshoe, so he was the last person who should pass judgment. It was damned hard to dash the hopes of someone who was important to you.

Stepping under the shower's spray, he emptied his mind while the refreshing needles of water pounded his body. A few minutes later he dried briskly, wrapped the towel around his waist and returned to the bedroom. Cassie had kicked off her shoes and was propped up against the headboard, legs stretched in front of her, ankles crossed, presenting the most appealing picture imaginable. It came to him with something of a start that he had spent most of his life wanting a woman like her. Once he'd thought he'd found her in Becky, and to a point he had. But his wife had always possessed that headstrong, almost wild streak he'd found so difficult to deal with. There wasn't a trace of that in Cassie, and she was without a doubt the most guileless person he had ever known, with the possible exception of his grandmother.

When she smiled radiantly, he closed the space between them and sat on the edge of the bed, leaning forward to kiss her.

"Am I nicer to be near now?" he asked.

"You're always nice to be near, but, yes, you do smell divine." Abruptly she grew thoughtful, and her gaze seemed to fasten on a point somewhere past his right shoulder. "Scott, why did you ask me about Rob's plans?"

He tensed, realizing too late that he had to be extra careful when he talked about Rob. Cassie was much too sensitive when it came to her son. The slightest casual remark would prompt a barrage of questions from her. "No reason," he lied. "It just seems that a sixteen-year-old would have plans galore."

"He'll be seventeen next week." She sighed. "He'll be eighteen before I know it. Time goes so quickly. I don't suppose any parents stop to enjoy the baby years the way they should. Eighteen seems like such a milestone."

She sounded so sad that Scott was deeply touched. He supposed one had to be a parent to fully understand, but he tried. "I guess it is. I remember that Granddad gave me a 'today you are a man' speech on my eighteenth birthday. I also remember that for a minute it scared hell out of me. I wasn't sure I wanted to be a man. I was having too much fun being a kid."

"I wonder if Rob is. Having fun, I mean. He's always been such a serious boy."

"People have fun in different ways. Fun doesn't always mean ha-ha."

"I know, but... Scott, I've never said anything to you about this, but sometimes Rob scares me. He behaves as though...as though he doesn't really care all that much about the ranch, doesn't really want to run it, and that's unthinkable!"

"Why?"

"Why?" she asked incredulously. "Because...because the DO is his heritage!"

"Funny. You sound like someone else I know."

It took her a minute to understand. "Your grandfather?"

"Exactly." Brushing at her hair, he held her face for a moment. "Speaking of serious, you're in a very pensive mood today."

She attempted a smile. "Oh, I guess that's because parenting is such serious business."

"I can imagine. Hard work, too. So why don't you stop being a parent for a little while and just be a lover? We'll think about supper later."

Expertly he drew her into his arms and began rubbing, petting, kissing. Within minutes Cassie's body had lost its tenseness and become pliant, unresisting. She laid her head on his chest and gave in to all the wondrous sensations he could arouse with only a touch. Her hand slipped under the towel to stroke his hard thigh, then moved between his legs to feel his instantaneous arousal. He was a powerful man, admirably virile and lusty, yet his lovemaking could be so tender it brought her to the edge of tears. She marveled at how attuned they were to each other, how their bodies matched so perfectly. He knew exactly how to stimulate her down to the last nerve end. He was good, very good, leading her to suspect he had known legions of women. Yet he maintained that it was she who inspired him, she who taught him new heights of desire. He knew all the right buttons to push, and he pushed them quite effectively. He also pushed them quite often.

"Do you suppose we make love too much?" she once asked him.

"I don't think that's possible. But if you want me to stop..."

"Never!"

Scott thought he knew her body as well as he did his own. He quickly got rid of her blouse and bra, for he loved her breasts, and she was very sensitive there. That was something she claimed not to have known before. His slightest touch and the nipples hardened like rocks. He knew she liked him to fondle them, kiss and suckle. He knew he could give her goosebumps by putting his tongue in her ear or letting it trail across the taut flesh of her stomach. He never got so caught up in his own passion that he forgot to do the things she liked. And she responded to him so fully, so naturally, giving herself without reservation. He could always tell when she was going to climax; she grew as still as death for a split second before the explosion began. He knew everything about pleasuring her, and he took great care with their lovemaking, for it was the most important part of his life. He thought that if ever there were two people who were made for each other, emotionally and physically, they were. Sometimes when he was buried deep inside her he thought he might expire from happiness. It wouldn't be a bad way to go.

BY THE TIME THE SUN cleared the horizon the following morning, Cassie and Scott were in the saddle, heading for the top country. When they were an hour away from DO headquarters, Scott no longer wondered why so much of the ranch's work was done on horseback. Whereas the Horseshoe occupied a stretch of territory known as The Flats, easy to work and to fence, the DO was an awesome spread of rolling pastures, brushy ravines, sheer bluffs and jagged canyons. Fences were impractical, and horses were a necessity since much of the ranch was accessible only by horseback. He was beginning to understand why the Ferenbachs chose to ranch the old-fashioned way. The land itself demanded it.

"Cabeza de Vaca camped here in 1535," Cassie remarked at one point.

Scott's eyes scanned the area. "Doesn't look as though it's changed much."

"It hasn't. That's what's so wonderful about it."

"I have no idea where I am. Which direction is the ranch?"

She pointed. "That way."

"I'll have to take your word for it. I've flown over this country dozens of times, but that doesn't give you a clear idea of how wild and vast it is. It's a little breathtaking. I'd hate like hell to be lost in it."

"That's easy to do if you aren't familiar with the territory. But don't worry, you're with me. I'll get you home safe and sound." She glanced at him anxiously. "You doing okay?"

"I'm fine. What's the matter? Do I look like a real greenhorn to you?"

Her eyes made a thorough and exaggerated survey of him from head to toe. She loved seeing him this way and thought he looked wonderful on horseback. He sat the horse well, had a good seat in the saddle, though he admitted it had been years since he had been in one. She just wondered if he was uncomfortable. For sure he wouldn't say anything if he was. "I can't tell if you're saddle-broke or not," she teased.

"Don't you worry about me. I might surprise you. A man who can wrestle thirty-foot lengths of pipe can do anything."

"Have you really wrestled pipe?"

"When I was sixteen, all summer. Wonderful work, if you happen to be fond of back-breaking labor. I told you—Granddad believes that work is the only reason for getting out of bed in the morning.''

He was a constant revelation to her. She always had to smile when she thought of her first impressions of Scott—a dandy, a rich man's son, spoiled rotten and no doubt a bit lazy. How wrong she'd been!

At noon they stopped for lunch, which was a simple affair of sandwiches from Cassie's saddlebag and iced tea from a vacuum jug. Scott had yet to spot any cattle or anything resembling a fence. They finally reached a place Cassie referred to as Number Seven, a flat, grassy crest from which one could see the mountains of the Big Bend to the south. Hundreds of white-faced Herefords ambled across the pasture, heads down, eating, eating, eating. The panorama was breathtaking. They were high above trees, streams, roads, anything that spoke of civilization. Scott felt he had somehow stumbled onto the set of an old John Ford Western movie. He was also sure that they must have covered most of the Ferenback spread that day, but Cassie assured him they had seen only a small percentage of it. "It would take days," she said. "There are some parts of it even I haven't seen since I was very young."

"But you have seen it all?"

"Oh, yes, at one time or another."

Scott was impressed; he couldn't help it. Cassie watched his expression of wonder with a great deal of personal satisfaction. It was precisely the reaction she had hoped for.

They spent the remainder of the afternoon making camp and tending to their horses. Then, when the sun was low in the western sky, Cassie set about building a fire and making their supper. Scott felt he should be lending her a hand, but she worked so efficiently, and he knew nothing about campfire cooking. "I might not be any great shakes in the kitchen," she said, "but out here I'm a regular Julia Child."

Everything came out of a can and was prepared with minimal equipment, but Scott wondered if anything had ever tasted so good. When the meal was over and the gear stashed, they opened their bedrolls and lay side by side, watching daylight fade. Night came very quickly in the mountains. One moment the sky was splashed a brilliant orange-red, then it faded to violet and darkness fell. They stared up at the stars, little sparkling diamonds that looked close enough to touch. Somewhere in the distance came the lowing of cows and a calf's frantic bleat. A mesmerizing kind of peace settled over Scott. Had he been asked to describe the scene, the atmosphere, the aura, he thought "lonely grandeur" might have been appropriate. This remote, grassy mountain crest seemed to have an uplifting effect on his spirit.

"When did the first Ferenbach show up in these parts?" he asked.

"Right after the Civil War, in 1870."

"Sure must have been one lonely place in those days. Why in the world did he come?"

"He had some idea about going into the real estate business," she said with a little laugh. "But the economics of the time being what they were, land was easy to acquire but hard to get rid of. When he found himself with all this land and no buyers, he decided to ranch. Believe it or not, the DO used to be a lot bigger than it is now. Pieces of it have been sold off through the years, and of course, there was the ancestor who lost the Horseshoe."

She smiled, and so did Scott. Then silence descended again while they studied the stars. "I know why you brought me up here," he finally said.

"Oh?" She looked at him with interest. "Suppose you tell me then."

"To seduce me."

Cassie chortled. "I certainly didn't have to come all the way up here to do that, love. You're easy."

"I mean, to seduce me to this way of life."

"So, you admit it's seductive."

"I'm beginning to understand the lure, why it holds so much appeal for some people. I've spent the night at remote drilling sites that seemed to be on the earth's edge, but there are lights on a rig and a road leading to it. When drilling's going on, there's always some activity. Here . . . I never dreamed the world could be so silent. It gets to you somehow."

Cassie was quiet for a moment. She'd had all this wild country to be free in all her life. She tried to imagine how it must look to someone seeing it for the first time, but it was impossible. "Of what avail are forty freedoms without a blank spot on the map?"

Scott raised one elbow to look down at her. "How eloquent."

"I read that somewhere once, I don't remember where. But I understood."

Folding her hands behind her head, Cassie stared up at the stars. She heard a rustle of movement beside her, but hypnotized by the night sky, she didn't turn for a moment. "Do you know where I'd really like to take you, Scott? Down to the Big Bend. We could take a raft ride down Boquillas Canyon. It's a two-day trip, and the campsites along the way are almost primitive, but, oh, it's spectacular! You get such a feeling of being close to nature. How does that sound?''

There was no reply. Cassie turned. Scott had crawled into his sleeping bag and was dead to the world. *Looks as though I am as safe as if I were in my granddaddy's lap,* she thought with a smile. *Not even a good-night kiss. Tomorrow he'll be so sore he'll barely be able to walk, but all in all he didn't do bad for a tenderfoot.* She decided that not much fazed Scott, that he could handle whatever life threw him.

Rolling over, she slipped into her own bag. It had been a glorious day, but all her days seemed to be now that Scott was part of them. Life was sweet and good. The world and problems were far away, and she didn't see any reason for them not to stay that way for a very long time.

CHAPTER THIRTEEN

THEY ARRIVED BACK at ranch headquarters in early afternoon the following day. Scott thought if he didn't get out of the saddle damned soon he was going to die. When he had crawled out of his sleeping bag at dawn that morning he was sure he was coming down with the flu. There wasn't a spot on his body that didn't hurt. He had experienced sore, aching muscles before, but never like this. Cassie had assured him it was a day in the saddle, not a germ, that was responsible for his discomfort, and she even admitted to being a bit stiff and sore herself. "Guess I'm getting soft in my old age," she said. They both were glad to see headquarters loom into view.

"I'll call you later," Scott promised, his mind focused on the steaming shower awaiting him at his house. "Maybe you'd like to drive into town or something."

"Right." She turned the horses over to one of the cowboys, while Scott made his rather painful way down the rise and over the fence. Picking up the two bedrolls, Cassie went into the house and headed straight for the bathroom.

An hour later, after a soak in a hot bath, a shampoo and a change of clothes, she felt her energy returning. The house was very quiet. Rob wasn't home from school yet, and she had no idea where her father was. From the kitchen came the muted sounds of Cora's activities. Cassie would have liked nothing better than to curl up on the sofa with a magazine. Instead, she went into her office to check the day's mail.

Most of the mail they received consisted of magazines, junk and official government bulletins, both state and federal. These she always read carefully, then gave the important ones to George for posting on the bulletin board in the bunkhouse office. She read two of them before coming to the one from their local congressman's office. She began reading, then stopped when she realized that what she was reading didn't make sense. Only when she turned over the envelope did she realize that the letter was addressed to Rob. Sitting back in her chair, she placed a hand over her mouth and reread the letter, disbelieving.

As best she could tell, Rob actually had contacted the congressman about an appointment to the Air Force Academy. The letter was to inform him that he would be required to take the civil service exam that fall, and it concluded by wishing him good luck. Cassie laid the letter down on the desk and stared vacantly across the room. She thought she could hear her heart knocking against her ribs. She felt as though she had received an unexpected shower of ice water. There had been some mistake. Rob wouldn't do that to them, to *her*. He knew what was expected of him, how much she depended on him.

She glanced at her watch. He wouldn't be home for an hour, and that was only if he drove straight home from school, which he rarely did. There always seemed to be something to stay after school for, or someone who needed a lift home. But when he got home, he'd have a logical explanation for this, Cassie was sure. He probably had made some casual inquiry, and it had gotten blown out of proportion.

She had lost interest in the rest of the mail. Getting to her feet, she restlessly paced back and forth for several minutes, warning herself not to jump to conclusions, reminding herself that anything that might have been done could be undone. If necessary, she would go to their congressman herself and have him squelch this. The man was a friend of J.B.'s. Rob wasn't leaving the ranch. He couldn't! Glancing at her watch, she paced some more.

"Oh, I'll go crazy if I continue to do this," she muttered to the walls. Slipping the letter in her shirt pocket, she left the house and went in search of George.

George had worked for Cassie long enough to know by the set of her shoulders or the tilt of her head if things were good or bad. Usually, if something was wrong, he already knew about it. Very little happened at the DO that the foreman wasn't aware of. When he looked up and saw Cassie marching purposefully toward him, he knew she was upset, but to his knowledge, everything was humming along fine and dandy.

"Afternoon, boss. What's up?"

"I want to talk to you."

"Sure."

"In private."

George frowned. That was odd. They usually had their discussion in her office. "Well, sure." He looked around. "This way. We'll use the bunkhouse office."

The small room at one end of the bunkhouse was occupied by four men playing cards. "Beat it, fellows," George ordered. "The boss and I have business."

It was like flushing a covey of quail. Leaving their cards where they lay, the men scurried out of the room without a word. Cassie scarcely noticed them. She grabbed the first chair she could find and sat down. George took the swivel chair in front of an ancient rolltop desk, folded his hands and waited. He was sure he had never seen the boss so agitated.

"I want to talk to you," she repeated.

"Okay."

"It's about Rob."

Wonderful, George thought. How he had allowed himself to be designated chief nursemaid he'd never know. No, that wasn't true. He did know. Cassie had asked him to. "Rob?"

"This past summer you spent more time with him than anyone else on the ranch, right?"

The foreman hadn't spent near as much time with Rob as Cassie thought he had, chiefly because the minute his back was turned, the boy often hightailed it. He hadn't, however, told Cassie that, and he saw no reason to now. "I guess so."

"Did he ever mention any future plans...college or anything?"

George thought about it. "I don't think so. Not that I recall, at any rate." Here he felt on safe ground. Rob didn't talk about personal things. George didn't know anything about anything, and when it came to the family in the big house, that was precisely the way he liked it. A fellow could get in a heap of trouble just by knowing too much about the people he worked for.

"Did he ever talk about going to Sul Ross?"

"No."

"Think hard."

"I'm sure he didn't, boss."

Cassie's heart sank. Any boy who was a high school senior and had plans for college would be chattering away about them by now. He would at least have mentioned them, for God's sake. Unless, of course, he didn't want anyone to know what those plans were. Looking away, she rubbed her temples.

George shifted uncomfortably. Here he was, confronted by a distraught boss who happened to be a pretty, and right now pretty miserable, lady, and he felt helpless. He wondered if it would be proper to inquire what the problem was. He had some rigid ideas about a boss-worker relationship, but, after all, Cassie had sought him out. If it was none of his business, she wouldn't hesitate to say so, knowing he wouldn't take offense. "Want to talk about it?" he asked quietly.

Cassie withdrew the letter from her pocket and handed it to him. George read it and handed it back to her. "That's too bad."

"Yes, it is." She could have kissed him for understanding her state of mind immediately. "The worst part of it is the fact that Rob's interested in something like that, that he even inquired."

"Yeah."

"Well, it's not going to happen, George. You can take that to the bank." Putting the letter back in her pocket, she got to her feet.

George stood also. "What are you going to do?"

"Put a stop to it, what else? And I'd appreciate it if you wouldn't mention this to anyone else. It'll all be over and forgotten soon, so the fewer who know about it, the better."

"Sure, boss."

The foreman watched her leave the office and shook his head sadly. He understood why she was upset, but she really ought to hang it up. There were wild critters out in the bush who were of more use to the DO than Rob was. George didn't know why he cared so much, but he did. He liked young Rob. He liked J.B. and he liked Cassie. He also felt damned sorry for her. But she really ought to give up.

Aw, what do I know? I'm not a parent, thank God. I'm not running a gigantic spread that's been in my family for generations. Also thank God. There was a lot to be said for being totally unencumbered, for being single and not owning more than you could carry.

AN HOUR LATER, Rob walked through the front door and headed for his room, but his mother's voice detained him. It came from her office. "Rob, come in here, please. I want to talk to you."

The boy tensed. There was something about the tone of his mother's voice that sent shock waves of uneasiness through him. But there was nothing he could do but go into the office, and when he saw the expression on Cassie's face, saw the taut line of her mouth, he steeled himself for what surely was coming. How in the devil had she found out?

He didn't have to wait long for the answer. Cassie had planned to ease into the confrontation gradually, but during the time she had waited for her son's arrival, her agitation had reached the boiling point. "I opened this by mistake," she blurted out harshly. "Suppose you explain it to me."

Rob crossed the room, took the letter from her hand and read it. He was surprised to realize he actually was glad to have it out in the open. "I tried to tell you, Mom. You just wouldn't listen."

"Of course I wouldn't listen, because the entire thing is ridiculous!"

"It's what I want to do."

"Well, it's not what you're going to do."

He brandished the letter. "This isn't the appointment. I might not make it."

Cassie wished she could believe that, wished it with all her heart. But she knew Rob too well. If he had been thinking about this very long, he would have prepared for it. Those superlative grades, his leadership ability, his prowess at track and baseball. Now she understood. He had been laying the groundwork. Oh, he'd get that appointment if he wanted it; she'd bet on it.

She also wished she knew what to do next. Put her foot down with firm authority? Grab him by the shoulders and shake some sense into his head? Try to reason with him? Rant and rave and cry, if necessary? She looked at her son and found that what frightened her most was Rob's quiet, confident manner. He wasn't seeking her permission or approval; he simply was telling her what he wanted to do.

"You will be betraying this family and your heritage," she said stiffly. "If you leave, what, may I ask, do you think will happen to this ranch that has belonged to the Ferenbachs for five generations?"

"For Pete's sake, Mom, it'll just keep on keeping on. I don't do a thing around here. I hate cows and horses and all the grubby chores you have to do in order to take care of the dumb things."

"It's life, Rob."

"Not mine," he said quietly. "It never has been."

Cassie felt disoriented, so confused and unhappy that she said the last thing she meant to say, the last thing she should have said. "You're too much like your father."

The room was absolutely silent for a minute. Then Rob said, "You've told me that before. I wish I remembered more about him. I don't, you know, not really. The only thing I really remember is that he once read me a story about some guy who climbed the Matterhorn. I thought that was so great, and so did he. I guess we had a lot in common."

Cassie's shoulders slumped. "I'm . . . sorry. I didn't mean that in a derogatory way. Your father was a fine man." She could feel defeat enveloping her like a shroud, and she couldn't let that happen, she couldn't. She had to take charge, be the head of this family of two. Throwing off the sense of doom, she straightened her shoulders and held her head too haughtily high. "You'll get over this nonsense, Rob. It's just a passing fancy, pie-in-the-sky dreams not based on reality. We all have them at one time or another. When I was your age I wanted to be a movie star." That was a lie. She'd never wanted to do anything but what she was doing. "But I'm confident you'll stay where you're needed, because you're a Ferenbach."

Rob's mouth was set as determinedly as her own. "Only half."

"What?"

"I'm only half Ferenbach. The other half of me is Tate."

Cassie was alarmed to realize she was trembling. She only hoped Rob couldn't see it. "This isn't going to happen, son. It can't."

"It's what I want."

The look of shock on his mother's face prompted Rob to try to explain further. "I've always wanted to fly, Mom. Not just fly, but fly the best and the fastest. And the academy is where it has to begin. It's the only place where I can learn to be what I want to be. Scott says..."

"Scott?" Cassie was on her feet, her eyes wide. "What does Scott have to do with this?"

"He has a friend in Fort Worth who graduated from the academy. He told the friend about me, and he says..."

"Scott knows about this?" She was white-lipped.

"Well...yes."

"Since when?"

Rob had to think. "Since that first day he took me up in his plane."

"That was over two months ago!"

"I guess so. Yeah, it was right after the Fourth of July barbecue."

Cassie sat down with a thud. Rob didn't understand his mother, not at all. He had fully expected her to be good and steamed when she found out he was actively seeking an appointment to the academy, but why did she give a hang whether Scott knew about it? She sure was one strange lady. The boy waited, but she continued staring across the room, her mouth slightly open. When a minute or two passed and she said nothing, he cleared his throat and asked, "Is that all, Mom?"

Cassie looked up, distracted but with eyes blazing. "Of course it isn't all. It's just . . . all for now."

Rob hurried out of the room at something just under a dead run. He knew this wasn't the end of it, not by any means. The worst was probably yet to come, but he'd worry about that when the time came. He supposed his grandfather would be the next to hear about it. Lord, he dreaded supper tonight.

Cassie was scarcely aware of his departure. *Scott knows about this!* That pounded over and over in her brain. *He's known all along and didn't tell me, didn't warn me. He knows how important this is to me. How could he keep it from me? I've told him all about my plans for the future, and he just listened, let me go on believing. I could have nipped this thing in the bud if I had known. How could Scott do this to me?*

To her tangled mind, it was one betrayal heaped upon another.

SCOTT COULDN'T HAVE BEEN more surprised to see Cassie standing at his back door. "Hi, sweetheart, come in."

She brushed past him, thrusting something in his hand as she did. "Read this," she said, then went to stand at the work island with her back to him.

He read the letter and sighed. "Well, it's about time you found out. Did Rob give this to you?"

"No. I opened it by mistake when I was going through today's mail."

"That's too bad. I'm sorry you had to find out that way. I kept hoping Rob would tell you."

She whirled to face him. "Why didn't you tell me? Rob says you've known about it for months."

"Cassie, it wasn't my place to tell you."

"Not your place? You knew how I felt about Rob and the ranch and...everything. How could you have kept it from me?"

It was beginning to dawn on him that not only was she upset over Rob, she was angry at him, too. And scared, sensing that she was impotent where her son was concerned, that all the arguments and threats in the world wouldn't dissuade him from what he wanted to do. Scott moved toward her and put his hands on her shoulders, unwilling to believe that her anger at him was serious and couldn't be calmed by some soothing words. "He promised he would tell you. He also made me promise that I wouldn't. I couldn't betray the boy's confidence."

Cassie was in no mood to be reasonable. She needed someone to blame, and Scott was handy. "You should have told me. If I had known about it, I could have done something."

"No," Scott said solemnly, "I don't think you could. He's growing up, Cassie, and he's going to do what he's going to do. In no time at all he won't belong to you in the sense that you can tell him what to do."

"Oh!" Impatiently she threw up her hands and tossed her head. "He's just a kid. He doesn't know what he wants."

"I'm afraid he does. You're upset because what he wants isn't what you want for him. But there's nothing you can do about that, sweetheart. Nothing."

"You don't understand. You never have."

"I understand, all right. What's more, I can see both sides of the thing. You can't."

"What in the world do you think will happen to the DO if Rob goes out into the wild blue yonder?"

"Why, I imagine it will just go on as it always has."

Cassie wasn't listening. "Rob is supposed to get married and have children and stay here."

"Oh, he'll get married and have kids someday. And he'll learn to fly airplanes and be stationed all over the world. Then, in about thirty years, he'll retire from the Air Force, and maybe he'll want to come back here. Who knows?"

She looked at him incredulously. "Thirty years? I'm supposed to wait and wonder for thirty years?"

"Cassie, simmer down. Accept the inevitable. There's nothing you can do except make yourself miserable. You've allowed this to become an obsession." Scott did his best to placate her. He stroked her arm and smiled tenderly. "You know, Rob's doing exactly what I'm doing. You think it's perfectly all right for me to turn my back on what my grandfather expects of me."

"No, I don't!" she cried irrationally. "I understand how he feels now, and I think it's terrible."

Scott's arm fell to his side, and his eyes narrowed. "Really? That's not the way you've been talking."

"I . . . didn't understand before. Now I do." Moving away from him, she began to pace and rub her hands together. "Rob's just got his head screwed on wrong, but it's only temporary. I'll get him straightened out if everyone will just leave him alone."

"Does that include me?"

She didn't answer.

"For God's sake, Cassie, let him go! You can't put the boy in a vault. Even if you could, you'd only make things worse. He'd just grow more restless and resentful. Then when he finally left—and he would, make no mistake about that—he'd never come back. Let him go with your blessing.''

She looked at him as though he were speaking a foreign language. ''You must be joking. Just say, 'Okay, son, run off and fly your jet airplanes and leave the ranch to your grandfather and me. Then when we're gone, some conglomerate will buy it and turn it into God knows what. Forget the generations of your ancestors who started with nothing and built the DO into what it is now.' That's what you advise me to do?''

Scott shrugged. ''You might as well. There's nothing else you can do.''

''Yes, there is. There has to be. And I'll find it. Rob is not going to the Air Force Academy or anywhere else. Scott, I...forbid you to take him up in that plane again.''

''Oh, sweetheart, that little puddle jumper of mine doesn't mean a thing to Rob. His dreams are focused on something so much bigger.''

''In fact, I want you to stay away from him altogether for the time being.''

The air around them grew tense and silent. Scott couldn't believe he had heard her right. ''What did you say?'' he demanded coldly.

''I said, stay away from him.''

He gripped her arm tightly. ''Now, listen, Cassie. I know you're upset—''

''You're damned right I'm upset.''

''—and in spite of what you think, I do understand. I'm trying my dead level best to be patient with you, but I'm rapidly becoming royally ticked off! Maybe I should shake you until your teeth rattle. I thought you and Rob were going to be very big parts of my life. I had some pretty big plans for the three of us. And, goddammit, I certainly don't plan to stay away from the boy! You might as well get that through your thick skull right now. You've gone off the deep end over this. Stop and think what you're saying. I'm the man you love."

"I *am* thinking, I am. How I feel about you has nothing to do with this. I'm facing a crisis, and you're the wrong sort of influence on him right now. You've something of the rebel in you, too."

Scott stared at her for a minute, then stepped back and squared his shoulders. "I see. All right, as you wish. But if I stay away from Rob, I stay away from you, too. You can't order me to stay away from your son and expect us to go on as before. Is that what you want?"

That was the time to stop and set things right before matters got out of hand, but Cassie was too self-involved to realize it.

When she said nothing, Scott expelled a labored breath. "Well, I guess I see where your priorities lie. If you ask me, you're the one who's got her head on crooked. You're not behaving like a responsible mother. You're behaving like a spoiled brat who isn't getting her own way. You should be thinking about what Rob wants, not what you want."

Cassie gasped. "Don't you dare tell me what I should and shouldn't do when it comes to Rob. What do you know? You're not a parent." Her heart was hammering like mad. She had never seen Scott angry, but he was good and angry now. His facial muscles were set like stone.

"It's impossible to talk to you about this." His voice was hard and grating. "You and those ridiculous tra-

ditions. You wear them like a holy mantle. You'll forgive me if I don't show you the door. I believe you
know your way out." He stomped out of the room,
full of masculine pride, more hurt than angry, his
heart lodged somewhere in his throat.

How had it happened, he wondered. How the hell
had it happened? From utter happiness to this in the
blink of an eye.

Cassie could actually taste the bleakness she felt.
Her first impulse was to run after him, apologize, do
whatever was necessary to put things right between
them again, but something prevented her from doing
so. Scott surely would forgive her. When he had a
chance to think about this, he would understand why
she had to focus all her time, all her energy on Rob
right now.

Besides, talking to Scott did no good. She suspected that his sympathies were all with Rob. Over and
over he kept telling her all the things she didn't want
to hear. Later there would be time to undo what had
been done, but not now.

Still, the physical act of putting one foot in front of
the other in order to walk out of that house was the
hardest thing she had ever done.

SUPPER THAT NIGHT was a strained, almost silent affair, and J.B. had no idea why. Cassie spoke in mono-
syllables, and her face was a study in unhappiness.
Rob spoke hardly at all. The minute the boy finished
his meal, he asked to be excused and made straight for
his room. Since George and two of the other men were
having supper with them, J.B. was forced to wait until they left before he could talk to Cassie. Sometime

later he found her sitting on the front porch, staring out into the black night.

"Did someone just die?" he asked.

She looked up. "What?"

"You could have cut the air in there with a knife," J.B. said. "What gives?"

Cassie told him. She expected a king-sized explosion. Not only expected it but hoped for it. She hoped her father would rave and rant; she needed an ally. But to her surprise, J.B. said nothing for a long time. Finally, heaving a sigh, he sank into the chair next to hers. "Guess I've known for some time that this was coming. Didn't know exactly what it'd be, but...reckon I never could see the boy staying here and taking charge. Don't worry. We'll make the best of it, you and I, just like we always have."

Cassie's mouth dropped in disbelief. "Don't worry? That's all you have to say about this?"

"Doesn't appear there's anything else I can say. Sounds to me like the boy's already made up his mind."

"I don't believe this!"

"Hon, what do you expect me to do?"

"Forbid this! Stop him! Thrash him if need be."

"He's a little old for that, don't you think? And I could beat him within an inch of his life, but it still wouldn't do any good."

Little by little, Cassie could feel herself slipping into abject despair, and she couldn't let that happen. If she allowed despair to take over, she would lose hope. "What, pray tell me, do you think is going to happen to this place if Rob leaves?"

"Oh, I imagine it'll survive. It's been through a damned sight worse than this, and it's still here. We'll just keep on running it, and he might come back one of these days. Or maybe he'll have a son or daughter who will. We'll just take it as it comes. To tell you the truth, the DO might be better off without him. It's not his fault that he doesn't have what it takes."

"Don't say that! He's...been temporarily side-tracked, but he'll come around."

"Sure wouldn't count on that, hon. Sure wouldn't. Don't let this thing get to be an obsession with you."

Obsession? That's what Scott had called it. Didn't anyone understand? The three most important people in her life had failed her. And she couldn't think about Scott now. Thinking about him clouded her judgment, and she needed all her faculties in order to deal with this.

"Dad, my son is not going to be the first Ferenbach to leave this land."

"He won't be. When I was a kid my granddaddy told me about his brother, the one who went to sea. Saw just about the whole world before he died. Their dad almost busted a gut when the boy left, but that didn't keep him from doing what he wanted to do. Might as well forget it, Cassie. Comes the day when a mama's gotta untie the apron strings. If you love something, you have to set it free, and that's the God's truth if ever it was told. When you think about it, we spend our whole lives giving up things and people we love. I'm thinking that the boy might love this place a whole lot more than he thinks he does, but there's something else he loves more. It'll be easier for him to leave if he thinks this place isn't so hot."

"Oh, spare me all this homespun wisdom, Dad. Rob's not going anywhere. I have no intention of forgetting it. And I have no intention of just going on as before, waiting and hoping that Rob will come back to the DO when I'm in my sixties and old and decrepit."

J.B.'s eyes narrowed to slits under his bushy white brows. "I got news for you, young lady. The sixties don't mean old and decrepit."

"Sorry," she said humbly. There were times when she honestly forgot her father's age. He was so active and vital. Damn, why couldn't Rob have been more like his grandfather? Then she dismissed the thought as unworthy and futile.

Cassie got a white-knuckled grip on the arm of the chair. The one person she had expected to back her to the hilt had backed off instead. Had she bothered to look, she could have seen the pain and disappointment in J.B.'s eyes, as acute as her own, but she didn't. She dwelled instead on her own misery. She was angry at both Scott and her father for deserting her, for not expending any effort on real understanding. She felt totally alone.

It would have been easy to give up at that moment, to give in to the tears that had been lurking just below the surface even since her argument with Scott. With the slightest nudge, she would have gone into the house, picked up the phone and dialed the Horseshoe, then done whatever was needed to put her own life in order. But she refused. A more sensible woman would have let go of the last fragile strands of hope and accepted the inevitable, but not Cassie. She wanted to scream, to throw things, to march upstairs and lay down the law to Rob. There was a solution to this, dammit, and she was going to find it.

But until she did, she was going to ride hard on that son of hers. No more giving him his head and looking the other way. She had been so wrapped up in Scott, she had all but ignored Rob. Perhaps her leniency was the source of the problem. She had always trusted that her son would feel the same way about this spot on earth as his ancestors had. But she had been wrong. Somewhere in the dim recesses of her mind she had imagined that love of the land was inherent, but perhaps J.B. had taught it to her in subtle ways she didn't remember.

So that was what she was going to do with Rob. This was serious business, and from that moment on, Cassie intended treating it as such.

CHAPTER FOURTEEN

ROB'S SEVENTEENTH BIRTHDAY came and went. It hardly was a joyous occasion, despite Cassie's efforts. She had Cora fix his favorite foods and organized a nighttime cookout with all his friends from school, and there were gifts galore. Still, the guests seemed to have a much better time than Rob did. There was a gift from Scott, although the boy didn't get it until four days after the event, when he managed to slip over to the Horseshoe for a quick visit with his idol. The gift was a copy of Jane's *All the World's Aircraft*. Getting it home without Cassie's seeing it presented something of a problem, but Rob managed, all the while feeling as guilty as a smuggler running contraband. He wasn't even sure why it was so important to him to keep the book a secret from his mother, but he didn't want her to know anything about it. Now it lay hidden under his bed, and every night he took it out and thumbed through its pages.

Most of all Rob dreaded the weekends when he was under his mother's watchful eye from the minute he got out of bed in the morning until he escaped to his room after supper. If he had believed in witchcraft, he would have thought Cassie was possessed by some kind of demon spirit. She was on him about something all the time, and once again poor George had a very unhappy and unwilling charge under his wing. It seemed to Rob that whenever he turned around there was either George or his mother bearing down on him, wanting him to do this and that. The boy felt almost as sorry for the foreman as he did for himself. If he hadn't been so miserable, he might have thought it funny. Did his mom really think that all this unwanted attention would magically change his mind about the appointment? *Lord,* he thought, *this senior year is going to be a bummer from start to finish.*

Fortunately he had Scott. Not that he got to see much of the man, but occasionally he would stop at the Horseshoe on the way home from school. And one Saturday morning when Cassie had gone into town, he simply walked down the rise, hopped the fence and went to Scott's house. "She's driving me nuts, Scott," Rob complained. "I don't think this year's ever going to end."

Scott was suffering, too. "Try to be patient, Rob. Nothing lasts forever. Nobody can continue to behave the way you say your mother is. She'll have to bend sooner or later."

"You don't know Mom."

No, Scott would give him that. He wouldn't have dreamed their estrangement would last so long, that she could be so confounded hardheaded. He ached to see her, but he wasn't about to put himself in the position of having her turn on him again. His sympathies were far more with Rob than with Cassie, and that would show.

"Let's have a root beer, okay?" Scott suggested.

"Okay."

"How's school?"

"Not too bad. Pretty good, I guess."

"Tell me something, Rob—have you ever had a serious girlfriend?"

"No, not really."

"That's a bit unusual for sixteen...no, seventeen."

Rob shrugged. "Maybe. I know some girls, but what's the point in getting serious about one of them? Girls mess up a guy's head and make him forget all the grand things he wants to do. I've known for a long time I wouldn't be hanging around here once I graduated, and Mom's tears are going to be hard enough to put up with without having some girl dripping all over me. Usually I date old friends, buddies, you know."

Scott smiled. "You may be a great deal like your father, but you certainly inherited your mother's single-minded determination."

"Single-minded. That's Mom, all right. Man, she's driving me nuts! Do this, do that."

"She won't hold you long, Rob. She can't. Just be patient. I can't say I've ever regretted it when I took things slow and easy."

"Yeah, I guess so. You know what's really strange, though? Granddad hasn't said one word to me about the academy, not one. And he has to know about it."

"Maybe your grandfather simply realizes there are some things you can't change."

"I wish Mom would."

"So do I, Rob. Believe me, no one wishes that more I than do."

Rob sighed and shook his head in bewilderment. "I'm really not supposed to be over here."

"I would have bet on that," Scott said, "and I dislike doing things behind your mother's back."

"How else can we ever see each other? Besides, Mom's not home now. She went into town and then was going to stop at Laurie Tyler's. So the prisoner's off the hook for a few hours."

Scott hesitated, wanting to ask Rob so many questions about Cassie. He finally settled for, "How is your mother these days? I haven't seen her in a spell."

"Really? I thought you guys had something going."

"I thought so, too."

"Had a fight, huh?"

Scott smiled ruefully. "Let's say there's been a slight difference of opinion."

"About me?"

"Partly."

Rob shook his head. "Man, she is acting wierd. All my friends think Mom is the greatest, but they don't have to live with the Ferenbach Traditions. I always think of that in capital letters." The boy took a last swallow of root beer and slid off the stool. "I hate to leave but guess I'd better. Mom might not stop at Laurie's after all. If she gets home and finds me gone, there'll be holy heck to pay."

"Thanks for stopping by. Always good to see you." Scott placed a companionable arm around Rob's shoulders. "This is going to pass. You'll see."

"I hope so. By the way, how're things going between you and your grandfather?"

Scott recalled his phone conversation with Theo only the day before, recalled his grandfather's testy voice and thinly veiled suspicions. But Theo had yet to come right out and demand that his grandson come back. "Oh, he's making overtures, and I'm stalling. I'm not too proud of myself for that, either."

Rob laughed dryly and rolled his eyes toward the ceiling. ''Parents!''

Scott stood on the deck, arms folded, and watched as Rob headed back home. He longed to follow him, to go over to the DO, to confront Cassie and make her talk to him. He missed her and needed her. He felt much the same as he had during those first awful, empty days after Becky's death, only this was worse. Then he had known Becky was gone forever, but Cassie was right over there, very alive... and as pigheaded as a mule. He wanted to rant at her. He wanted to make love to her. He wanted to do all those erotic things that she had always liked so much. He wanted to feel her shuddering with ecstasy beneath him. He wished he could stop thinking about it. His nights had become a torment.

And he wondered how long it would take for this thing to be resolved. He refused to entertain the notion it might never be. She had to feel bad about this. Even though it was her doing, she couldn't just walk away from what they'd had and not feel a terrible sense of loss. He wondered if she felt as awful as he did. He certainly hoped so.

ROB BARELY BEAT CASSIE HOME. Rather than meet her and have to answer a lot of dumb questions about what he'd been doing, the boy went in search of George, the only person on the ranch who gave him some space. Curiously, Rob thought he and the foreman had become friends. Rob stayed out of everyone's way as much as possible, and in return, George didn't try to transform him into Cowpoke of the Year.

He found the foreman in the bunkhouse office packing a duffel bag. "Hi, Rob," George greeted. "Come on in. How's it going?"

"Okay, I guess. Mom's home, so I'm hiding out."

George grinned. He really felt sorry for Rob. Cassie had been riding him pretty hard, as if that would change anything. The boy was what he was, and what he was wasn't too bad. He just wished the boss would lay off. She was making her son's life miserable.

"What are you doing?" Rob asked.

"Heading out to spend the night in the top country."

"Why?"

"It rejuvenates my soul."

Rob made some sort of disdainful sound.

"Want to come along?" George asked. That was an afterthought. He would have preferred going alone since that was part of the rejuvenation process. His idea of heaven was to ride to a remote part of the ranch and spend the night under the stars with only his thoughts and his horse for company. But the weekends were difficult for Rob. The boy might like to get away.

Rob's first impulse was to say no. He never had been crazy about sleeping on the ground with the smell of cows and horses nearby, to say nothing of manure. Though he had been riding since he could walk, he'd never even been all that wild about being on horseback—something he wouldn't dare breathe to a soul since it amounted to overt heresy at the DO.

But on second thought the invitation took an appeal. What would he do if he stayed at the house? A big lot of nothing, that's what. He should have gotten a date for tonight, but he hadn't, and it was too late now. And George was an all right guy who didn't treat him like an inept kid. But most of all, spending the night in the top country would give him a chance to get away from his mother's stultifying protection. "Sure you don't mind?"

"Not at all," George fibbed. "I'll enjoy the company. I'll get enough grub for two. You just bring a heavy jacket and a bedroll. That is, if your mom says it's okay."

Of course Cassie said it was okay. She would have allowed Rob to go to the ends of the earth with George. "And pay attention," she said. "You can learn a lot from George."

"Yeah. Sure, Mom."

As the two of them rode away from ranch headquarters, negotiating the canyons and draws, Rob allowed the foreman to lead the way. He couldn't remember the last time he'd been up to the top country, but it had been years and years. However, he saw no reason to tell George that. Twisting in his saddle, he got his bearings. He didn't know the ranch nearly as well as he should have, he supposed, but that didn't bother him at all. In a matter of months the DO simply would be the place he was from.

Their trail dropped into a canyon and topped off through a pass, then down a smaller canyon and up a hill. George followed it as easily as if they were on a clearly marked highway. From the crest of the hill they could see a broad valley and a dirt road worn smooth by pickup trucks, and Rob thought the road led to ranch headquarters. So why, he wondered, had they taken such a roundabout, rugged path? Part of the cowboy mystique, he supposed. He had never understood why the men on the ranch would ride a horse up a steep embankment when a fairly smooth trail was available only a few yards away.

At the floor of the valley, near a water tank and a corrugated tin shed, they made camp. The shed was a welcome sight to Rob, just in case those thunderheads he saw building in the south moved up their way. Daylight was fading fast, so George set about building a fire and unpacking the supper Cora had prepared for them. The fire was for warmth and light; the food was served as is. Rob hadn't realized he was as hungry as he was, and he admitted there was something about a campfire that made anything taste good.

He watched the foreman work, noticed his spare, efficient movements. George was different from the other men who worked on the ranch. A nice-looking guy, well-mannered, neat. Talking to him, one knew he had some education under his belt. And Rob realized that he really didn't know much about the foreman, his background, so when George handed him a tin plate piled high with food, he asked, "How did you get interested in this kind of life?"

"Oh . . . I didn't want to farm cotton."

"Is that what your folks did?"

George nodded.

"Did anybody holler his head off when you left?"

"No, not really."

"You're lucky."

George immediately knew what had prompted that remark. "Well, Rob, my situation was entirely different from yours. It wasn't as though the farm had been in my family for generations or anything like that. I don't remember my mother since she died when I was just a kid. Then my dad married a woman named

Anna, and the farm belonged to her. No one expected either my sister or me to get all choked up over it. The situation was just different. I think I can understand how your mom feels, but I understand how you feel, too.''

Rob forked in a mouthful of food, chewed slowly, then shook his head. ''Lord, as long as I can remember, I've been smothered by family. Not just Mom and Granddad, but all those Ferenbachs all the way back to that guy in Germany who lit out just ahead of the law. I can't remember what he did that got him in trouble, but Mom could tell you, right down to the last tiny detail.''

''Yeah, well, some people get all caught up in that sort of thing.''

The two of them ate in silence for a few more minutes before Rob remembered his original question. ''So you didn't want to be a farmer, but why a cowboy? Doesn't seem to me there's a whole lot of difference.''

''You're wrong. I'm not tied down to the land the way a farmer is. I can pick up and go anytime I please.''

''And that's important to you?''

''Yeah, that's important to me. Itchy feet, wanderlust, call it whatever you like. I've got a bad case of it. When I got out of high school, I went to Oklahoma State for a year, to please my dad, but it didn't take me long to figure out that school and I just weren't meant for each other. When summer came, I signed on at a ranch in the Panhandle, the greenest greenhorn you ever saw. It was just a lark, something to do until I decided what I wanted to do. I sure never meant to stay. But when fall came around, I wanted to stay on for roundup. Then the boss sent me out to one of the winter camps. I stayed there all alone for a month. The first week I was so lonesome I thought I was gonna die. But one day my mind just turned a corner, and I didn't care if I never saw another person as long as I lived. I've been punching cows ever since."

Rob chuckled. "Takes all kinds, I guess."

"That it does," George agreed. "There's no accounting for tastes, that's for sure. For instance, there's nothing on earth that would make me go through the regimentation of a service academy. Nothing! I'd as soon be in prison."

Rob's head jerked up. "You know about that?"

"Yep, and frankly it sounds awful to me. But, like you said, it takes all kinds. You want to be an astronaut or something?"

"Maybe, but first I want to be a fighter pilot."

"Well . . . good luck."

They finished their meal and stowed the gear. After all that time in the saddle, Rob could barely restrain himself from crawling into his bedroll and calling it a day. He did have some pride, however, and George looked as full of energy as if the day had just begun.

Rob scanned the sky. The thunderheads had stayed safely to the south and now were dispersing. He never could look at a clear night sky without envisioning himself up there one day, streaking along faster than the speed of sound, leaving a contrail that earthbound people could see for hundreds of miles. That was a long way down the road, though, and the way wouldn't be easy. First the Academy and then pilot training. And then the cockpit of a F-16, or whatever was tops then. It never occurred to him that he might not hack it, that he could wash out. He'd see to it that nothing liked that happened. He wouldn't get that far and then fail. He was going to be the best. Lord, the wonders he would see before it was all over. The mere thought gave him goosebumps.

"What are you going to do with the rest of your life, George?" Rob suddenly asked.

The foreman frowned thoughtfully. "Don't know. Can't say I give too much thought to that kind of thing."

"Do you ever want to get married and have kids?"

"Don't know that, either. A wife and kids mean a house, one place. Never could see me standing still that long."

"Almost everybody gets married," Rob said.

"Yes, almost everybody."

"Have you ever had a girl?"

George looked at him. "What do you mean by 'had?'"

Rob shook his head. "Not that. I reckon you've been in the sack with a girl a few times. But have you ever been serious about one particular one?"

"Once."

"What happened?"

"She married some guy who owned a hardware store and could build her a nice house."

Rob was enjoying this campfire gossip tremendously. "Where was that?"

"Wyoming. An ol' cowpoke I worked with up there signed on at the DO for the roundup last year. He told me she's got three kids . . . bam, bam, bam. Sure hope the guy she married sells a lot of hardware."

"Were you sad when she got married?"

"Not really. I figured any gal who wanted a hardware salesman wasn't my type, anyway. By the way, do you think your mom's going to marry Maitland?"

Rob uttered a derisive sound. "Not if she keeps on acting so goofy. What guy's gonna get tied up with a goofy woman?"

George laughed, then silence descended. The world was unbelievably quiet. A minute or so passed before Rob asked, "How's Laurie?"

The question seemed to take the foreman by surprise. "Laurie? Well...she's just fine, I think. Why?"

Rob smiled and shrugged. "Just wondered." He had chanced to overhear a conversation between his mother and the school teacher that had led him to think Laurie might have the hots for George. He bet George didn't even know it. Folding his hands behind his head, Rob lay still, contemplating the sky for a few more minutes. Then he felt his eyelids growing heavy, and he yawned. There wasn't much sense in fighting sleep any longer. Sitting up, he pulled off his boots, huddled deeper into his jacket and crawled into his bedroll. "'Night, George. Thanks for asking me along."

"You're welcome, kid. Anytime."

Long after the boy had fallen asleep, George hunkered around the fire, watching it burn itself out. He was in his rightful element, alone, with nothing but the stars and his horse for company. He glanced at Rob's sleeping figure. Well, almost alone. Up here a man could think. He had grown to love the High Country and would miss it when he left.

Pushing his hat farther back on his head, he stared into the flames. Lately it had occurred to George that it might be time to be moving on. Four years was a

long time to stay in one place. A person started form-
ing attachments. He thought it odd that Rob had
asked him about Laurie, because George had found
himself thinking about her a lot lately. Too much. He
rationalized that it was because she had so damned
many problems, and he could be of only so much help
to her, but that wasn't entirely true. He thought about
her, about the way she looked, the things she said.
That hadn't happened to him since the woman in Wyoming, and sometimes when he recalled how near he'd
come to being roped and tied, he broke out into a cold
sweat. Women had a way of getting under a man's
skin before he knew what was happening. So maybe
it was time to be moving on. Right after roundup. He
was way past due for a visit with the family. After that,
he might head for . . . oh, Montana. He'd never been
there. That might be a good idea.

WHEN ROB WOKE the following morning, the sky was
pink with the first rays of dawn, but George was already stirring, building a fire and making campfire
boiled coffee. Rob hated the stuff. The rest of breakfast was beans out of a can and bread. The ''adventure'' was beginning to pall, so he hoped George was
ready to head on back home. The boy had to fight
back his dismay when the foreman said, ''I've been
scouting the area and found a bunch of strays that
have wandered up here again. I hate to leave 'em up
here for the mountain lions and coyotes to get to. A
big bunch of the herd is holed up around Number
Five. I think we ought to try to drive 'em down there.''
    George seemed to have forgotten that he didn't have
a seasoned cowboy on his hands, but Rob was reluctant to beg off. He'd felt a comfortable sort of com-

munion with the foreman the night before, campfire camaraderie, and he hated to diminish himself in George's eyes. Perversely, considering his less than enthusiastic feelings about ranch life in general, he was rather pleased that the foreman had asked for his help. "Well . . . sure," Rob said. "Just tell me what to do."

"When we break camp I'll swing wide to the west, and you go to the east. Round 'em up as you go, then drive them to Number Five. They ought to stay put until roundup. We'll meet there and head for the house."

"Sure," Rob said confidently. It sounded simple enough, and the operation would gobble up most of the day. Once they got home and he'd had a bath, it would be fairly close to suppertime, and he would have made it through another weekend.

It was a splendid morning, clear and bright with the promise of fall in the air, and Rob began to enjoy himself. He rode slowly, letting his horse have his head, thinking of almost everything under the sun but rounding up strays. He had been riding for perhaps half an hour before he saw any livestock. Suddenly three calves appeared, seemingly from nowhere, and his sure-footed horse scampered up a brushy ravine in pursuit. The calves apparently were reluctant to leave their private playground. They bolted, and the horse gave chase. The playful animals dashed this way and that until the horse managed to corral them into a tight group. In the saddle, Rob grinned foolishly, enjoying the game. That, he realized, was most of his problem. He had always looked on ranching as something of a game. He simply couldn't think the way his mother and grandfather did, that cattle represented money in the bank.

He and the horse "played" the morning away, and by midday they had a grand total of nine calves to show for their efforts. "Shoot, that's enough," Rob muttered. "I'm tired of this, and I'm starving to death, to boot. Let's take them in."

If he remembered correctly, there was a line shack at Number Five, and that's what he was looking for. But when he had been riding for some time and hadn't encountered it, he began scanning his surroundings. Everything just looked like more of the same. There wasn't a landmark of any kind. He supposed there were men on the DO, men like George, who knew these ravines and draws like streets of a town, but he wasn't one of them. The only thing he was sure of was that he was riding west, so it stood to reason that he would meet up with George. Unless, of course, he had gone farther north than the foreman had. Too late he decided it might have been a good idea to tell George he wasn't familiar with the territory.

Nudging his horse's flank, he continued on, hoping any minute to see something, anything that would clue him in on where he was. People were always talking about how big the DO was. "Awesome" was a word often associated with it. Now Rob knew what they meant. It was vast and spectacular. He topped a hill and looked down into a grassy ravine so untamed that one could well imagine no human foot had ever trod in it. Lifting his eyes, he saw a flat expanse of valley, a lofty peak rising off in the distance. Nothing stirred ahead or below, not man nor beast. He might as well have been plunked down on a distant planet. The first twinges of real trepidation twisted his insides, and a shiver ran up his spine.

Where in hell was Number Five, and more importantly, where in hell was George?

He glanced at his nine charges. They were old enough to be weaned or they wouldn't have strayed from their mamas, so that was one thing he didn't have to worry about. He looked down into the ravine again, and that was when he remembered he had noticed it once while flying over the area with Scott. Shading his eyes with his hand, he peered up at the sun and guessed at the hour.

Well, for sure he had to do something. He didn't dare let the sun set on him, and he wasn't the least worried that George couldn't take care of his own hide. Circling the calves, he formed them into a tight group again and, without too much difficulty, drove them down into the ravine.

GEORGE WAS AS NEAR full-swivel panic as he'd ever been in his life. He'd been searching for Rob for over an hour with no results. He didn't dare stray too far from Number Five for fear they'd never rendezvous. He had covered the entire area, even backtracked, yelling at the top of his lungs, but he'd seen nothing, heard nothing.

Finally he decided he needed help. He wasn't accomplishing anything up here alone, and the sun wasn't going to cease its relentless journey through the sky. Not much really threw him, but this did. The thought of Rob's wandering aimlessly alone in these mountains made George shudder with dread. Why, oh, why had he brought a tenderfoot up here? Why had he suggested rounding up the strays? He needed his head examined, and the sickest feeling he had ever experienced hit his stomach and lay there like so much lead. God a'mighty, he was going to have to go back to headquarters and tell the boss he had lost her son.

CHAPTER FIFTEEN

SUNDAY DINNER hadn't been the big occasion it normally was. None of the married men had brought their wives out. Rob and George were away. Laurie and one of J.B.'s old cronies had been the only guests, and the mood simply hadn't been right somehow.

Being honest, Sunday dinners were always dull affairs without Scott. Life was dull without Scott. Cassie's throat tightened. She hadn't seen him in so long. She often found herself standing on that spot of the rise where she had a clear view of the Horseshoe, hoping for a glimpse of him, wishing she knew what she could do to put things right with them again. She had behaved abominably, but admitting that to him would solve only part of the problem. Until he truly understood the business with Rob, until the entire affair became as vital to him as it was to her, she didn't see how they had much of a future. He had to understand, and when she thought about it long enough, she could conveniently become irritated with him all over again. *If something were this important to Scott,* she would seethe, *it would be that important to me, too.*

But, oh, she missed him! It was a dull ache that she lived with from morning until night. The longing threatened to eat her alive. She was grateful that J.B. hadn't quizzed her about Scott, but her father had to know she was miserable. She wondered if he suspected that she and Scott had been lovers. Probably. Not much got by J.B., and anyone would assume that when a man and a woman spent that much time together, they went past the hugs-and-kisses stage.

Laurie left early, so Cassie went into her office to do some reading. It was four o'clock when George rushed through the door. "Hi," she said. "Glad you're back." Then she noticed the frantic look on the foreman's face, and her heart leaped right up into her throat. "George, what's wrong?"

"Boss . . . please tell me Rob's here."

"Here?" Her eyes widened as she shot to her feet. "Of course he isn't here. He's with you!"

"Damn! I've been looking for that kid since noon. We were supposed to meet at Number Five . . ."

"Oh, God, you didn't let him out of your sight, please, you didn't! He doesn't know the first thing about this ranch." Her voice was frantic. "I doubt that he's even been up to the top country in five or six years."

"Well, for God's sakes, why didn't someone tell me that? The kid's lived here all his life."

"What happened?"

Succinctly George told her about their mission to round up the strays. "But he never showed up at Number Five. I waited and waited, finally went out looking for him, but I was afraid to wander too far from camp. After so much time passed, I figured he must have headed on home. It never occurred to me he might not know where the camp was."

"Oh, my God, we've got to do something! Get everyone available saddled up."

George put a restraining hand on her arm. "We could ride for days and not find him. You know that.

I know you're worried, but we've got to keep our heads. I think we ought to inform the sheriff. Maybe get the Civil Air Patrol. We've got about four hours of daylight left. There's time."

"Air?"

"It's the best way, don't you think?"

Cassie's heart was beating rapidly, and her mind whirled. She had to think. Fear was doing such crazy things to her. "Air," she repeated. "Yes, yes, that would be the best way, but forget the sheriff for now. I've got a better idea. It's quicker, too. Come with me, George, and let's go out the back way. Dad and his friend are on the front porch, and I'd just as soon he not know about this yet."

"Where're we going?"

Already she was leaving the house with George quick on her heels. "To Scott's place. Hurry."

Cassie didn't bother with a vehicle. She sprinted across the yard, down the rise and over the fence. They moved at a dead run, George following her unquestioningly. Dozens of "what ifs" ran through her mind. What if Scott was in Fort Worth? What if the plane was broken or out of gas or at an airport somewhere being worked on? Never once did she wonder if he would help her. Of course he would. He might be angry at her, he might never want to see her again—she couldn't blame him—but he would want Rob found.

Scott happened to look through the kitchen window and saw them coming. Cassie and George Whittaker, both running across his property like the Devil himself was chasing them. A knot of fear rose up in his stomach. He rushed out on the deck to meet them.

"Cassie, what . . ."

"Oh, Scott, it's Rob!" She practically fell against his chest, and he placed his hands beneath her arms to steady her. She was gasping for breath.

"Rob? What . . ." He shot a quizzing glance toward George.

"We got separated up in the top country," the foreman explained. "I didn't know the boy's not familiar with the lay of the land."

"Scott, please, help us." The tears had begun streaming down Cassie's cheeks. "George thought . . . the Civil Air Patrol, but I thought of you, and . . . if the sun goes down . . ."

"I'm way ahead of you. Let me get the keys." He rushed into the house, calling back over his shoulder, "You two get her out of the hangar."

Cassie wondered how he expected the two of them to move an airplane, but there was a hand-held portable tug attached to the nose wheel. George seemed to know what it was and how to use it. Scott came running toward them, and when he'd unlocked the passenger door, Cassie stood aside to let George in the back seat.

The foreman balked, his eyes widening. "Me? You want me to go up in this thing?"

"George, you have to! You're the only one who knows exactly where the two of you were."

Reluctantly, he climbed in, but as Scott was going through his preliminary checks, George confessed, "I think it's only fair to warn you that the only other time I was in one of these things I got awful sick."

Cassie closed her eyes. "Oh, beautiful!"

But Scott was undaunted. He'd had airsick passengers before. "There's a barf bag in the seat pocket in front of you. Better get it out and have it ready. And there's a headset, too. Put it on so we can talk to each other.'' He turned to Cassie and patted her knee reassuringly, his eyes soft and kind, completely unaccusing. ''Don't worry. We'll find Rob and lead him home if I have to fly this thing through the treetops.''

She nodded numbly and tried to smile. She really did feel more confident now that Scott was in charge.

''Are you two buckled up?'' he asked. When assured they were, he reached across Cassie to make certain her window was securely shut and said, ''Okay, here we go.''

As they lifted off the ground, George uttered a heartfelt, ''Sonofabitch!'', which carried loud and clear to the two people in the front seats. Cassie didn't think she had ever heard anything stronger than an occasional ''damn'' from George.

The wheels were scarcely in the well before the plane was flying over the spot where George said he and Rob had camped the night before. ''Okay, George,'' Scott said. ''I'm going down lower. I want you to get your bearings.''

''You mean, I gotta look out of this thing?''

''Yes!''

Cassie cast an anxious glance over her shoulder. George's face was absolutely white. ''Please,'' she said plaintively and reached to give his hand a squeeze.

That simple gesture plus the pleading look on her face were all George needed to galvanize his courage. He'd be damned if he was going to fail her now, not when she was counting on him. Scott banked the plane to the left. George's stomach made a couple of sickening revolutions, then settled. He looked down at the ground and discovered he wasn't going to pass out or throw up or anything like that.

"Okay, there's the water tank and the shed," he said. "That's where we spent the night." Scott circled the area to give him plenty of time to get his bearings. "The strays were scattered just to the north. I swung west and Rob went east. The plan was to gather up as many as we could and drive them to Number Five, which is south and slightly to the east of our campsite."

Scott flew as low as he dared, but it was like searching for the proverbial needle in a haystack. Occasionally they spied a group of livestock, but there was no sign of human life. Cassie kept swallowing to keep down the fear-induced nausea that churned in her stomach. *Please, God, please let us find him and lead him home. Just let him be safe, and I promise...he can be anything he wants to be, go anywhere he wants to go. Everyone else was right, and I was wrong. Rob's heart and mind lie elsewhere, so he doesn't belong here. Just let him be safe. And I'll make it up to Scott, too. I'll atone for the miserable way I've treated him, even if I have to get down on my hands and knees and beg his forgiveness.*

Scott was beginning to get worried. He'd pretty well covered the entire area, and right now he was keeping a watchful eye on the gas tank. The last time he'd come back from Fort Worth he'd meant to land at the little airport in Alpine and get the tank topped off, but he'd been racing the sun and anxious to get home. For sure he couldn't tool around in these mountains until dark. Ten more minutes, fifteen tops, and he would be forced to tell Cassie they were going to have to land and gas up. That might scare hell out of her. She looked like she was going to crack any minute. Reaching over, he rubbed her neck gently. "It's all right," he said. "We'll find him." He wished his voice could have carried more conviction.

"Hey!" George yelled from the back seat. "Turn around. I think I saw something. Over to the east."

The three of them anxiously scanned the tangled wilderness that seemed to stretch on all sides to infinity. Scott saw nothing, Cassie saw nothing, but George saw something. "Look down there in that ravine. What's that?"

What it was was one boy on horseback driving nine calves in single file through a narrow winding ravine. And from the air, it could be clearly seen that the ravine, which obviously had been a riverbed many eons ago, led almost to DO headquarters.

"Well, I'll be!" George exclaimed. "He's heading for the house."

"Are you sure?" Cassie asked.

"Sure I'm sure. He can't go anywhere but home."

"What's he doing with those calves?" she wanted to know.

"I guess he couldn't find Number Five and didn't know what else to do with them. Pretty smart if you ask me. He's got 'em down in that ravine where they're halfway manageable."

Scott circled overhead and dipped his wings. Rob waved. Cassie expelled her pent-up breath and closed her eyes, offering a prayer of thanks. George just laughed.

"Okay, we're going home," Scott said, turning toward the Horseshoe. "He's okay. No search party needed."

When they landed, Cassie was limp. The adrenaline that had been rushing through her veins was abating, and she felt absolutely exhausted. Now she wanted to cry with relief and gratitude instead of fear. Resting her head on the back of the seat, she felt Scott reach across her to flip open the window, and he loosened her seat belt.

"Thanks," she said lifelessly. Then she focused her gaze on the windshield. There was so much she wanted to say to him, needed to say to him, and she didn't know where to begin. "That was above and beyond."

"No, it wasn't," Scott insisted. "It was neighbor helping neighbor."

"It was marvelous the way you jumped in to help without question after... You should have told me to buzz off after the way I've treated you."

"Hey, I was worried about Rob, too. You don't have a monopoly on caring about the boy." He put a gentle hand on her shoulder.

The tears she had been struggling with splashed out of her eyes and ran down her cheeks. "Oh, Scott, I'm so sorry. I've behaved terribly."

He didn't deny it. "We all do sometimes, sweetheart."

She turned to look at him. "You can still call me sweetheart after..."

"I've thought of you as sweetheart for a long time."

They heard the sound of a throat being cleared loudly. Swiveling, they stared into George's grinning face. They both had forgotten he was with them. He looked like a mischievous boy who had been caught eavesdropping on adults. "If you two will excuse me, I'll leave you to have this fascinating discussion in private."

Cassie scooted her seat forward as far as it would go to give him room to get out the door. Then, when George placed his foot on the step, she made a surprising move. Placing her hand on his arm to get his attention, she leaned and kissed him on the cheek. "Thanks, George. You were wonderful, too."

The foreman couldn't have been more surprised by a gesture if she had slapped him. Then he recovered, and his grin returned. "Yeah...ah, well...I'll see you all in a bit." Hopping off the wing, he strolled off in the direction of the DO, thumbs hooked into the pockets of his jeans.

Cassie's seat went sliding back to its original position. "Scott, I made a promise while we were up there looking for Rob. I vowed that if he was safe I was going to back off. He can do anything he wants to do, go anywhere he wants to go. And I intend keeping the promise."

The smile he gave her would have melted an iceberg. "That's the best thing to do, Cassie. He'll flourish and you'll survive."

"It's going to be hard to let go."

"I can imagine. But all parents have to sooner or later."

"I also swore I'd make it up to you for the dreadful way I've treated you, no matter what it takes."

His eyes twinkled. "Mmm, that could be interesting."

"It was never you I was ranting at, do you understand that? I was railing at fate, at the death of all my hopes and dreams. But I swore I'd even get down on my hands and knees and beg forgiveness."

Scott tried to envision a totally supplicant Cassie, but it was useless. No picture would form. "Down on your hands and knees begging? I don't know, sweetheart. That doesn't sound like you."

His hands framed her face, stroking her hair, then her cheeks. "There are so many more delightful ways to seek forgiveness. A couple have already occurred to me." He pulled her as close as the cramped confines of the cockpit would allow and kissed her tenderly.

She laid her cheek against his chest. "I've been miserable without you."

"It hasn't exactly been fun and games over here, either." He clung to her, and she to him. "I know you think I don't understand, but I do, really I do. It's tough seeing dreams die."

Cassie sighed. "I guess deep down in my heart I've known for a long time that Rob wouldn't stay here. I just wouldn't admit it. Funny, Dad gave up so easily, and he still hasn't said a word about it."

"I know. Rob told me."

She looked up at him with a slight frown. "When have you seen Rob?"

"Cassie, he comes to see me all the time. I want you to know that I've never actively sought him out, but when he came to see me, I damned sure wasn't going to tell him to leave. I like to think Rob is my friend."

She thought about that and nodded. "He adores you. It was ridiculous to demand you stay away from him. Just part of my refusal to face facts. You were right when you said I don't own him anymore. He'll be a man soon, and I can't tell him what to do. The raising years are over. Guess they have been for some time."

Scott said nothing for a minute, knowing she had come to a pivotal part of her life and needed time to adjust. Her eyes were fixed on a spot over his shoulder, so he gave her a few moments with her own thoughts. Finally he spoke. "Don't you think we ought to be there to greet Rob? He'll be showing up anytime now."

Cassie shook herself out of her reverie. "Oh, yes, of course."

"Afterward we'll come back over here for . . . a nice long chat."

"Chat?"

"Well, it won't all be talk."

"Oh, Scott," she breathed, her heart in her eyes, "I've missed you so. And I . . . need you."

"Lady, I think those might be the nicest words I've ever heard."

WHEN ROB ARRIVED at the DO with the nine calves, he caused quite a stir out in the yard. "Hey, Robbie boy!" one grizzled old-timer called. "Where'd you get the little ones?"

"Just found 'em," he said nonchalantly as he dismounted. "Didn't know what else to do with 'em, so I brought 'em with me. Stupid things. Why anyone would spend his life taking care of those dumb creatures is beyond me."

George sauntered up. One would never know it by his casual expression, but he was so glad to see Rob, he could have hugged him. "What the hell happened to you?"

"I couldn't find Number Five, so I came home."

"Just like that, huh?"

"Just like that."

"I have you to thank for the worst day of my life." Then the foreman smiled. "You'd better get on inside. There are a bunch of people waiting to see you."

"Oh, wonderful. I guess the fat's in the fire."

"Don't know. Go find out for yourself."

All he owned, which wasn't much when you got right down to it, Rob gladly would have given to be spared whatever was waiting for him inside the house. When he walked into the living room all heads turned—his mother's, his grandfather's and Scott's. Then, to his everlasting embarrassment, his mother raced across the room and enveloped him in a hug. She started to cry. Rob couldn't remember the last time he had seen his mother cry, but it might have been when his dad was killed.

"We were worried sick about you," she sobbed.

"Why?"

"Why?" J.B.'s voice boomed across the room. "Thunderation, boy, you don't know this ranch near as well as you should."

"But I wasn't really lost. When I came to the ravine I remembered seeing it from the air one day when Scott and I were just fooling around in his plane. I remembered that it led to the house, so I followed it. Hi, Scott. What the devil were you doing skimming through the treetops?"

"Looking for you," Scott barked.

"Oh, Rob, you took a chance and won," Cassie said, "There are dozens of ravines and gulches on this ranch."

The boy shook his head. "No, it had to be the same one 'cause it ran southeast. I couldn't find Number Five, but I always knew where the house was."

"How could you possibly have known?" Cassie asked.

He reached into his pocket and withdrew something, which he held out to his mother. It was a compass. "I carry it with me all the time. How do you think Lindbergh found his way across that ocean in

1927? He sure didn't have radar. You worried for
nothing, Mom. I'm sorry I couldn't meet up with
George, and it was dumb of me not to tell him I wasn't
sure where Number Five was, but I always knew I
could find my way home."

Cassie stepped back, suddenly aware that she was
making her son uncomfortable with this outward display of emotion and affection. She looked at him and
saw what she'd been denying for a long time—he already was a man. And he had a whole lot more common sense and real intelligence than she'd ever wanted
to give him credit for. Lord, he was going to look
splendid in a uniform!

"Rob, come into my office for just a minute, will
you? There's something I want to tell you."

AN HOUR LATER Scott pushed open the door to his
bedroom with his elbow, then pushed it closed again
with his foot. He was carrying two long-stemmed
glasses of wine. Walking to the bedside, he handed one
of the glasses to Cassie. She was stretched out on the
bed with her back resting against the headboard, the
way he had seen her so many times, the way he had
feared he might never see her again. She smiled radiantly and took the glass. With her free hand she
grasped his arm and encouraged him to sit down beside her.

Scott felt an enormous sense of contentment as he
gazed at her face in the shadowy room. "There's only
one thing wrong with this whole scenario," he said.

"I can't imagine what it would be. Everything seems
absolutely perfect to me." Cassie sipped slowly from
the glass, looking at him over it's rim.

"You're not spending the night."

"I'd like to, but..."

"But you'd feel funny because of your dad and Rob. I understand."

"I'm sure Dad knows that you and I do more than kiss each other, but I don't like being so obvious. Old-fashioned, I guess." Her look bordered on being sultry. "But, I certainly don't have to go home early. We have time for...oh, all sorts of things."

Scott smiled. "Minx."

Cassie laughed lightly, then asked. "How are things going with your grandfather?"

His eyes clouded. "I haven't quite gotten around to telling him I'm staying here, if that's what you mean. But I will, soon."

"Dreading it?"

"Wouldn't you?"

Cassie grew thoughtful. "Yes, I guess I would. I think I know how Rob must have felt. He was so happy when I told him that I wasn't going to object to his trying for the appointment. I could see his Adam's apple bobbing up and down, like he was trying to keep from crying. It made me feel terrible about the way I've acted. Talk about guilt heaped upon guilt."

"Forget it, sweetheart. It's all behind you now." He took a drink of wine and then glanced around. "Does this room suit you?"

Cassie's eyes followed his. "Suit me? It's a wonderful room. I've spent a lot of happy hours in this room. Why?"

"I just wondered. It's a little on the masculine side."

"Why not? It's a man's room. The whole house is beautiful."

"You wouldn't make any changes?"

"Nary a one that I can think of off-hand. What is all this?"

"Surely you know. I want you with me all the time. No more of this getting up and going home."

Cassie tilted her head, smiling at him. "If this is a proposal, it's a mighty strange one."

"We belong together," he said simply. "Are you going to marry me?"

"I think I'd better."

"I love you."

"And I love you." Her voice was a little high and not quite steady. "Lord, it's scary."

"Scary?"

"The two of us, at our advanced ages, learning to live with someone all over again."

Scott chuckled. "We'll make mistakes and hurt each other without realizing we're doing it, just like everyone else does, but all in all, I imagine we'll get along better than most. Don't you?"

Cassie looked at him with absolute adoration. "I'm sure of it. Funny that I should be so sure, but I am. I always thought we weren't well suited. So why am I so sure that living with you will be the easiest thing I've ever done? I wonder if our marriage will send out shock waves that will be felt round the world."

"Maybe not round the world, but I'm sure it'll feed the local gossip mill for quite some time. Imagine…Cassie Tate and that crazy Maitland fellow! Odd the people some folks are attracted to."

"The reaction I'm most curious about are the ones from your grandfather and my dad."

"Do you care how they feel, one way or another?"

Cassie shook her head. "Surprisingly, no. I've spent way too much time worrying about others. From now on, I worry about us."

Scott scooted closer, and she laid her head against his chest, hearing the reassuring steadiness of his heartbeat. His warmth seemed to seep right through her, bringing a slow flush to her skin. How wonderful it felt to have him hold her. He rested his cheek against her hair, and they sat that way for a long time, watching the room sink deeper and deeper into shadows as sundown approached. When they had come over from the DO earlier, she had thought that the minute the doors were closed behind them they would fall into wild, intense lovemaking. Instead, just being together and talking had so far been enough. They were sharing the most calming sort of peace.

She felt his chest expand as he took a deep breath. Her free hand moved to rest on his knee. A moment ticked by. Then Scott set his wineglass on the bedside table, took hers out of her hand and placed it beside his. He drew her to him and held her tightly until he could feel the warmth of her body through her clothing. "There were a lot of long, lonely nights in this room when I thought and thought about this," he finally said. "I'm very grateful to Rob. Sorry that he scared you, of course, but at least he brought you over here."

Cassie lifted her head and looked into Scott's solemn, clear eyes. "Something would have brought me back, I'm sure of it. I wouldn't have stayed away forever. I went through some long lonely nights, too."

"Good." He smiled tenderly. "Serves you right."

"I am sorry, Scott. So very, very sorry."

"Forgiven and forgotten." His fingers reached for the first of her shirt buttons and freed it. The back of his hands brushed her velvety skin. Another button gave way, and his hand slipped inside to cup a breast. His thumb teased its bud to hardness. Her reaction was immediate and predictable. Her lips parted in expectation, and a tiny sound escaped—part moan, part sigh. Her tongue skimmed along her bottom lip. Scott was drawn to the movement as if he'd never seen anything so fascinating in his life. Bending, he brushed her lips, then his tongue sought hers, gently, tentatively.

That simple gesture was the kindling needed to ignite the smoldering fire that had slowly been building in Cassie. Suddenly impatient, she fumbled with the buttons of his shirt, and there seemed to be a hundred of them. When the last was undone and the shirt pulled free of his waistband, she pushed the garment off his shoulders. Then, with great deliberation, she undressed him, garment by garment, kissing and murmuring sweet words all the while.

Scott was transfixed, hypnotized, almost crazy with sensations. He had envisioned this throughout many a lonely night, but in his dreams he had been the orchestrator, the agressor, the seducer. In reality, she was taking charge. Cassie's hands worshipped him. Totally aroused, he was turgid and pulsating with desire. He wanted to feel her naked body beneath his, to thrust inside her once more, but that would have to wait. Apparently she had something else in mind.

When she had removed the last of his clothing, she knelt on the floor between his legs. Beginning with his feet, she kissed him—his calves, his knees, the inside of his thighs, while her hands stroked his bare hips and

the length of his legs. He wanted to taste every part of
her, too, but that also would have to wait until later,
after she had finished performing this exquisite tor-
ture on him. A strange garbled sound came out of his
throat as he felt her fingers close around him. His
stomach muscles, so hard they hurt, contracted
sharply. He wondered if it were possible to die from
pleasure, if absolute ecstasy could be fatal. Closing his
eyes, he laced his fingers through her lustrous hair and
gave himself up to pure bliss, while she made love to
him.

CHAPTER SIXTEEN

AUTUMN CAME to the High Country. The fall roundup was behind them, and spirits were high. Most of the area's ranchers were enjoying the fruits of the best year they had known in a decade. On a bright afternoon in early November, Cassie sat in her office, working on her year-end financial statements. She heard the front screen door slam and the staccato rhythm of boot heels crossing the hall. She glanced up in time to see George pause on the threshold.

"Got a minute, boss?" the foreman asked.

"Of course."

He crossed the room to stand in front of her desk. "I've got something to tell you, and believe me, it isn't going to be easy."

Cassie laid down her pencil. "Oh?"

He looked down, then at her. "Guess I'll be leaving right away."

"George!" Cassie was thoroughly stunned by the announcement. For a minute she didn't know what to say. "I . . . don't understand. Are you unhappy here? If you've had grievances, you should have let me know. We could have worked out something."

"Aw, boss, it isn't anything like that. This is the best outfit I've ever worked for, you know that." George wished with all his heart that this could be short and sweet, but he guessed he'd known there was no chance it would. He'd become a fixture around the DO. That was the problem, the thing he was fighting. He'd simply been around too long.

"Then I really don't understand," Cassie said. "Please tell me why you want to leave us." Her thoughts immediately flew to Laurie.

The foreman's reasons for wanting to leave were complicated and impossible to explain. For one thing, he imagined there were going to be some changes at the DO, changes he wouldn't like. Now that Cassie was married to Scott Maitland, George could envision a time when the DO was more concerned with the bottom line than with ranching. Even though Cassie had assured all the regulars that things at the DO would go on as before, George had his doubts.

But that wasn't the only reason he needed to be on his way. "It's just the restless itch, I guess. I haven't been back to visit my family in a long time, and . . ."

"Then take a vacation, take as long as you need. When you're all finished visiting, come back."

George shifted his weight to the other foot. This was even harder than he had imagined it would be. No boss had ever asked him to stay before. In this business, when a man decided to move on, he just did it. The boss gave him his pay and a handshake, and that was it. This was awful. He looked at Cassie and realized he was going to miss the Ferenbachs, and that was the real reason he had to leave. "It's just time, boss. There are a lot of places I want to see before I die."

He didn't sound convincing, and he didn't look very happy. "George, are you running away from something?"

His eyes widened. "Running away?"

"Never mind. It's none of my business. Tell me, have you told Laurie you're leaving?"

"No. I wouldn't tell anyone before I told you."

"But you are going to tell her?"

"Sure. I wouldn't just not show up one day. That's where I'm going when I leave here." It occurred to him that this was the first time he'd ever had people to say goodbye to.

"You're going to leave her in the lurch, I hope you know that."

Jeez, he thought. "It isn't as though I've been a lot of help to her, boss. In fact, I haven't been able to do much at all. I've just cleaned up her place a little and made some repairs. Laurie needs a whole lot more than me."

Cassie looked down at her hands. *Oh, George, you are so incredibly dense. Nice, but dense.* He didn't know how much Laurie cared for him, because he wouldn't look. And he wouldn't look for fear of what he might see—a beautiful woman with soft eyes who might get under his skin and put an end to the antiquated way of life he had chosen for himself. She raised her eyes. "Your mind's make up?"

George nodded.

"When will you be leaving us?"

"Tomorrow, if that's all right. I have some loose ends to tie up."

Cassie wondered how Laurie would feel about being categorized as a "loose end." "No need for me to say good luck. You know I wish it for you."

"Thanks, boss. Would you mind if I take one of the trucks over to Laurie's? I won't be gone long."

"No, that's fine. Don't you dare leave tomorrow without saying goodbye."

"I won't. See you in a bit."

Cassie stared after him and sighed. Laurie would survive. There had been no passionate love affair to get over, so she would survive. Cassie suspected her friend had been expecting something like this all along. Only a week ago Laurie had said, "George is the worst kind of man to fall for. He'll never get attached to a woman, because he doesn't want to. I've got plenty of problems without adding George to the list."

So Cassie decided to save her pity for George. He had missed out on something wonderful.

LAURIE GLANCED OUT the window when she heard the sound of an approaching vehicle. She saw that it was one of the DO's pickups, so she assumed it was Cassie. Opening the door, she walked out onto the porch in time to see George climbing out of the cab. Her heart gave a little leap.

"Well, good afternoon," she said, shading her eyes with a hand. "Did you get your days mixed up? I wasn't expecting you."

"Hi, Laurie. No, I know what day it is. I..." He stopped at the foot of the steps, thinking it would be easier with some distance between them. *Why am I doing this, he wondered. Why in hell didn't I just pack and catch the first bus heading north?* It had been difficult enough saying goodbye to Cassie. There had been a lump in his throat when he'd left her office. Now it was back. "Actually, I came to say goodbye."

Laurie's hand dropped, and she steadied herself. Outwardly her composure was intact, but inside she felt something die. A dream, she supposed. A foolish, unrealistic dream. "Oh? Going anywhere in particular?"

"To Oklahoma to see my family for a while, and then . . . I don't know. Thataway." He pointed west.

"I see." She drew a deep breath. The announcement was unexpected but not particularly surprising. Men like George never had any reason to stay in one place. They made sure of that. "Good luck."

"Thanks."

"It was nice of you to take the time to say goodbye."

George felt like a heel . . . and he didn't even know why. "Don't mention it."

"And thanks for all your help around here."

His eyes swept his surroundings. Lord, there was a lot that needed doing. The house for one thing. He'd meant to get around to painting it. "Wish I could have done more. What you really need is a full-time man around here."

Laurie uttered a dry, mirthless laugh. "Yes, I guess I do. I surely could use one of those."

George kicked at the ground with the toe of his boot, then looked at her. "Laurie . . . ah, there's something I've always wanted to ask you, but I figured it was none of my business. Still isn't, I reckon."

"That's okay. Ask whatever you like."

"How come a pretty woman like you never got married?"

There was a tense moment of silence. The expression on her face was indescribable. Then she stared him straight in the eye. "Oh, obligations, duties, people who needed me. All those things you've been running away from." Her gaze did not falter.

George felt as though a knife was slicing through him. Cassie had accused him of running away, too. He tried to smile, found he couldn't, so he only nodded. "Yeah. Guess you've got me pegged, all right. Well . . . so long." He touched the brim of his hat and turned away from the intenseness of her eyes.

"George, wait a minute. There's one more thing."

He turned to see Laurie coming down the steps. She walked up to him and stood so close he could smell her perfume. "I hope I'm not entirely out of line, but . . ." She raised her face to his and placed a light, melting kiss on his very startled mouth. "Goodbye. Have a safe journey. I hope you find whatever it is you're looking for in the next place. Send me a postcard." Then she smiled, turned and went up the steps, crossed the porch and disappeared behind the front door.

George stood in the dusty yard for a minute, staring at the closed door, grappling with an emotion he couldn't name, because he'd never felt it before. Finally he got back in the pickup and started the engine. Attachments, he thought. They were something he'd never formed until he'd come here, and they were something he could do without, thanks.

BACK AT THE DO Cassie glanced at her watch. It was four-thirty, time to close up shop. She straightened her desk, locked it and gathered up the financial statements that Scott wanted to see. Her very dear but very stubborn husband insisted they carry out the terms of that ridiculous bet to the letter. Cassie didn't see the point since their marriage had brought about a merger between the DO and the Horseshoe. "A bet's a bet," he had said, so she'd play the game. Just wait until Scott saw her statements. It had been a long, long time since the DO had shown a three-hundred-thousand-dollar profit.

Out in the hall she called to her father. "I'm leaving now, Dad."

"Okay, hon. See you tomorrow."

"Rob won't be home until after five. When you see him, you might tell him his mother would appreciate it if he would take a few minutes out of his busy life and pay her a visit."

J.B. chuckled. "I'll relay the message."

Cassie left the house and climbed into the new sedan Scott had bought her. Then she drove to the Horseshoe where she now lived as Mrs. Maitland. It had been the only major change in her life since her marriage. She continued to run the DO as before, and Scott continued to run the Horseshoe, which had become sort of a satellite operation within the larger ranch. It had proven to be a perfect arrangement.

Everything was perfect, or as perfect as life ever got. Rob had chosen to continue living in the big house with J.B., even though both Cassie and Scott had asked him to live with them. "Aw, shoot, Mom. You two guys need to be alone for a while. Besides, Granddad'll be lonesome all alone," the boy had said. Rob, Cassie knew, was eternally grateful to his grandfather for not raising a ruckus over the academy. She wished she had shown as much good sense. Her son was happier than she had ever seen him. He'd taken the civil service exam, and now they all were just waiting for the congressman to make his appointments. Scott had been through his confrontation with Theo, and they'd both survived. There were even plans afoot for Theo and Norma to spend Christmas at the Horseshoe. All of the problems and worries that had

seemed so monumental two months ago had been resolved, one by one.

Parking beside Scott's Mercedes, Cassie took the
front steps two at a time and entered the house.
"Scott!" she called.

"In here, sweetheart." His voice came from his office. She followed it and found her husband seated
behind his desk. Crossing the room, she slid her arms
around his neck and bent for a kiss. "Missed you,"
she cooed.

"You saw me at noon."

"Ah, the honeymoon's over. You're not supposed
to be able to stand being away from me longer than an
hour."

He laughed and patted her rump. "So, what's
new?"

Cassie straightened, her smile fading. "George is
leaving us."

"Oh? That's a surprise, isn't it?"

"More like a shock. I hate to see him go."

"You'll find someone else."

"I know." She brightened. "So, anything new in
your world?"

"Yeah, and I want to talk to you about something.
A honeymoon."

"Oooh, that sounds nice. Where would you like to
go?"

"I'm thinking about Italy."

Cassie's eyes widened. "Italy?"

Scott nodded and thumped a letter on his desk.
"This is from my folks. They want us to come for a
visit. How does that sound to you?"

"Well, of course I'd love to meet them, but . . . my
goodness, Italy!"

He laughed. "Sweetheart, it's not the moon. You're such a provincial creature. It's time you saw something of the world. The Mediterranean in winter. Sounds good to me. Will you at least think about it?"

Cassie was thinking about it. For someone who'd never strayed very far from home, Italy sounded so far away and exotic. "It might be nice," she mused. "And we'll be together, far from everything familiar. Yes, let's go."

"Done. We'll go right after the first of the year. I'll get a letter off to Dad tomorrow. Now, what's that you're clutching so tightly?"

Cassie had forgotten the folder of papers. Now she handed them to him with a broad smile. "The DO's year-end statement. You insisted."

"That I did." He leafed through the papers, then set them on his desk. "Nice," he commented.

"Nice?" Cassie's mouth dropped. "Is that all you can say? That may look like pocket change to you, but three hundred thousand dollars is the biggest profit the DO's shown in years. What about you? Did that accountant come by this afternoon?"

Scott nodded and pointed to a large manila envelope that was lying on the desk. Cassie picked it up. "I'll just skip the finer points. I'm only interested in the bottom line."

She gasped when she read it. She looked at Scott's grinning face, then back at the report. "This is ridiculous! Six hundred ten thousand?"

"Right."

"That isn't possible. You didn't even have any cattle to sell."

"Hey, I made twenty-four dollars an acre on my hay operation."

"Don't be cute. You had that accountant do this as a joke, right?"

"Wrong. It's all certified, verified, et cetera. I don't joke about income, sweetheart. I don't want Internal Revenue on my ass."

Cassie stared at the figures in disbelief. "But . . . where did all this money come from?"

"Read the statement. I'm going to get a beer." He got up and headed for the kitchen. "Want something?"

"What? Oh . . . ah, yes, a glass of wine would be nice, thanks." While he was out of the room, she studied the statement with new interest. It didn't take her long to discover the main source of the Horseshoe's enviable income. Eleven investors had paid one-hundred-thousand dollars apiece for one-twelfth of the rights to Trendsetter's semen. Scott retained the other twelfth. Cassie could hardly believe it. The bull he had paid half a million dollars for had more than doubled in value . . . and Scott still owned him!

Her husband came up behind her, a glass of wine in one hand and a can of beer in the other. Bending, he nibbled at her earlobe. "Guess I win the bet, huh?"

"In a big way!"

"So pay up." Handing her the glass of wine, he clicked his beer can against it. "I want to hear you say my methods work."

"Work? Scott, darling, you are a blinking financial genius!"

He chuckled. "Is this the woman who staunchly believes there's a reason for everything under the sun, including drought? The very same woman who believes in letting nature have its way? What about tradition and all that garbage?"

She smiled at him sheepishly and lifted her glass in a salute. "Well, love, I think you and I are about to establish some new traditions of our own. I want to talk to you seriously. About next year...do you really think the Horseshoe can run thirty cows a section?"

EPILOGUE

ONE WEEK AFTER CASSIE AND SCOTT had returned from visiting his parents in Italy, Cassie walked into her office at the DO and found a letter lying on her desk. It was addressed to Rob, so he obviously had placed it there when he left for school. The letterhead read, "Congress of the United States, House of Representatives." Picking it up, she began reading it.

Dear Rob,
Congratulations! I am pleased to inform you that you have been selected...

From that point on, the print swam in and out of her vision. "The broad range of interests and leadership abilities you have shown... Your commendable characteristics... The years ahead will be exciting for you... You have my best wishes..." It was signed by the congressman from their district.

Cassie set the letter down and brushed at her eyes. So there it was, undeniable, and though she had expected it, a pang or two still squeezed at her heart. She glanced out the window, across the side yard in the direction of the corrals. There was little activity on the ranch this time of year. The day was cold and overcast, but spring wasn't far away. Before long, patches of green would begin to appear here and there. It would be branding time again, and the unending cycle would begin anew, fascinating in its repetitiveness. Rob would never be a part of it, but then, he never had been, not really. Everyone had known that but her. She had fought it so long that she hadn't been willing to admit the battle was lost.

Still, she refused to think of this as an ending. He might come back to them someday, or perhaps one of her grandchildren would. That was a thought she had to cling to.

But if that didn't happen, well...the DO simply would renew itself with unknown people, and the cycle would go on. She could no longer be worried about what would happen after she was gone. Scott had such plans for them, such plans!

She reread the letter, then shoved it aside. She didn't in the least feel like working today. She guessed she wasn't quite over the excitement of Italy, and Scott already was talking about taking her to Australia next winter. There was so much she hadn't seen, and the trip to Italy had made her realize what a tiny part of the universe the ranch was. At that moment, more than anything, she didn't want to sit in this office.

Well, where was it written that she had to? *You're the boss here, remember.* Standing up, she started to leave the room, but something occurred to her. Returning to the desk, she tore a sheet off a notepad and grabbed a pencil. On the paper she wrote: "I'm very proud of you. Love, Mom." Clipping it to the letter, she left the room and went home to Scott.

TEARS IN THE RAIN

STARRING
CHRISTOPHER CAVZENOVE AND
SHARON STONE

BASED ON A NOVEL BY
PAMELA WALLACE

PREMIERING IN NOVEMBER

TITR-1

ATTRACTIVE, SPACE SAVING BOOK RACK

Display your most prized novels on this handsome and sturdy book rack. The hand-rubbed walnut finish will blend into your library decor with quiet elegance, providing a practical organizer for your favorite hard-or soft-covered books.

Only $9.95

Approximately 16" x 8" when assembled

Assembles in seconds!

To order, rush your name, address and zip code, along with a check or money order for $10.70* ($9.95 plus 75¢ postage and handling) payable to *Harlequin Reader Service*:

Harlequin Reader Service
Book Rack Offer
901 Fuhrmann Blvd.
P.O. Box 1396
Buffalo, NY 14269-1396

Offer not available in Canada.

BKR-1A

*New York and Iowa residents add appropriate sales tax.